Praise for the novels of
New York Times and USA TODAY
bestselling author

DIANA PALMER

"The popular Palmer has penned another winning novel, a perfect blend of romance and suspense."
—*Booklist* on *Lawman*

"Diana Palmer is a mesmerizing storyteller who captures the essence of what a romance should be."
—*Affaire de Coeur*

"Readers will be moved by this tale of revenge and justice, grief and healing."
—*Booklist* on *Dangerous*

"Diana Palmer is one of those authors whose books are always enjoyable. She throws in romance, suspense and a good story line."
—*The Romance Reader* on *Before Sunrise*

"Lots of passion, thrills, and plenty of suspense… *Protector* is a top notch read!"
—*Romance Reviews Today* on *Protector*

"A delightful romance with interesting new characters and many familiar faces. It's nice to have a hero who is not picture-perfect in looks or instincts, and a heroine who accepts her privileged life yet is willing to work for the future she wants."
—*RT Book Reviews* on *Wyoming Tough*

DIANA PALMER

WYOMING RUGGED

HQN™

ISBN-13: 978-0-373-77973-4

Wyoming Rugged

Recycling programs
for this product may
not exist in your area.

www.HQNBooks.com

Printed in U.S.A.

WYOMING RUGGED

CHAPTER ONE

NICOLETTE ASHTON'S FATHER was always trying to get her to go out on dates. She loved rocks. Men, not so much. She was an introvert, shy and quiet with people she didn't know. She had a lovely face, a complexion like peaches and cream with long, soft, platinum-blond hair and eyes the color of a foggy September morning. Her figure was equally pretty. But she refused dates right and left. There was a man in her life. He just didn't know it. He thought she was too young. Sadly, that didn't keep her from longing for him.

Because of that, she kept to herself. She'd avoided dating all through college by going out with her girl-friends. But her friends said she needed involvement. They insisted that she needed to get out in the world and date somebody. They meant well. Perhaps she did need to get out more. It wasn't as if the object of her affections was ever going to reciprocate them.

So as the end of the semester neared, they set her up with this man. She didn't know him. He wasn't from Catelow, Wyoming, where she lived on her father's cattle ranch. Her date was from Billings, Montana, where she went to college. At the moment, she wished she'd never agreed to the blind date.

He was inconsiderate and frankly rude, especially when she insisted on being brought home to the fam-

ily ranch, instead of going to her date's apartment.
The ranch wasn't so far away, just about a twenty-
minute drive. But Niki knew what was likely to happen if she agreed to go home with the man. However
out of fashion it might be among her fellow college
students in Billings, she didn't go with the crowd.
Harvey, her date, refused to believe that any girl
would refuse his advances. After all, he was a football star at the college both he and Niki attended, and
he was very good-looking. He was used to women
falling all over him. But Niki wouldn't.

"You have to be out of your mind," the young man,
Harvey, muttered as he pulled into her driveway and
raced up to the front steps of the grand Victorian
mansion. "There aren't any women left in the country
who don't sleep around these days, for God's sake!"

"There are some. I'm one," she said. "I agreed to
go to dinner with you, Harvey. Only to dinner."

He made an angry sound in his throat. He pulled
up at her door. He studied her in the light from the
front porch.

"Your old man home?" he asked.

"Not yet," she said without thinking. "He had a
business meeting. But a friend of his is coming to
stay with us for a few days. He should be here any
minute." It was a calculated lie. There was a friend,
named Blair Coleman, who owned a multinational oil
corporation. Niki had seen him infrequently when he
came home with her father. In fact, she'd had a flaming crush on him since she was seventeen, but he
treated her like a child. So Blair Coleman was coming to stay. She just wasn't sure when. "I have to go
in," she added.

"I'll walk you to the door," he said. He even went around the car to open her door for her. There was a calculating look on his face, but Niki was too relieved to notice it. She'd unlock the door, go inside and she'd be free.

"Thanks," she said.

"No problem," he said, with an odd, smug little smile.

She put her key into the lock, noticing with a frown that it wasn't needed. The door was unlocked. Maybe her father was home after all.

She turned to tell Harvey good-night and found herself pushed inside the house. He closed the door behind them.

"Now," he said menacingly, "you frigid little tease! Girls who date me always give out. Always!"

He grabbed her and wrestled her into the living room, down onto the sofa.

Niki was frail from a hospital visit that had left her weak and breathless. Even though she wasn't a tiny girl, she was slender, and she had no martial arts skills at all. Harvey was a football player, with the muscle that came with the game. He had her on her back on the sofa, her long blond hair fanned around her oval face with its delicate complexion and pale gray eyes. She was flushed from the illness, and breathless from the aftereffects of it. She did fight him, but she knew she'd never get away in time. He was trying to take something from her that should be her right to give. She was furious. Being helpless made her even more angry.

"Let go of me!" she raged. "You idiot! I am not going to let you…!"

"You can't stop me," he panted, ripping the bodice of her dress as he held her down with his formidable weight. "And there's nobody home who can."

"Oh, I wouldn't bet good money on that," a deep, gravelly voice mused from the doorway.

Niki glanced toward the voice. And there he was, larger than life. The reason she never dated. Blair Coleman.

Harvey was just tipsy enough not to realize how much trouble he was in. At least, not until a man the size of a wrestler jerked him off Niki by his collar and slammed him down onto the floor.

"You can't do that to me! I play football! I'll put you through the wall!" Harvey raged as he jumped to his feet and went for the big man.

There was a deep chuckle. Harvey's rush was met with a fist the size of a ham. It inserted itself into Harvey's diaphragm and sent him to his knees.

While he was trying to recuperate from that, the big man jerked him up by his collar, drew back his fist and knocked the younger man over the back of the sofa that a shocked Niki was still lying on.

"I'll tell my dad!" the football star raged. "He's got all sorts of lawyers."

"I have a few of my own. Get your butt back here and apologize to this girl for what you tried to do," he added in a voice like a grater.

"I...will not," the boy faltered.

"Your choice. I don't really mind involving the sheriff's department." He was pulling out his cell phone as he spoke.

"Nicolette, I'm very sorry," the boy said at once, his face red as he stared at Niki.

She was on her feet by now, clutching her torn bodice together. Her pale eyes were blazing with outraged modesty. "Not as sorry as you're going to be when I tell my father what you tried to do, Harvey," she promised. "He has some good lawyers, too."

"I was drunk!" Harvey exclaimed. He glared at her. "And you can read about yourself on my Facebook page," he added with a sarcastic smile.

The big man moved closer. Harvey backed up a step.

"Let me give you some advice," Blair said quietly. "Don't think about getting even with her online. I'll have my people checking, just in case. The first time I see anything posted about her, you'd better be on your way out of the country before any of my security people can find you. Are we clear?" he added, his stance as threatening as his deep voice.

"Y-yes. Very clear. Very."

Blair jerked his head toward the door.

Harvey took the hint. He didn't quite run for his car. But he got down the driveway in a hurry.

Niki got a better look at her rescuer when he came back from the window, making sure Harvey left.

He was dressed casually, but in designer slacks that clung to his broad, muscular thighs, and an expensive green knit shirt that outlined formidable muscles. He had a broad face with a big nose and a beautiful, wide, chiseled mouth. His complexion was olive. His hair was wavy and jet-black, with a few strands of silver. His eyes were large and black as jet. They were deep set, under thick eyebrows. His feet looked as oversize as his hands. He was very fit for a man his size. There wasn't an ounce of fat showing anywhere on him. Niki had adored him from the day her father brought him home to visit, years ago. But since she'd been seventeen, there had been no man in her life at all. This one colored her dreams, made her ache for things she couldn't quite grasp.

"Thanks," Niki said in her soft voice. "I couldn't stop him." Her breathing was jerky and shallow.

He scowled. "You have asthma, don't you?"

She nodded. "And I'm just getting over pneumonia." She smiled at him. "Thanks, Mr. Coleman."

He smiled gently, and the fierce look left his face. "Just Blair," he corrected. "It's nice to see you again, Niki," he added. "Well, I would have preferred different circumstances," he amended as he looked at her.

She managed a breathy laugh. "Me, too. I'm just glad you were here when I got home." She was still clutching her dress.

"Did he hurt you?" he asked gently.

"I don't...think so."

"Let's see." He drew her down on the couch and his big hands moved gently to the torn fabric. "None of that," he chided when she flushed, mistaking her reaction for shyness when it was actually excitement at the touch of his fingers instead. "I'm way too old to make a pass at a girl your age. Besides, I'm engaged."

"Oh." *Story of my life*, she told herself, *that the only man I'm even interested in thinks of me as a child*. And he was getting married. She felt her heart break right in two. But she didn't let it show. She relaxed her death grip on the fabric. "Sorry. I've had a bad night."

"I noticed." He drew the fabric away from her lacy little bra. But it wasn't the undergarment he was looking at. It was the bruises on what he could see of her pretty little firm breasts just above the cup of the bra. She had beautiful little breasts. He clamped down hard on feelings he shouldn't even entertain, especially now. There were more bruises on her thin shoulders. He winced.

"I wish I'd hit him harder," he said in a cold, biting tone.

"He was so shocked when you showed up," she recalled with a laugh like tiny bells. "He's a football star, you know." She grimaced. "Goodness, I must be an idiot. I didn't even realize that he felt entitled to anything he wanted in life."

"Sadly, some men think that way. Turn around, honey." He moved her so that he could draw the dress down and look at her back. There were more bruises there.

"Is it bad?" she asked.

He drew in a breath and turned her back to him. His black eyes were glittery. "I think we need to take you to the emergency room, and then talk to the sheriff. These bruises are an outrage."

"It would be my word against his," she said quietly, searching this big man's eyes.

"I saw most of it," he reminded her.

"Yes, but you weren't with us in the car. He could say I promised him whatever he wanted and then got cold feet."

He cursed under his breath. "I don't like letting him get away with this."

"He'll be much too busy explaining his bruises," she said with a flare of humor. "And when I go back to school, I'll swear to everyone I know that I gave them to him!" she said with a little laugh.

He chuckled. "He'll be a legend in his own time."

"Yes, he will," she promised. She cocked her head and looked at him curiously. "You don't look like a man who gets into many fights," she said.

He shrugged and smiled at her. "My...father—" odd how he hesitated on the word, Niki thought "—founded an oil company. He built it into a multinational corporation and groomed me to run it. But his idea of management was to teach me the job from the bottom up. I started out as a roughneck, working on oil rigs." He pursed his lips. "The boss's son wasn't the most popular guy around. Plenty of other men thought I'd be a pushover."

"I imagine it didn't take them long to learn the lesson," she said, smiling up at him.

"Not long, no," he agreed. "You'll have bruises, Niki. I'm really sorry."

"It would have been much worse if you hadn't been here," she said. It began to catch up with her and she shivered. "I've been on blind dates before, in high school, but nobody ever tried to..." A sob broke from her throat. "Sorry," she faltered.

He bent and scooped her up in his big arms. He sat down in an armchair and cuddled her in his lap. "Get it out of your system, Niki. I'm not afraid of tears," he said softly, brushing his mouth over her hair.

She bawled. It was a rare thing, comfort. Her father had never been a physical sort of man. He loved her, but he never kissed bruises or offered much comfort. Like Blair, he was an oilman, and he'd worked on oil rigs in his youth, too. Her mother had died when she was in grammar school, so it had just been her and Daddy, most of her life, here on the enormous cattle ranch he'd inherited from his father. She was nine-teen, almost twenty, and this was the first time she'd ever had anybody offer her a shoulder to cry on. Well, except for Edna Hanes, the housekeeper.

She pressed close to Blair's broad chest and mourned the loss of him. He was going to get married. She'd had this stupid idea that one day she'd grow up enough for him to finally notice her. That was a pipe dream, and it had gone up in ashes tonight. At least, she thought, he'd saved her from that overly muscled brute.

"Poor little thing," he murmured against her fore-head. "I'm sorry."

"I didn't know men could be like that," she said brokenly. "I don't date much. I like to live in the past. I'd have been right at home in the Victorian age. I don't...fit in in the modern world."

"Neither do I," he confessed. He lifted his head and searched her wet eyes. "Still a virgin?"

She nodded. Oddly, it wasn't at all embarrassing to talk to him like this. She felt as if she'd always known him. Well, she had, for several years, if dis-tantly. "Daddy took me to church every Sunday until I went off to college," she confessed. "Some of the other girls at school say I'm stupid to think any man would want to marry an innocent woman. They say I need experience, so I'll appeal to a man." She looked at him like a curious little bird. "Is that right?"

He smoothed the damp hair away from her cheeks. She was almost otherworldly. He ached in inconve-nient places and chided himself for that reaction to her. She was a child, compared to him, even if she was in college. "I think innocence is a rare and beautiful thing," he said after a minute. "And that your husband will be a very lucky man."

She smiled shyly. "Thanks." She pursed her lips.

"A question?" he teased. "Ask away."

"Will your wife be a very lucky woman?" she asked outrageously.

He burst out laughing. "No. Emphatically, no." He searched her shimmering eyes. "You really are a pain, aren't you?"

She linked her arms around his strong neck. "I truly am." She smiled at him. "What's she like, your fiancée?"

"Black hair, blue eyes, beautiful, sophisticated, very artistic," he summed her up.

"And you love her very much."

He smiled back. "She's the first woman I ever asked to marry me. I've been too busy making money to think about a private life. Well, about a permanent one, at least."

"Is she nice?"

He frowned. "What a question."

"I mean, will she take care of you if you get sick, and stay home and take care of the babies when they come along?" she asked, because she realized if she couldn't have him, she wanted happiness for him, above all things.

The questions made him uncomfortable. Elise was uncomfortable with illness. She avoided it like the plague. And she'd already said that if she agreed to have a child, there would be a price, and it would be years from now. Why hadn't he considered that before? In fact, he'd been so busy that he'd fallen into the engagement without much consideration about compatibility or children. He was so hungry for her that he'd have done anything to get her, including getting married. She kept him at fever pitch, always backing away just in time…

"Do you want children?" she asked.

He tucked a strand of hair behind her ear. "Yes," he said, but he sounded troubled.

"Did I put my foot in my mouth?" she prodded when he scowled.

"No. Of course not." He smiled faintly. "I'd never considered those things. I'm sure she'll take care of me when I'm sick, though."

"That's good, then." She smiled up at him. "You'll be a good husband, I think."

He looked down at the torn dress and winced. "You poor little creature," he said softly. "I'm sorry you had such a bad night."

"It ended better than it began," she replied.

The front door opened and Todd Ashton, Niki's father, walked in. He stopped dead in his tracks when he saw his friend and his daughter in the big armchair. Niki was sitting in Blair's lap. Her dress was torn. And she looked…

"My friend Laura set me up on a blind date with Harvey the Horror," she told her father, not budging out of Blair's lap. "He dragged me in here, after I refused to go to his apartment with him, and if Mr. Coleman hadn't been here to stop him, he'd have…" She stopped, swallowing hard.

"I'll have my lawyers contact his parents," Todd said icily.

"I offered to take her to the emergency room and call the sheriff," Blair sighed. "She wouldn't."

"My poor girl," Todd said, grimacing. "I'm sorry. I should have been home, but this damned budget crunch drew me into an emergency meeting at work."

"I know how that feels," Blair agreed. He looked down at the girl in his lap. "Better now?" he asked softly, and he smiled.

"Much better. Thank you for what you did," she added as she got reluctantly to her feet. It was nice, being held.

He chuckled. "I'm glad to know I haven't forgotten how to punch a man," he said.

"You hit him? Good for you!" Todd said shortly.

"I'm going on up," Niki said wearily. "I really am tired."

"You shouldn't have gone back to classes so soon," Todd said.

"I couldn't afford to miss finals," she protested. "I did the last one today. Just before Laura hooked me up with Harvey for a dinner celebration." She sighed. "Some celebration."

"When you graduate, Elise and I will take you out for champagne and lobster," Blair promised.

She forced a smile and tried to pretend that her heart wasn't breaking. "That won't be for another year or two, but thanks. That would be nice."

"Elise?"

"My fiancée," Blair said with a chuckle. "We're getting married in two months, in Paris. I'll make sure you two get an invitation."

"I doubt we can make it. But I'll send a present," Todd said, grinning. "Something tasteful, I promise."

"Good night," Niki said.

They echoed the words.

"Damned bounder," Blair muttered when he and Todd shared snifters of cognac. "I brought him to his knees and made him apologize. She was pretty shaken."

"I haven't been much of a father," the older man confessed. "She's been on her own a lot. Too much, probably."

"How old is she?" Blair asked.

"Nineteen. Almost twenty."

"I remember being nineteen." The other man chuckled. He put aside the brief hunger he'd felt while Niki was in his arms. She was years too young. And besides, he was getting married. "Back in the Dark Ages. She's a nice girl. You've done a good job raising her."

"Thanks. And thanks for saving her from the football hero."

He shrugged. "What are friends for?" he asked, with twinkling black eyes.

IT WAS A year later when Blair came back to the ranch to spend a few days. He and Todd had seen each other socially on occasion, but he hadn't come to the ranch since the night Niki had her bad encounter.

He and Elise were having problems. Big problems. He was broody and wouldn't talk to Todd. But he talked to Niki. It was the Christmas holidays, and the tree was glorious. Despite a few sick days, Niki had managed to do all the decorating herself. The tree was nine feet tall, decked out in red beaded strands and red velvet bows, with every sort of ornament imaginable, especially mechanical ones. There were trains that ran, dancers who danced and starships that made blast-off noises. It was glorious.

"I've never had a Christmas tree," Blair had to confess. "But I'm tempted, after seeing this one."

Niki laughed softly. "You should have Elise decorate one for you."

His face closed up. "She's not much for the holidays."

She cocked her head and looked up at him with warm, curious eyes. "Aren't you?"

He shrugged. "I like Christmas. It was my mother's favorite holiday. She was forever buying decorations. I still have them, in storage."

"You sound sad," she said.

"She died over a year ago. It's been lonely."

"No brothers or sisters?"

He shook his head. "My...father died ten years ago." Again, that odd hesitation. "It was just my mother and me."

"Now it's Elise and you," she said, lowering her eyes. "So you still have family."

"Yes."

His tone wasn't pleasant. She wondered why. He'd been so happy the last time they'd seen each other, talking about his upcoming marriage, bragging about his fiancée. And now he was somber, quiet.

"They say marriages sometimes start rocky and end happy," she blurted out.

He glanced down at her, his black eyes twinkling. "Do they, now?"

"Okay, I'm no authority on couples. You might remember my first and last attempt at that," she added with a little laugh.

"Don't tell me you haven't been out with anyone since," he said, surprised.

She grimaced. "Well, I was sort of afraid to try again," she confessed. "I wasn't sure you'd be around to rescue me when my date brought me home," she added with a smile. She couldn't confess that no man in the world could compare to Blair, in her mind or her heart.

He stuck his hands in his pockets. "How did the football hero fare?" he asked.

"He went back East rather suddenly after my father's attorney had a talk with his father," she said. "Strange, isn't it?"

"Very."

"If he tries it again, I hope the girl's father belongs to the mob and they find him floating down some river in an oil drum," she said firmly.

He laughed under his breath. "Vicious girl."

"You're right. That wasn't nice at all. Can you put this on for me? I can't quite reach." She indicated a spot high on the tree where she wanted one last red velvet bow.

"You can reach." He caught her small waist and lifted her easily within reach of the branch. She was so slight, it was like lifting a feather. The feel of her, the scent of her, was disturbing.

She laughed. "You're awfully strong," she remarked when he set her down again.

He moved away from her rather quickly. "It comes from wrestling with my board of directors," he replied drily.

She moved back and looked at the tree. "Will it do, you think?"

"It's lovely." He frowned. "Do you and your father have any other family?"

"Not really. He has an aunt, but she lives overseas. He didn't have brothers and sisters. My mother did, but her only brother died when I was in grammar school." She looked up at him. "Didn't Elise want to come with you?" she asked. "I'd love to meet her. I'm sure Daddy would, too." She was lying through her teeth. She never wanted to meet Elise, if she could help it.

"She's in Europe with some friends," he said.

"Oh." She didn't really know what else to say. She went back to her decorating.

His voice sounded raspy.

"Are you all right?" she asked.

He drew in a breath and grimaced. "My chest feels a bit tight. I think it's allergies. I get them this time of year."

"Me, too," Niki confessed. "But mine usually lead to pneumonia. I had it in my early teens. I guess it repeats. It's so unfair. I don't even smoke."

"Neither do I," Blair replied. "People around me do, however. I came here by way of Saudi Arabia. I was coughing before I got on the plane. It's probably just the allergy."

She nodded. But he sounded the way she did when she was coming down with a chest infection. Men never seemed to want to admit to illness. Perhaps they thought of it as a weakness.

BLAIR DIDN'T GET up for breakfast the next morning. Niki was worried, so she asked her father to look in on their guest. She wasn't at all sure if he wore pajamas, and she didn't want to walk in on him if he didn't.

Her father was back in a minute, looking concerned. "I think I'd better ask Doctor Fred to come out and check him. He's got a fever, and he's breathing rough. I think it's bronchitis. Maybe something more."

Niki didn't have to ask how he knew. He'd seen her through pneumonia too many times to mistake the symptoms.

"That might be a good idea," she agreed.

DR. FRED MORRIS came out and examined Blair, prescribing a heavy cough syrup along with an antibiotic.

"If he isn't better in three days, you call me," Fred told Niki's father.

"I will."

"And you stay out of his room until the antibiotic takes hold," Fred told Niki firmly. "You don't need to catch this again."

"It might not be contagious," she protested.

"But it might be. Humor me."

She managed a faint smile. "Okay, Dr. Fred."

"Good girl. I'll be in my office until late, if you need me," he told her father as they shook hands.

"Okay. Thanks."

"No problem."

NIKI INSISTED THAT her father call Elise and tell her that Blair was sick and needed her. Todd was reluctant, but he badgered Blair until he got the number. He called her.

Niki never knew what was said, but her father came out of his office cold-eyed and angry.

"Is she coming?" she asked.

Her father made a rough sound in his throat. "She said that's what doctors are for, getting people well. She doesn't do illness, and she doesn't want to be exposed to what he's got anyway. There's a ball tomorrow night in Vienna. A friend is taking her."

Niki felt sick to her stomach. What sort of woman had Blair married, for heaven's sake?

"It's not our business," her father reminded her.

"He was so kind to me, when Harvey attacked me," she recalled. "I thought he'd found a nice woman who'd want to have children and take care of him."

"Fat chance, that woman ever having a child," her father scoffed. "It might interfere with her social plans!"

She sighed. "Well, we'll take care of him."

"Mrs. Hanes and I will do that, until he's no longer contagious," her father emphasized. "I'm not risking you. Don't even ask."

She smiled and hugged him. "Okay, Daddy."

"That's my girl." He kissed the top of her head. "Poor guy. If it's this bad and they've only been married a year or so…" He let the rest of the sentence taper off.

"Things might get better," she said. But she didn't really believe it.

"They might. Let's have Mrs. Hanes fix us something to eat."

"I'll ask her."

EDNA HANES HAD been the Ashtons' housekeeper for over twelve years. She was as much a mother as a housekeeper to Niki, who adored her. When Niki had her sick spells, Mrs. Hanes was the one who nursed her, even when her father was home. He was a kind man, but he was out of place in a sick room. Not that he'd ever been unkind to his daughter. Quite the opposite.

"She's not coming, then?" Edna asked Niki about Blair's wife.

"No. There's a dance. In Vienna," she replied with a speaking glance.

Edna made a face. "He's a good man, Mr. Coleman," she said, pulling out pans to start supper. "I hate to see him married to someone like that. Wants his money, maybe, and not him, as well, but had to take the one to get the other."

"He said she was beautiful."

"Beautiful isn't as important as kind," Edna replied.

"That's what I think, too."

"Pity you aren't older, my girl," Edna said with a sigh.

"Why?" Niki asked, smiling.

Edna forgot sometimes how unworldly the younger woman was. "Nothing," she said quickly. "I was just talking to myself. How about mincing some onion for me, and I'll get this casserole going!"

"I'd be happy to help."

BLAIR WASN'T DOING WELL. Niki managed to get into his room the next day while her father was out talking to his foreman and Edna went shopping.

His chest was bare, although the covers were pulled up to his diaphragm. He had a magnificent chest, she thought with helpless longing, broad and covered with thick, curling hair. Muscular and manly.

He opened bloodshot, feverish eyes to look at her as she touched his forehead. "You shouldn't be in here," he said in a gentle tone. "I might be contagious."

"I'm not worried. Well, not about me. You should be better by now. When an antibiotic starts working, you can feel the difference."

He drew in a raspy breath and grimaced. "He gave me penicillin. It usually does the trick."

"Maybe not this time. I'm calling him right now."

She went out the door and phoned the doctor.

He was perturbed that she was trying to nurse Blair. "Listen, if you get it again, it might go into pleurisy," he argued.

"Now, Doctor Fred," she teased softly, "you know I've just finished a course of antibiotics. I'm not likely to pick anything up. Besides, there's nobody else to do this. Edna has her hands full just with meals, and Daddy's in the middle of a business deal. Not that he's a nursely sort of person," she laughed.

He sighed. "I see your point. Isn't Coleman married? Where's his wife? Did you call her?"

"There's a ball someplace in Europe where she has to go dancing," she said, the contempt in her voice unmistakable.

"I see." His tone was noncommittal. "Well, I'll phone in another prescription, something stronger, and a stronger cough syrup, as well. Try to get some fluids into him. And I don't want to have you wind up in my office…"

"I'll be very careful, Doctor," she promised, thanked him quickly and hung up.

LATER, SHE SENT one of the ranch's cowboys into town to get the new medicines, which she'd coaxed out of the poor, harried pharmacist, a friend from high school.

Blair grumbled when she came in with more medicine. "Niki, you're going to come down with this damned stuff," he complained.

"Just be quiet and take the nice tablet," she interrupted, handing him a glass of orange juice with crushed ice.

He frowned. "How did you know I like this?" he wondered.

She laughed. "I didn't. But I do now. Come on, Blair. Take the pill." She coaxed his mouth open and dropped the large tablet in.

"Bully," he muttered in his deep voice.

She only grinned.

He sipped the juice and swallowed. He winced.

"Oh, gosh, it's acidic. I'm sorry. I'll get you something less abrasive. Gatorade?" she suggested.

"I'd rather have the juice, honestly. I do wish I had—"

"Some cough drops?" she finished, digging in the prescription bag. "How fortunate that I asked Tex to bring some. And you can have the cough syrup, too."

She pulled a spoon from her pocket and poured out a dose of the powerful cough syrup the doctor had prescribed.

He took it, his dark eyes amused and affectionate

as they met hers. "Your father's going to raise hell if he catches you in here."

She made a face at him. "Edna asked me earlier if you'd like something light for dinner. An omelet? She makes them with fresh herbs."

He hesitated. "I'm not really hungry," he said, not wanting to hurt Edna's feelings. He hated eggs.

"I like eggs. We have fresh ones most of the year, when our hens aren't molting." She paused, her eyes narrow on his broad, handsome face. "You don't like eggs, but you don't want to trouble anyone," she blurted out. "How about chicken noodle soup instead?"

He laughed. "Damn. How did you figure that out?"

"I don't know," she said honestly.

"I'd really rather have the soup, if it's not too much trouble," he confessed. "I hate eggs."

She grinned. "I'll tell Edna."

He studied her soft face with narrow, thoughtful eyes. "When do you start classes again?"

"January," she replied. "I've already decided what I'll take."

"How do you get back and forth when the snows come?" he wondered.

She laughed. "Dad has one of the boys drive me back and forth. We have a cowboy who grew up in northern Montana. He can drive through anything."

"It might be more sensible to get you an apartment near campus," he said.

"I don't like being on my own," she said quietly.

He reached out a big hand and tangled her fingers in it. "All men aren't animals, Niki."

She shrugged. "I suppose not. I keep thinking what

would have happened if you hadn't been here that night."

His face tensed. So did he. She was so fragile. Like a hothouse orchid. It bothered him that she was in here risking her own health to nurse him while his wife was off having a wild time in Europe and couldn't be bothered to call him, let alone look in on him.

He'd never told Niki why he'd really married Elise. It had less to do with who she was than who she re-sembled. He'd just lost his mother, whom he'd adored, and Elise looked just like her. She'd come up to him at a party while he was grieving, and he'd fallen for her at first sight. Elise looked like his mother, but with-out her compassion and soul. Niki, oddly, reminded him more of her even than Elise, although Niki's col-oring was very different. Elise had the compassion of a hungry shark.

"You're very quiet," she commented.

He smiled gently. "You're a nice child," he said softly.

"I'm almost twenty-one," she protested.

"Honey, I'm almost thirty-seven," he said, his voice deep with tenderness.

"Really?" She was studying him with those wide, soft gray eyes that were silvery in the soft light of the bedside lamp. She smiled. "You don't look it. You don't even have gray hair. Don't tell me," she mused wickedly. "You have it colored, don't you?"

He burst out laughing and then coughed.

"Oh, gosh, I'm sorry," she said at once, wincing. "I shouldn't have opened my mouth!"

He caught his breath. "Niki, you're a breath of spring," he said. "No, I don't color it," he added. "My

father was from Greece. His hair was still black when
he died, and he was in his sixties." He didn't tell her
that his real father was from Greece. He didn't know
or care where his stepfather, the man who'd raised
him, came from.

"I remember my grandfather..."

"What in the blazes are you doing in here?" Todd
ground out when he saw Niki sitting on the bed beside Blair.

"Well, darn, caught in the act," Niki groaned.

CHAPTER TWO

"I DID TRY to chase her out," Blair told his friend rue-fully. "She wouldn't go."

"I called Doctor Fred," Niki told her dad. "Blair wasn't getting better. By the second day, I'm usually bouncing off the walls. Doctor Fred called in some new meds, and I had Tex go pick them up in town."

"You'll get sick again," her father said solemnly.

"I will not," Niki replied. "I'm just off antibiotics myself. And it isn't as if I'm kissing him or anything," she added indignantly. "I'm only pouring medicine into him. Well, that and orange juice," she added. She grinned at her father.

Blair, looking up at her, had a sudden stark urge to drag her down into his arms and see if her mouth was as soft and sweet as it looked. That shocked him into letting go of her hand. He must be losing his mind. Well, he was sick. If that was an excuse.

"I'm sorry to stick you with an invalid over the holidays," Blair began.

Todd cut him off, chuckling. "Niki's almost always sick at Christmas," he replied. "We're used to it."

He frowned. "At Christmas?"

"Yes," Todd said with a sigh. "Last year we made sure she wasn't around anyone who had a cold. She got pneumonia anyway."

Blair's dark eyes narrowed. "You have a live fir tree downstairs."

"Yes. We always do," Niki said, smiling. "I love live trees. It's in a ball, so that we can plant it after…"

"A live tree," Blair persisted. "Some people are allergic to them."

Niki and her father looked at each other in confusion.

"We had artificial trees until about three years ago," Todd said. "You wanted a live tree like your girlfriend had at her home."

Niki grimaced. "I started getting sick at Christmas three years ago. I never connected it."

"I'll have Tex come and take the live tree out," Todd said. "We'll get a pretty artificial one from the hardware store in town, and you can decorate it again."

Niki laughed. "I guess I'll have to." She glanced at Blair. "Leave it to you to see the obvious, when both of us miss it."

"Good for me," he mused.

"I'll go talk to Edna about that soup," Niki said. She put the bottle of cough syrup on the bedside table and picked up the spoon. "Want some more juice?" she added.

He shook his head. "I'm fine. Thanks, Niki."

She grinned and left the men to talk.

"I couldn't stop her," Blair said quietly. "She's formidable when she makes up her mind. I didn't encourage her to come in here."

"I know that." Todd dropped into the chair beside the bed. "Her mother, Martha, was just like that," he told the younger man. "She'd go out of her way to help sick people. Niki worries."

"Yes."

Todd's eyes narrowed. "I called Elise."

Blair's face closed up. "She can't bear illness."

Todd didn't say a word. But his expression was eloquent.

Blair just shrugged.

"She reminded you of Bernice, didn't she?" Todd asked, because he and Blair had been friends for a long time. He'd been the one they'd called when Blair was going out of his mind after the accident that left his mother first paralyzed, and soon after, dead.

Blair's face grew hard. "Yes."

Todd didn't know what else to say. "I'm sorry."

"So am I. But I'll make the best of it," he added. "No woman is going to be perfect."

THE NEXT DAY, Blair was feeling better. He sat up in bed to eat the food on the tray Edna brought him, and he was smiling when Niki peered in to check on him.

"I'm not going to die anytime soon," he assured her with a grin.

She grinned back. "Okay. Nice to see that you're better. I won't have to worry Doctor Fred again."

"Are you all right?" he asked.

She nodded. "I don't think I'm going to catch whatever you've got. I don't even have a sore throat."

"I'll keep my fingers crossed," he said. "I don't want to be responsible for putting you back in bed again."

"Thanks. But I'm good. Want some more orange juice?"

"Please."

"I'll be right back."

SHE SAT WITH Blair from time to time while he recovered. Once, she brought in her iPad and presented him with a graphic novel from the *Alien vs. Predator* series, one they both enjoyed.

"This is cool," he chuckled. "You can carry graphic novels around without having to lug a suitcase full of them."

"I thought so, too. I've got a Calvin and Hobbes collection on there, as well. It's one of my favorites."

He nodded. "Mine, too. Thanks, Niki."

"No problem." She got up. "I have to help Edna and the two temporary cooks with the breads. We have a huge spread for Christmas dinner."

"That's on Thursday," he pointed out.

"Yes, and today is Tuesday. We start baking breads today for the dressing, and cooking giblets for the gravy and making pies and cakes. It takes a while. We set the big fancy table in the dining room, and we have the cowboys and their wives come by, in shifts, to share it with us. That's a tradition that dates back to my grandfather's time here."

"It seems like a nice one," he commented.

She smiled. "They work very hard for us all year. It's little enough to do. We have presents for them, and their children, under the tree. It's usually a madhouse here on Christmas Day. I hope you'll be up to it," she added with a grin.

"I've never been involved in Christmas celebrations," he commented.

"Not even when you were a child?" she asked, surprised.

"My...father was an agnostic," he said, hating the

memory of his stepfather. "We didn't celebrate Christmas."

She hesitated. "Was your mother like that, too?"

His face was hard. "She did what he told her to do. It was a different generation, honey. He was old-school. God bless her, she put up with a lot from him. But she missed him when he died."

"I'm sure you did, too."

"In my way."

Eager to lighten the atmosphere, because his face was painfully somber, she said, "We have eggnog on Christmas Eve. I make it from scratch."

He made a face.

She grimaced. "I see. You don't like eggs, so you won't like eggnog, right?"

"Right. I'll just have my whiskey neat instead of polluting it with eggs," he said, tongue in cheek.

She sighed. "Are you always such a demanding dinner guest?" she despaired.

He chuckled. His black eyes twinkled at her. "I like pretty much anything except things with egg in them. Just don't forget the whiskey."

She sighed. He was very handsome. She loved the way his eyes crinkled when he smiled. She loved the strong, chiseled lines of his wide mouth, the high cheekbones, the thick black wavy hair around his leonine face. His chest was a work of art in itself. She had to force herself not to look at it too much. It was broad and muscular, under a thick mat of curling black hair that ran down to the waistband of his silk pajamas. Apparently, he didn't like jackets, because he never wore one with the bottoms. His arms were muscular, without being overly so. He would have delighted an artist.

"What are you thinking so hard about?" he wondered aloud.

"That an artist would love painting you," she blurted out, and then flushed then cleared her throat. "Sorry. I wasn't thinking."

He lifted both eyebrows. "Miss Ashton," he scoffed, "you aren't by any chance flirting with me, are you?"

"Mr. Coleman, the thought never crossed my mind!"

"Don't obsess over me," he said firmly, but his eyes were still twinkling. "I'm a married man."

She sighed. "Yes, thank goodness."

His eyebrows lifted in a silent question.

"Well, if you weren't married, I'd probably disgrace myself. Imagine, trying to ravish a sick man in bed because I'm obsessing over the way he looks without a shirt!"

He burst out laughing. "Go away, you bad girl."

Her own eyes twinkled. "I'll banish myself to the kitchen and make lovely things for you to eat."

"I'll look forward to that."

She smiled and left him.

He looked after her with conflicting emotions. He had a wife. Sadly, one who was a disappointment in almost every way; a cold woman who took and took without a thought of giving anything back. He'd married her thinking she was the image of his mother. Elise had seemed very different while they were dating. But the minute the ring was on her finger, she was off on her travels, spending more and more of his money, linking up with old friends whom she paid to travel with her. She was never home. In fact, she made a point of avoiding her husband as much as possible.

This really was the last straw, though, ignoring him when he was ill. It had cut him to the quick to have Todd and Niki see the emptiness of their relationship. He wasn't that sick. It was the principle of the thing. Well, he had some thinking to do when he left the Ashtons, didn't he?

CHRISTMAS DAY WAS BOISTEROUS. Niki and Edna and three other women took turns putting food on the table for an unending succession of people who worked for the Ashtons. Most were cowboys, but several were executives from Todd's oil corporation.

Niki liked them all, but she was especially fond of their children. She dreamed of having a child of her own one day. She spent hours in department stores, ogling the baby things.

She got down on the carpet with the children around the Christmas tree, oohing and aahing over the presents as they opened them. One little girl who was six years old got a Barbie doll with a holiday theme. The child cried when she opened the gaily wrapped package.

"Lisa, what's wrong, baby?" Niki cooed, drawing her into her lap.

"Daddy never buys me dolls, and I love dolls so much, Niki," she whispered. "Thank you!" She kissed Niki and held on tight.

"You should tell him that you like dolls, sweetheart," Niki said, hugging her close.

"I did. He bought me a big yellow truck."

"A what?"

"A truck, Niki," the child said with a very grown-up sigh. "He wanted a little boy. He said so."

Niki looked as indignant as she felt. But she forced herself to smile at the child. "I think little girls are very sweet," she said softly, brushing back the pretty dark hair.

"So do I," Blair said, kneeling down beside them. He smiled at the child, too. "I wish I had a little girl."

"You do? Honest?" Lisa asked, wide-eyed.

"Honest."

She got up from Niki's lap and hugged the big man. "You're nice."

He hugged her back. It surprised him, how much he wanted a child. He drew back, the smile still on his face. "So are you, precious."

"I'm going to show Mama my doll," she said. ".Thanks, Niki!"

"You're very welcome."

The little girl ran into the dining room, where the adults were finishing dessert.

"Poor thing," Niki said under her breath. "Even if he thinks it, he shouldn't have told her."

"She's a nice child," he said, getting to his feet. He looked down at Niki. "You're a nice child, yourself."

She made a face at him. "Thanks. I think."

His dark eyes held an expression she'd never seen before. They fell to her waistline and jerked back up. He turned away. "Any more coffee going? I'm sure mine's cold."

"Edna will have made a new pot by now," she said. His attitude disconcerted her. Why had he looked at her that way? Her eyes followed him as he strode back into the dining room, towering over most of the other men. The little girl smiled up at him, and he ruffled her hair.

He wanted children. She could see it. But apparently his wife didn't. What a waste, she thought. What a wife he had. She felt sorry for him. He'd said when he was engaged that he was crazy about Elise. Why didn't she care enough to come when he was ill?

"It's not my business," she told herself firmly.

It wasn't. But she felt very sorry for him just the same. If he'd married *her*, they'd have a houseful of children. She'd take care of him and love him and nurse him when he was sick… She pulled herself up short. He was a married man. She shouldn't be thinking such things.

She'd bought presents online for her father and Edna and Blair. She was careful to get Blair something impersonal. She didn't want his wife to think she was chasing him or anything. She picked out a tie tac, a *fleur de lis* made of solid gold. She couldn't understand why she'd chosen such a thing. He had Greek ancestry, as far as she knew, not French. It had been an impulse.

Her father had gone to answer the phone, a call from a business associate who wanted to wish him happy holidays, leaving Blair and Niki alone in the living room by the tree. She felt like an idiot for making the purchase.

Now Blair was opening the gift, and she ground her teeth together when he took the lid off the box and stared at it with wide, stunned eyes.

"I'm sorry," she began self-consciously. "The sales slip is in there," she added. "You can exchange it if…"

He looked at her. His expression stopped her tirade midsentence. "My mother was French," he said quietly. "How did you know?"

She faltered. She couldn't manage words. "I didn't. It was an impulse."

His big fingers smoothed over the tie tac. "In fact, I had one just like it that she bought me when I graduated from college." He swallowed. Hard. "Thanks."

"You're very welcome."

His dark eyes pinned hers. "Open yours now."

She fumbled with the small box he'd had hidden in his suitcase until this morning. She tore off the ribbons and opened it. Inside was the most beautiful brooch she'd ever seen. It was a golden orchid on an ivory background. The orchid was purple with a yellow center, made of delicate amethyst and topaz and gold.

She looked at him with wide, soft eyes. "It's so beautiful…"

He smiled with real affection. "It reminded me of you, when I saw it in the jewelry store," he lied, because he'd had it commissioned by a noted jewelry craftsman, just for her. "Little hothouse orchid," he teased.

She flushed. She took the delicate brooch out of its box and pinned it to the bodice of her black velvet dress. "I've never had anything so lovely," she faltered. "Thank you."

He stood up and drew her close to him. "Thank you, Niki." He bent and started to brush her mouth with his, but forced himself to deflect the kiss to her soft cheek. "Merry Christmas."

She felt the embrace to the nails of her toes. He smelled of expensive cologne and soap, and the feel of that powerful body so close to hers made her vibrate inside. She was flustered by the contact, and uneasy because he was married.

She laughed, moving away. "I'll wear it to church every Sunday," she promised without really looking at him.

He cleared his throat. The contact had affected him, too. "I'll wear mine to board meetings, for a lucky charm," he teased gently. "To ward off hostile take-overs."

"I promise it will do the job," she replied, and grinned.

Her father came back to the living room, and the sudden, tense silence was broken. Conversation turned to politics and the weather, and Niki joined in with forced cheerfulness.

But she couldn't stop touching the orchid brooch she'd pinned to her dress.

TIME PASSED. BLAIR'S VISITS to the ranch had slowed until they were almost nonexistent. Her father said Blair was trying to make his marriage work. Niki thought, privately, that it would take a miracle to turn fun-loving Elise into a housewife. But she forced herself not to dwell on it. Blair was married. Period. She did try to go out more with her friends, but never on a blind date again. The experience with Harvey had affected her more than she'd realized.

Graduation day came all too soon. Niki had enjoyed college. The daily commute was a grind, especially in the harsh winter, but thanks to Tex, who could drive in snow and ice, it was never a problem. Her grade point average was good enough for a magna cum laude award. And she'd already purchased her class ring months before.

"Is Blair coming with Elise, do you think?" Niki asked her father as they parted inside the auditorium just before the graduation ceremony.

He looked uncomfortable. "I don't think so," he said. "They've had some sort of blowup," he added. "Blair's butler, Jameson, called me last night. He said Blair locked himself in his study and won't come out."

"Oh, dear," Niki said, worried. "Can't he find a key and get in?"

"I'll suggest that," he promised. He forced a smile. "Go graduate. You've worked hard for this."

She smiled. "Yes, I have. Now all I have to do is decide if I want to go on to graduate school or get a job."

"A job?" he scoffed. "As if you'll ever need to work."

"You're rich," she pointed out. "I'm not."

"You're rich, too," he argued. He bent and kissed her cheek, a little uncomfortably. He wasn't a demonstrative man. "I'm so proud of you, honey."

"Thanks, Daddy!"

"Don't forget to turn the tassel to the other side when the president hands you your diploma."

"I won't forget."

THE CEREMONY WAS LONG, and the speaker was tedious. By the time he finished, the audience was restless, and Niki just wanted it over with.

She was third in line to get her diploma. She thanked the dean, whipped her tassel to the other side as she walked offstage and grinned to herself, imagining her father's pleased expression.

It took a long time for all the graduates to get through the line, but at last it was over, and Niki was outside with her father, congratulating classmates and working her way to the parking lot.

She noted, when they were inside the car, that her father was frowning.

"I turned my tassel," she reminded him.

He sighed. "Sorry, honey. I was thinking about Blair."

Her heart jumped. "Did you call Jameson?"

"Yes. He finally admitted that Blair hasn't been sober for three days. Apparently, the divorce is final, and Blair found out some unsavory things about his wife."

"Oh, dear." She tried not to feel pleasure that Blair was free. He'd said often enough that he thought of Niki as a child. "What sort of things?"

"I can't tell you, honey. It's very private stuff."

She drew in a long breath. "We should go get him and bring him to the ranch," she said firmly. "He shouldn't be on his own in that sort of mood."

He smiled softly. "You know, I was just thinking the same thing. Call Dave and have them get the Learjet over here. You can come with me if you like."

"Thanks."

He shrugged. "I might need the help," he mused. "Blair gets a little dangerous when he drinks, but he'd never hit a woman," he added.

She nodded. "Okay."

BLAIR DIDN'T RESPOND to her father's voice asking him to open the door. Muffled curses came through the wood, along with sounds of a big body bumping furniture.

"Let me try," Niki said softly. She rapped on the door. "Blair?" she called.

There was silence, followed by the sound of footsteps coming closer. "Niki?" came a deep, slurred voice.

"Yes, it's me."

He unlocked the door and opened it. He looked terrible. His face was flushed from too much alcohol. His black, wavy hair was ruffled. His blue shirt, unbuttoned and untucked, looked as if he'd slept in it. So did his black pants. He was a little unsteady on his feet. His eyes roved over Niki's face with warm affection.

She reached out and caught his big hand in both of hers. "You're coming home with us," she said gently. "Come on, now."

"Okay," he said, without a single protest.

Jameson, standing to one side, out of sight, sighed with relief. He grinned at her father.

Blair drew in a long breath. "I'm pretty drunk."

"That's okay," Niki said, still holding tight to his hand. "We won't let you drive."

He burst out laughing. "Damned little brat," he muttered.

She grinned at him.

"You dressed up to come visit me?" he asked, looking from her to her father.

"It was my graduation today," Niki said.

Blair grimaced. "Damn! I meant to come. I really

did. I even got you a present." He patted his pockets. "Oh, hell, it's in my desk. Just a minute."

He managed to stagger over to the desk without falling. He dredged out a small wrapped gift. "But you can't open it until I'm sober," he said, putting it in her hands.

"Oh. Well, okay," she said. She cocked her head. "Are you planning to have to run me down when I open it, then?"

His eyes twinkled. "Who knows?"

"We'd better go before he changes his mind," her father said blithely.

"I won't," Blair promised. "There's too damned much available liquor here. You only keep cognac and Scotch whiskey," he reminded his friend.

"I've had Edna hide the bottles, though," her father assured him.

"I've had enough anyway."

"Yes, you have. Come on," Niki said, grabbing Blair's big hand in hers.

He followed her like a lamb, not even complaining at her assertiveness. He didn't notice that Todd and Jameson were both smiling with pure amusement.

WHEN THEY GOT back to Catelow, and the Ashton ranch, Niki led Blair up to the guest room and set him down on the big bed.

"Sleep," she said, "is the best thing for you."

He drew in a ragged breath. "I haven't slept for days," he confessed. "I'm so tired, Niki."

She smoothed back his thick, cool black hair. "You'll get past this," she said with a wisdom far beyond her years. "It only needs time. It's fresh, like a raw wound. You have to heal until it stops hurting so much."

He was enjoying her soft hand in his hair. Too much. He let out a long sigh. "Some days I feel my age."

"You think you're old?" she chided. "We've got a cowhand, Mike, who just turned seventy. Know what he did yesterday? He learned to ride a bicycle."

His eyebrows arched. "Are you making a point?"

"Yes. Age is only in the mind."

He smiled sardonically. "My mind is old, too."

"I'm sorry you couldn't have had children," she lied, and felt guilty that she was glad about it. "Sometimes they make a marriage work."

"Sometimes they end it," he retorted.

"Fifty-fifty chance."

"Elise would never have risked her figure to have a child," he said coldly. "She even said so." He grimaced. "We had a hell of a fight after the Christmas I spent here. It disgusted me that she'd go to some party with her friends and not even bother to call to see how I was. She actually said to me the money was nice. It was a pity I came with it."

"I'm so sorry," she said with genuine sympathy. "I can't imagine the sort of woman who'd marry a man for what he had. I couldn't do that, even if I was dirt poor."

He looked up into soft, pretty gray eyes. "No," he agreed. "You're the sort who'd get down in the mud with your husband and do anything you had to do to help him. Rare, Niki. Like that hothouse orchid pin I gave you for Christmas."

She smiled. "I wear it all the time. It's so beautiful."

"Like you."

She made a face. "I'm not beautiful."

"What's inside you is," he replied, and he wasn't kidding.

She flushed a little. "Thanks."

He drew in a breath and shuddered. "Oh, God…" He shot out of the bed, heading toward the bathroom. He barely made it to the toilet in time. He lost his breakfast and about a fifth of bourbon.

When he finished, his stomach hurt. And there was Niki, with a wet washcloth. She bathed his face, helped him to the sink to wash out his mouth then helped him back to bed.

He couldn't help remembering his mother, his sweet French mother, who'd sacrificed so much for him, who'd cared for him, loved him. It hurt him to remember her. He'd thought Elise resembled her. But it was this young woman, this angel, who was like her.

"Thanks," he managed to croak out.

"You'll be all right," she said. "But just in case, I'm going downstairs right now to hide all the liquor."

There was a lilt in her voice. He lifted the wet cloth he'd put over his eyes and peered up through a growing massive headache. She was smiling. It was like the sun coming out.

"Better hide it good," he teased.

She grinned. "Can I get you anything before I leave?"

"No, honey. I'll be fine."

Honey. Her whole body rippled as he said the word. She tried to hide her reaction to it, but she didn't have the experience for such subterfuge. He saw it, and worried. He couldn't afford to let her get too attached to him. He was too old for her. Nothing would change that.

She got up, moving toward the door.

"Niki," he called softly.

She turned.

"Thanks," he said huskily.

She only smiled, before she went out and closed the door behind her.

"CAN WE HIDE the rest of the liquor?" she asked her father with a grin.

He chuckled. "He'll leave it alone now. I imagine his head is two sizes too big, and he's sick as a dog."

"He certainly is," she agreed. Her face hardened. "That horrible woman! If she wanted money, why didn't she just get a job and make her own living?"

Todd looked at her with pride and affection. "That's you, Niki. Elise is cut from a different sort of cloth. She wanted to have a life in the fast lane. She charmed Blair into thinking she wanted him." He shook his head. "I think Christmas was the last straw. He was in bad shape, and she didn't give a damn and made it obvious. She'll fight him in court for alimony, of course," he added harshly. "To the death, I imagine."

"I imagine it'll only last until she marries again," she said. "That might not be long."

He gave her an odd look. "I seriously doubt she'll ever remarry."

"Life goes on," she said.

"Inevitably." He kissed her on the forehead. "Happy graduation day, sweetheart," he said softly. "I'm very proud of you. Sorry it ended in such misery."

"I'm glad we brought Blair here," she said. "God knows what he might have done, left alone with too much liquor." She shivered inside. He must have loved Elise greatly. She said the last aloud to her father.

"He was infatuated with her, certainly. He's not a playboy. He never was."

"You've known him a long time, haven't you?"

He nodded. "He's a good man. Best friend I've ever had."

"He's been my friend, too," she pointed out, smiling. "I don't know what I'd have done if he hadn't been here that night Harvey brought me home after our date." She drew in a breath. "I'm still afraid to try dating again, you know."

"Sweetheart, you can't carry it around like a burden for the rest of your life," he pointed out. "You'll never be happy without a husband and children. You know that."

She wrapped her arms around herself. "I'm not in good health," she said slowly. "It...puts men off."

"It won't matter to any man who loves you."

"You think so?" She had her doubts, but she smiled. "I'm going to help Edna in the kitchen."

"Okay, Tidbit. I think I'll watch the news."

"Will you check on Blair, on your way to bed? Just in case?" she added.

He smiled. "Of course."

She wanted to do that herself. But that look Blair had given her hadn't been one of encouragement. She found him attractive, and she couldn't manage to hide it. She knew it was going to cause problems.

CHAPTER THREE

BLAIR WAS BARELY able to get out of bed the next day. His head hammered, and he was wobbly on his feet.

"Serves me right, I guess," he said when Niki brought him hash browns and bacon in bed.

"Don't say that," she chided softly. "You were entitled. I'm sorry life is so hard for you right now. But it will get better. Really, it will."

He looked up at her quietly. "You're an optimist, Niki. I'm not. I see things from a different perspective. So will you, when you're older," he added in a faintly bitter tone.

"For heaven's sake, I'm going on twenty-two," she burst out. "I just graduated from college!"

"And there's a big world out there, just waiting for you," he said. "New people, new places. New men," he added deliberately.

She wrapped her arms around her chest. "No."

He scowled, pausing with hash browns on his fork. "What do you mean, no?" he asked.

She bit her lower lip. "How do I know what men are going to be like when I'm alone with them? I know I haven't dated much, but that was one heck of a wake-up call, you know. If you hadn't been there…" Her eyes were tormented, and she shook her head.

"Come here."

She sat down beside him on the bed.

He took her hand in his and held it. "You have to know, very few men ever resort to force. He'd been drinking pretty heavily."

"I know. I tried to get him to stop. He said I was backward." She sighed. "I guess I am. I don't keep step with people in the modern world. I live in the country, I like wildflowers and little children, I don't drink or smoke or do drugs…" She made a face. "It's just a pity I wasn't born a hundred years ago. I'd have been right at home."

"There are other people like you in the world," he said softly. "You'll find them. You have to take chances, Niki. You have to get out in the world to cope with it. You're hiding here, honey. You're running away from life. It's cowardly. That's not like you."

Her face flamed. She got up and moved away from him, like a child burned by contact with fire. How could she tell him that she was in love with him, that she wasn't hiding from life? She was waiting, hoping, praying that one day…

His heart sank when he saw her face. He'd been too harsh. "Niki, I'm sorry."

She swallowed, hard. He was like an adult with a small child, and it hurt to be thought of that way. She stood up from the bed. "I have to help Edna clear up in the kitchen."

She was out the door before he could curse himself for bringing that look into her soft face. He felt guilty for the rest of the day, more so when she didn't come near his room again.

She kept to herself for the rest of the day. She was polite to Blair at dinner, but he saw right through her.

"You're very quiet tonight, Niki," her father said, frowning. "Everything all right?"

She toyed with her food. "Of course. I'm just not very hungry, that's all." She added a smile so that her father wouldn't get suspicious.

Blair sipped black coffee. "I thought I might drive over to Yellowstone tomorrow and see the sights. Want to come, Niki?" he added without looking at her.

She felt her heart trying to climb out of her throat. The invitation was unexpected.

"Go with him," her father said firmly. "You need to get out of the house for a while. It will do you good. Just be sure to take your inhaler with you," he added wryly. "Everything's just starting to bloom. You don't want another chest infection."

"Worrywart," she chided.

"I'll take care of her," Blair said quietly.

"I know that." Her father finished his coffee. "Got a minute?" he asked Blair. "I want to talk to you about that new drilling site I'm going to lease."

"Sure." Blair got up and followed him into the study.

Niki helped Edna clear away the dishes.

"You can hide it from your father, but not from me, young lady," Edna chided when they were putting dishes into the dishwasher. "What's wrong?"

She moved one shoulder a little. "Blair says I'm hiding from life. From men." She was, but she couldn't tell Edna why.

"He's right," was the unexpected reply. "You're letting that one bad date tie you up like a knot. Honey, not all men are going to try to force you. It was an unfortunate thing, what happened."

"I couldn't have stopped him," Niki recalled with disgust. "If Blair hadn't been here…"

"I know." Edna stopped and hugged her, smoothing her long, soft hair. "But he was. You can't go through life looking behind you. The future is bright and sweet, my darling. You have to look ahead."

Niki sighed and smiled against the older woman's shoulder. "Dad and I are so lucky to have you," she said. "I don't know how either of us would have coped. Especially Dad. He loved my mother so much."

Edna drew in a long breath. "Yes. He was crazy about her." She smiled sadly. "I loved my husband that way. When he died, I thought my life was over. Then Mr. Ashton offered me a job, and you were in grammar school…" She swallowed, hard. "You see, I was never able to have a child of my own. It was such a privilege, a blessing, to take care of you."

Niki drew back, her eyes soft and misty as she met those of the older woman. "You've been like a mother to me," she said. "God knows how I'd have turned out if it had just been me and Dad," she added with a laugh, lightening the atmosphere. "I guess I'd have learned to play poker and drink whiskey and get in fights with the cowboys."

Edna chuckled as she let Niki go. "He did a lot of that. Got stinking drunk and stayed that way for a whole month after the funeral. Most of the cowboys learned to hide in the barn until he had enough and passed out. To give them credit, none of them resigned."

"He's calmed down a bit," Niki said.

"Not a lot. He and your friend Blair are cut from

the same cloth." She winced. "Hurts me, to see poor Mr. Coleman like that. His wife was a piece of work."

"He really loved her," Niki said. "I remember when they were just engaged. When he talked about her, his face almost glowed, like his eyes." She glowered as she finished rinsing a plate to go in the dishwasher and handed it to Edna. "Imagine a woman who thought going to some stupid party was more important than taking care of her sick husband."

"She had her priorities," Edna said curtly. "Money and other men. What a shame. She's ruined him for marriage. He'll never take the chance again."

"He waited a long time to get married," Niki said thoughtfully.

"Yes. Your father said he took the loss of his mother particularly hard. He was vulnerable. That's probably how that she-cat got her claws into him. Playing up to him, pretending to be concerned, vamping him."

"What's vamping?" Niki asked curiously.

"Tempting him," Edna explained. "Most men are weak when a woman uses her body blatantly to tempt them. An experienced woman can make a plaything of a man, if he's vulnerable."

"It's hard to think of Blair Coleman being susceptible like that."

"He's a man, honey," Edna chuckled. "They're all susceptible."

"I don't know much about that."

"You'll never learn, staying in this house all the time," Edna continued. "You have to get out into the world and meet people. Meet men. Honey, you were made for a home and children."

Niki made a face. She couldn't tell Edna about her

hopeless passion for Blair, so she improvised. "I'm sick all the time. What sort of man wants a woman like that?"

"Your mother was sickly, too," Edna said. "But your father loved her madly. It made no difference to him, except that he spent a lot of time taking care of her." She smiled gently. "You love people for what's inside them. You live with the problems they have. That's what a good marriage is all about."

"I'm not sure I'll ever get married," Niki said. "I don't mix well with other people. Especially men."

"You get along fine with Mr. Coleman," Edna pointed out.

"Yes, but I'm not—what was that word you used, *vamping*? I'm not trying to vamp him."

"Just as well," Edna chuckled. "He'd put you down pretty quick if you tried. He thinks you're way too young for him."

"I know," Niki said, averting her eyes so that Edna didn't see the flicker of pain in them. "I guess I could get a job. There's an opening at the company Blair owns in Catelow, that mining office. They were advertising for a clerk."

"You have a degree in geology," Edna began. "I heard Mr. Coleman say they had an opening for a field geologist, too."

"Yes, they do," she replied. "Can you really see me going out into the field and working? I'd have to wear masks and carry all sorts of inhalers and medications, and I'd probably still get sick."

Edna grimaced. "I'm sorry. I wasn't thinking."

"It's okay. I'm glad you don't think of me as disabled. But in that sense, I am. My lungs won't let me do a lot of things. I even have trouble sitting in church next to women who think wearing a bottle of perfume is the way to attract attention."

"Never have understood that," Edna agreed. "I have a friend who has migraine headaches constantly. She never sees a connection between the thick perfume she wears and the headaches. She wears a layer of bath powder that's as bad as the perfume. Even started me sneezing in church last week," she laughed.

"I suppose we're all blind to our own faults," Niki had to agree.

"You going to Yellowstone with Mr. Coleman, then?"

Niki shrugged. "I guess I am." She didn't add that she was nervous of being alone with him. Not because she didn't want to be. But he was experienced, and she had no way to hide the effect he was starting to have on her. She'd have to try, though. It would just be too humiliating to have him know that he was the star in her sky.

THEY LEFT EARLY the next morning in the luxury car Blair had rented at the airport. He glanced at Niki to make sure she had her seat belt on. He smiled to himself at the picture she made in that soft yellow sundress with its spaghetti straps and long full skirt. She was wearing her beautiful blond hair down. It reached to her waist in back. She was very pretty. Very fragile. He frowned.

"Got your meds?" he asked suddenly.

She grimaced. "Yes."

"Sorry. I don't mean to sound like an overprotective parent."

"It's okay." She didn't mind if he treated her like a child. Of course she didn't. She worried her shoulder bag in her lap and looked out the window.

"I'm sorry that I said what I did yesterday, too," he added curtly. "But I meant it, Niki. You can't spend your life hiding from the world because of one stupid drunken date."

She drew in a long breath. "I guess not."

"A man who cares about you won't be rough," he added. "He won't try to force you."

"I know."

She didn't know. He wondered just how much experience with men she really had. She'd told him that she was still a virgin the night he saved her from the overbearing date. But that had been before she graduated, two years ago. He shouldn't be curious. It wasn't his business, but...

"Have you ever been intimate with a man?"

Her faint gasp told him everything. His teeth ground together. "Maybe that brooch I gave you was more accurate than I realized. You really are a little hothouse orchid, aren't you?" he asked through his teeth.

She bit her lower lip. She couldn't look at him. "I go to church," she began.

"A lot of people do. It doesn't mean that you have to live a life of total chastity," he said curtly.

She frowned. "I don't...feel things. With men, I mean."

His heart jumped. "What do you mean?"

She kept her eyes on the passing scenery. Far in the distance were the blue outlines of the Rockies. Closer, lodgepole pines grew in clumps across open pasture.

She saw a deer leaping through the underbrush, then disappear into the forest.

"Niki?"

"I haven't ever dated much," she confessed. "Boys in my high school teased me just because I went to church at all," she said. "One boy propositioned me right in the hallway, and he didn't lower his voice. When I got flustered and blushed, everybody laughed."

His heavy brows drew together. "That must have been awful."

"It got worse. He thought it was so funny that he posted it on his Facebook page." Her eyes closed. She didn't see the expression on Blair's face. "My dad found out. He called our attorneys. The post got removed. In fact, the boy had to close down his account. Dad has a really mean temper."

His hand tightened on the steering wheel. "Good for him."

"Anyway, that was the only really bad thing that happened. Until I went out with the football player in college."

"You dated other guys before him, didn't you?"

"Well, I went to the senior prom with my best friend and her boyfriend, in high school. I danced a lot, but I didn't have an actual date." She grimaced. "Word got around school, about the Facebook thing."

"Damn."

She leaned back against the seat. "Dad was very protective of me," she said. "There was an inspector for the cattleman's association who used to come out to the ranch, and a vet who did vaccinations for us. They both asked me out, but Dad got to them." She laughed. "He said the inspector was married, and the vet had a reputation that made him blush."

Blair didn't comment. Todd had always been protective of her. He would have felt the same way. She was fragile. Beautiful. Sweet. A world away from that vicious, cold woman he'd been married to for two years.

"It's funny," she said suddenly.

"What is?"

"How I can talk to you about things like this. I can't even talk to Edna about them."

"I'm not judgmental. And I'm old. Compared to you, at least, Tidbit," he added with a tender smile.

She sighed. "You're too gorgeous to be old, Blair, even if you think you are. Look, isn't that a buffalo?" she exclaimed, too occupied to notice the sudden flush on his high cheekbones at what she'd said. No woman in his life had ever talked to him like that.

He glanced out the window and smiled. "That's a buffalo, all right."

"I went with Dad to a buffalo ranch one time. There were warning signs everywhere," she added. "And the area they were kept in was double-fenced. The owner said that they were a lot more dangerous than people thought they were. He was always cautioning guests not to get too close to the fence."

"They can be dangerous," he agreed. "But any wild animal can be."

"And some people, too," she added.

"Yes. And some people."

It was a long drive to Old Faithful once they were inside the park. Periodically, cars stopped in the middle of the road and parked while their owners got out and ran to look at one of the park's residents. Once it was a moose, another time a small herd of bighorn sheep. Another time, it was an antelope.

Niki was laughing, the sun shining out of her, at the antics of a couple of small deer following their mother.

Blair looked down at her radiant face, and every part of his body clenched. She was unspeakably beautiful. That dress fit in all the right places. It was discreet, but the top of her breasts showed. Her skin was creamy. Her shoulders were lightly tanned, her arms softly rounded. He imagined how they might feel climbing around his neck.

"Aren't they cute?" a man about Niki's age enthused, joining her. His eyes were eating her up. "I used to work in a wildlife park, taking care of the abandoned babies. I love animals."

"So do I," Niki agreed, but she wasn't responsive. In fact, she moved back against Blair for security, tucking herself against one broad shoulder.

He melted inside. His big hand slid around her waist and pulled her back against him, closer than he meant to.

Niki fought to keep her heartbeat steady. It was sheer heaven to be so close to him.

"We're on a day trip to see the geyser," Blair told the young man. He was pleasant enough, but his eyes made threats.

"Are you? I'm here with my brother and his wife. We're camping for a few days. Well, have fun," he said, with one last longing glance and smile at Niki as he left.

Blair's hand rode up her side, to rest just under her

breast. He could feel her heart pounding. Her breath was wispy and quick.

"Be careful," he said in a strange, deep tone.

"Careful?" she asked, fighting the urge to lean back against him, to coax that big hand to move up just a little, just an inch, just a breath higher...

He felt her body arching helplessly. He felt her reacting to him. He was reacting to her, too, but he didn't dare let her feel how much.

"The cars are moving again. We have to go."

He let her go at once and guided her back to the car. He put her in, got in himself, and drove slowly behind the line of cars.

She was still trying to catch her breath. She was flushed and nervous.

"Sorry," she said in a thick tone. "He made me nervous."

"You're beautiful," he said through his teeth. "You can't expect men not to notice."

"I didn't flirt with him!"

"That isn't what I meant." He took a deep breath. "This is why you stay at home all the time, isn't it, Niki?" he added. "Men react to you. You don't like it."

She grimaced. "I feel...hunted." By every man except the one she wanted, she could have added, but she didn't dare.

It was an odd way to put it, but he understood. He glanced at her. She was fidgeting, uncomfortable.

"I wouldn't have let him near you," he said.

"I know that." She swallowed. "Thanks."

He was overly possessive of her. He'd wanted to punch the boy just for trying to flirt with her. She was years too young, but he wanted her. God, how he wanted her! "Hell," he burst out.

Her head turned. His face was rigid. "What's wrong?" she asked.

"Nothing. Not a damned thing. There's the turn-off, if we ever get to it," he added, noting a sign in the distance that pointed to Old Faithful. "Now all we have to do is hope that we're in time for the next eruption. They're spaced hours apart. We won't be able to wait for it."

She knew that. It was a very long drive. As it was, it would be dark before they got back home to the ranch.

He pulled into the parking lot and drove around to find a spot near the enormous hotel and gift shop.

"I'd still be driving around half an hour from now looking for a parking spot," she said with an attempt at humor. "You always hit a great spot."

"Luck," he said.

He got out, helped her out and locked the car. They walked to the spot where the geyser was located and read the sign. It gave approximate eruption times. The next one was in a half hour.

Niki looked up at him with a question in her soft eyes.

He got lost in them. His hand smoothed down her windblown hair. His face was impassive. "We can get coffee and look through the gift shop while we wait," he said.

She smiled. "Sounds great. Thanks."

"Why haven't you ever been here before?" he asked on the way inside.

"I have, actually. I took a course in anthropology

in college. Our class came here. But we didn't get to see the eruption."

"I minored in anthropology, back in the Dark Ages," he said with cold humor.

She stopped just inside the gift shop and looked up at him. Niki's slight figure was dwarfed by his height. The top of her head barely came to his nose. He was broad, like a wrestler. He moved with sensuous grace, and she remembered with some embarrassment how he looked without his shirt. She'd wanted so badly to touch him there, when he'd been sick and she'd nursed him.

He reached out and drew his thumb softly over her lips, parting them. Her reaction was arousing. He knew without asking that she was attracted to him. No woman could fake these signs, and they were blatant. His face hardened. He couldn't afford to indulge her hunger. She was very young, just feeling her power as a woman, and she was innocent. He couldn't take advantage of something she couldn't even help. Worse, those years between them were like a stone wall.

He dropped his hand as if her mouth had burned it and turned away. "Let's have coffee."

He didn't say another word until he was halfway through with his coffee.

"You're brooding again," she accused.

He looked up, both eyebrows arching.

She made a face. "We can go back now, if you want to. I don't want to make you wait for the eruption of Old Faithful. I imagine you've got things to do."

"I don't mind waiting," he replied. His narrowed eyes were on her face. "I've never seen it go off, either."

Something in the hardness of his face made her curious. "You've been here before, haven't you, Blair?" she asked softly.

His jaw hardened. "I spent my wedding night here."

She caught her breath and looked guilty. "Oh, darn, I'm sorry!"

"You didn't know." He looked away. "It was my idea to come, anyway, not yours."

That made it worse, somehow. He was reliving a failed marriage. Niki hadn't known about the connection to Yellowstone. Impulsively, she slid her small hand over his.

"You're always saying that I've let a bad experience lock me up in the past. Aren't you doing that, too, Blair?" she asked quietly.

His eyes were troubled. He felt the coldness of her hand. He turned it, locking it with his own. "I had great expectations."

"Did you?"

"She was beautiful, cultured, experienced," he said, smiling wryly. "She said she loved me. I married her and brought her here—" he looked around them "—to let her prove it."

She waited, just watching him, curious.

He laughed coldly. "She smiled. All the way through it. The whole time."

Her lips turned up. "She enjoyed it. Why should that make you unhappy?"

He stared at her. Gaped at her. She had no clue what he was talking about. He swallowed, and averted his eyes. "Drink your coffee. We can look around the gift shop until it's time to go."

He'd let go of her hand. She didn't understand

why he was so disturbed. Perhaps it was one of those male things, a broodiness that women didn't understand. She finished her coffee, waited while he paid the check then followed him out into the huge gift shop.

SHE FOUND A bracelet she loved, rawhide with a small round piece of deer's horn attached.

"They have silver and turquoise," he reminded her, puzzled by her delight with the simple, very inexpensive trinket.

"I like this. It's elemental, isn't it?" she added. "A piece of life itself."

She was a constant puzzle to him. Her father was well-to-do, but nowhere near as wealthy as Blair was. She could have picked the most expensive thing in the store, and he'd have bought it for her. She had to know that. But she was like a child in her desires; she liked the simple things. He remembered his wife and her greed, the way she searched out the most expensive diamonds she could find in a jewelry shop and begged for them when he was dating her. She'd found a very expensive set of turquoise jewelry here, in fact, and demanded that Blair buy it for her. He'd been so smitten that day, just after they were married, that he'd have bought her the entire inventory. Then he'd taken her to bed, and all his dreams had died…

"You're doing it again," she said when they were walking out toward Old Faithful.

"Doing what?" he asked abruptly.

"Brooding."

He stopped and turned toward her. "You don't really like expensive things, do you?" he asked bluntly.

She blinked. "Well, I'm partial to emeralds and pearls," she said. "But my jewelry box is full of them. And I really love this bracelet." She was puzzled.

"My wife picked up a squash blossom necklace, earrings and bracelet set here," he said, referring to the highly expensive pieces of Native American jewelry, silver and turquoise, that had been in the display case, probably from a Navajo artist even though it was a Wyoming shop. "And had me buy it for her."

She searched his black eyes quietly. "You loved her very much, didn't you?" she asked softly.

His face hardened. "Yes. At first."

"I'm so sorry that it didn't work out for you."

He was scowling. His hands, in his pockets, were clenched. He hated the memories, especially how it had been here, in this hotel, with his wife that first night. He hated the humiliation, the crushing blow to his pride, his manhood. He hated how it had locked him up inside himself.

"You have no idea, do you? About life?" he wondered aloud. His face hardened as he looked down at her. "You're still in patent leather shoes and frilly little dresses, gathering Easter eggs in the park."

Her eyes widened. "Excuse me?"

He turned away. "It's going off."

She followed him to the geyser, adrift. She didn't understand what he was saying, what it meant. He was sad. She wondered why.

Then she remembered what he'd said about his wife. Why did it make him angry that she'd smiled at him? For heaven's sake, didn't he want her to enjoy what happened between them on their wedding night? Men were so odd.

She put it to the back of her mind as the wind blew the spray from the geyser into her face, and she laughed like a delighted child.

CHAPTER FOUR

BLAIR LOOKED DOWN at Niki, at the glorious beauty of her young face, when the spray from Old Faithful hit her and she laughed. She held up her hands, enjoying the mist. She was so young. His heart clenched at the sight she made. Other men, even married ones, were staring at her, their expressions as revealing as Blair's. Niki was like spring personified.

The spray was making patterns on her bodice. Under it, her nipples were hard from the cool sting of the water. She laughed, glancing at two young men nearby who were staring at her so intently that Blair felt himself bristle. The way they were staring at her was disturbing. One of them started to move closer, smiling like a predator. She stopped what she was doing and glanced at Blair worriedly.

"Come here," Blair said in a hushed tone, and curved her into his side, holding her so that her soft breasts were pressed gently into the warmth of his broad chest. He gave the approaching man a glare so hot that he went back to his friend, and they quickly left the geyser.

"Why were they staring at me like that?" she asked under her breath.

He looked down into her wide, curious gray eyes.

Eyes like a September fog, he thought to himself. Soft and warm, full of dreams.

"Blair?" she prompted.

He bent his head so that his lips were right against one small ear. "Your body is reacting to the mist, but they thought it was them." He said it through his teeth. He didn't like other men staring at her. "Especially the one who started to talk to you."

"I don't understand," she whispered, shaken by the feel of his powerful body so close to her own, by the heavy thud of his heartbeat right against her.

He drew back. The black eyes that stared down into hers were narrow and glittery with some undefined emotion. "Don't you?" he asked, and he moved away from her just a breath, his eyes on her bodice.

She looked down at herself, but she didn't see anything that should disturb someone. Her wide eyes searched his.

She was so damned innocent that he wanted to throw back his head and scream. She didn't know. She had no idea what secrets her body was betraying.

He half turned toward the erupting geyser. "I'll explain it to you when we get back to the car. Watch the geyser."

His arm contracted. She pressed her cheek against his broad chest, aware of hard muscle and soft, cushy hair under his cotton shirt. She loved the way it felt, being close to him. The people around them vanished. The geyser was erupting, and she hardly noticed it. Blair's arm was strong and comforting, and just for these few minutes, there were only the two of them in the whole world. It was a moment out of time, out of space, when the impossible seemed possible. She

closed her eyes, savoring his breath against her forehead, drinking in the sexy, masculine scent of his
cologne, loving the warmth of him against the faint
chill of early spring air.

Blair was trying not to notice his own body's reaction to Niki. She was sixteen years his junior. They
were a generation apart. But her breasts were firm and
soft, and he wanted to touch them with his mouth. She
needed a younger man. Her heartbeat was so strong,
she was shaking, he could feel it. She was struggling
to breathe normally. He looked down at her pretty
bow-shaped mouth and wondered if she'd ever been
kissed by anyone who knew how.

"Gosh, that was great!" a young boy exclaimed
from nearby. "Can we stay until it goes off again,
Dad? Please?"

There was a deep chuckle. "Sorry, kiddo, we've
got hotel reservations in Billings, and it's almost an
eight-hour drive."

"Awww, Dad…"

The voices drifted away.

Blair moved back from Niki, averting his eyes.
"We'd better get moving, too," he added. "It's a long
drive home."

"It really was something to see," she said, not quite
meeting his eyes as she smiled. "I'll remember it all
my life." Truth be told, the geyser wasn't what she'd
remember, but she wasn't about to confess that to him.

HE PUT HER into the car and slid in beside her.

"You said you'd tell me what happened, at the geyser," she reminded him.

He stared at her quietly, his black eyes narrow and

somber. "Niki, what you know about men could be written on the head of a straight pin," he sighed. "You don't have a clue what was going on."

"You could just tell me," she prompted with a smile.

His big hand touseled her long, pale blond hair affectionately. "It will sound stark."

"So?" She searched his eyes. "You're my friend."

"I am." He drew in a long breath. "Honey, a woman's body gives away secrets. The spray hit your blouse, and the tips of your breasts went hard."

She flushed, but she didn't look away. "And...?"

"And cold water isn't the only thing that makes them that way. Desire has the same effect. You were getting some pretty intense attention from two men nearby, especially when you smiled at them. They thought it was a come-on," he added quietly.

"I...didn't know!" She averted her eyes and folded her arms across her breasts. "Oh, gosh!" She grimaced. "I went all the way through college, and I didn't know that, about my own body," she added miserably.

"I shouldn't have said anything," he said roughly. "Niki, I never meant to embarrass you. I'm sorry."

She shifted, her eyes out the window as she fought down raging self-consciousness. "They never talked about things like that in health class," she said. "Dad never had that sort of conversation with me, and Edna's just as repressed as he is. I didn't know!"

He pulled her into his arms and wrapped her up tight, burying his face in her throat, against her soft hair that smelled of wildflowers.

"You're so uninhibited," he groaned. "I love it.

Men want you, honey. It's a very natural reaction. You're very pretty."

She drew in a breath, so happy that she could have died of it. She sheltered in his arms, feeling safe, secure. Her face nestled in his warm throat. She had to fight the hunger to kiss it.

She breathed in the male scent of him, heady and delightful. "Does it always happen, when women feel desire?" she asked in a husky, shy tone.

"Yes."

"Does it happen to men, too?" she asked suddenly.

He chuckled. "Yes. But men swell in other places, as well."

Her face was flaming. "Blair! I'm not that dim!"

"Never mind," he mused. "We'll leave that discussion for another time. Right now," he said, moving her away, "we need to get home. It will be dark before we get there."

She buckled her seat belt. "Thanks, Blair," she said without looking at him.

"For what?"

"Explaining it to me." She shrugged. "I'm just grass-green."

"We all were, once, Niki. Don't sweat it."

She drew in a long breath, and her fingers went to the bracelet he bought her. "Thanks for my bracelet, too." She glanced at him. "I'm sorry the hotel brought back sad memories for you."

"I went into it thinking it would be the perfect marriage," he sighed.

She smiled. "I remember. You were engaged, and you were so happy. I hoped that it would be a good marriage, that you'd have kids and she'd take care of you…" She stopped when she saw his expression. "Sorry," she said quickly. "Will there be any more animals in the road to stop and look at, do you think?" she asked, changing the subject.

"Some, perhaps. But we're going back another way. We probably won't see many."

"I'll keep my eyes peeled for deer, just the same," she added. "I remember one of Daddy's friends ran into one on the highway. It totaled his car and almost killed him. The deer ran away, but he found it dead the next day in a ditch near the accident."

"They can cause serious injuries," he agreed.

"Do you hunt?" she asked.

He smiled. "I don't have the time," he said. "Business takes up most of my life." His face hardened. "I haven't had time for a lot of things."

"If I'm hiding at home, from men, aren't you hiding in your business from life?" she wondered aloud, then ground her teeth together at having made such a personal remark. "I'm sorry, Blair. I shouldn't have said that."

His hand had contracted on the steering wheel until the knuckles were white. But it slowly relaxed. "The one time I didn't hide, I had my heart torn out of me," he said coldly. "Never again."

She winced at the raw anguish in his tone. He'd loved his wife. It must have been pure hell to end up like this, to lose her. But it hurt to hear him say that, about Elise. Niki loved him, and he was never going to love her back.

She swallowed. She hated his wife for the way she'd treated him, but there was no accounting for human emotions. People couldn't help who they loved. She glanced at him. "Isn't there a chance that she might come back?" she asked quietly. She wanted him to be happy, even if it wasn't with her.

"I don't want to talk about it anymore." The way he said it went through her like an arrow. He'd never used that tone with her in all the time they'd known each other.

She started to apologize again and thought better of it. She turned her attention out the window and watched the landscape passing by until darkness fell over it.

IT WAS A long, silent ride home after that. He pulled up in the driveway of the Ashton ranch. She didn't wait for him to open her door. She climbed out and went ahead of him through the front door. The television was on in the living room. She had a glimpse of her father's blond hair before Blair caught her arm and pulled her right back out the door.

He closed it again and looked down at her in the dim light from the windows. "It's hard for me to talk about her," he said after a minute. "I'm not used to sharing things, personal things, with anyone. But that's no excuse for snapping at you the way I did. I'm sorry."

"It's okay," she managed. "I won't do it again." She forced a smile, moved away from him and went inside. She called to her father before she made an excuse and went up to her room. She managed to hold the tears back until then.

WHEN SHE GOT up the next morning, after a sleepless night, her face showed the ravages she couldn't camouflage even with makeup.

She went downstairs and hesitated at the dining room door. Nobody was up except Blair. He was sitting at the table, dressed in gray slacks and a yellow knit designer shirt, sipping black coffee.

He looked up when he heard her. His own face looked worn, as well.

"Good morning," he said.

"Good morning," she replied. "Is Edna up?"

He shook his head. "I made coffee."

"Thanks." She went into the kitchen and fetched a cup from the cupboard. She was pouring herself a cup of coffee when she felt the warmth of his big body behind her. His hands went to her waist and tightened. She felt his breath at the back of her head.

"You didn't sleep, did you?" he asked deeply.

She swallowed. "I said stupid things…"

He turned her around to face him. He didn't let go of her waist. "So did I," he said curtly. "Stupid, hurtful things. I can't leave like this. Not with you hating me."

"I don't…hate you," she managed.

He smoothed back her long blond hair, his black eyes intent on hers. "It's hard for me to share things," he began. "I keep it all inside. I hate my marriage. I hate remembering it."

"I know. It was my fault. I should never have brought it up."

He drew in a long breath. His eyes had dark circles beneath them. He looked so tired. She reached up impulsively and smoothed the frown between his eyes. "Don't brood so much," she said softly, her eyes adoring him. "Life is sweet. Every day is a miracle. You have to look ahead, not back, Blair."

One big thumb smoothed over her soft mouth. His eyes were oddly intent on it. "So they say," he replied quietly.

"I'm going to apply for that job at your mining company," she said with a pert grin. "There. How's that for getting out of the house?"

The frown came back. "Niki, that's a field geology position. The pollen…"

"No, not that one," she corrected. "The clerk's position. You know, filing and stuff in an office."

"You're overqualified for it."

She shrugged. "Hey, it's a job, right?" she teased.

He drew in a breath. "It isn't a clerk's position. It's a personal assistant position, in the vice president's office. He hasn't started interviewing for it. If you want the job, it's yours."

"That wouldn't be fair…"

He put his thumb squarely over her soft mouth. "I own the damned company. I can hire who I please."

His thumb was disturbing. Her heart kicked into overdrive. She laughed. "All right. But if the knives come out from other women who wanted the job…"

"Send them to me. I'll deal with it."

"Okay. Thanks."

His eyes narrowed. "You haven't worked before, have you?"

"I've worked for Dad," she countered. "Keeping the books at home, filing, doing computerized searches, things like that. I type very fast."

"That isn't what I mean," he said. "You haven't had

to hold down a nine-to-five job, five days a week."
He looked concerned. "It's a grind, even for someone in good health."

Her chin came up. "Teddy Roosevelt had terrible
asthma. He exercised and pushed himself and did
amazing things. I can follow his example."

He lifted an eyebrow and grinned. "Okay. But try
not to overdo it."

"You make me the same promise, then," she chided.

His black eyes softened. "You're the only confidante I have," he said after a minute. "I don't want
to lose you."

Her heart jumped, but she tried not to read too
much into the impulsive comment. She grinned back
at him. "I'm not robust, but I'm stubborn. I'm not
going anywhere."

"Okay, then."

"Have a safe trip home."

He nodded and searched her eyes. "We'll go back
to Yellowstone another time and see the mud flats and
the other geysers. Maybe up to Hardin, Montana, and
walk over the Little Bighorn battlefield."

"I'd like that."

"Maybe you're right," he conceded. "Maybe I do
hide behind my business."

She smiled. "If I can stop hiding, so can you."

He laughed mirthlessly. "Easier said than done."

"Drive safely."

"I'm flying," he pointed out.

"Well, fly safely."

"I will."

He hesitated and started to say something else,
when he heard footsteps. He let Niki go and opened

the door. "I hear breakfast making its way to the table," he mused.

She laughed. "So do I. Let's go grab it!"

IT WAS SEVERAL weeks before she saw Blair again. He was in the middle of a conference in Colorado and stopped by to talk to her father about a new drill site.

"You should stay overnight," Niki said, worried by the gaunt look of him.

He shrugged. "Don't have time, honey. I'm between meetings."

She frowned. "When's the next one?"

"Monday. In Los Angeles."

"It's Saturday," she reminded him. "You can get up early tomorrow and fly out, can't you? That gives you a whole day before the meeting."

He drew in a breath and glowered at her. "Worry-wart."

She grinned.

"How's the new job?" he asked.

She smiled. "It's nice," she said. "Mr. Jacobs is a wonderful boss. His old assistant still works for the company, just in another office, as an executive. She's been teaching me the job in her spare time. I like the people there, too."

"I handpicked Jacobs for the job, mainly because he knows how to keep his mouth shut," he said pointedly.

"I see," she teased. "That would include secrets like how I got my job."

He chuckled softly. "Something like that. Not that I think there would be gossip. Most of the executives know I'm best friends with your father. They'd figure I owed him a favor, if anything was said about it."

She just nodded.

He cocked his head. "Any nice, single men over there?" he asked with a twinkle in his black eyes.

"There's a guy from San Francisco," she said. "He sits with me at lunch in the cafeteria sometimes."

He didn't like that, but didn't dare let it show. "Young guy?" he asked pointedly.

She smiled. "Well, a few years older than me," she said.

"Yes, but in the same generation, I gather," he added. He stretched and groaned. "God, I hate flying!"

"No wonder, if you have to be all scrunched up in a seat for hours on end, even in an executive jet," she added.

"If I didn't own the jet already, I'd buy one," he said flatly. "I hate commercial flights. The last time I had to take one, the only seat available was in Economy." He made a face. "I sat next to a woman with a baby in one seat and a five-year-old in the seat beside her. He talked nonstop, and I mean nonstop, from Seattle to Fort Worth!"

She laughed out loud. "Oh, you poor man," she said.

"It almost put me off kids for good."

"Almost?" she probed.

He shrugged and smiled at her. "I love kids, usually. I hadn't slept in twenty-four hours, and I had a sinus infection at the time, as well."

"Flying didn't do that any good," she guessed.

"No good at all."

"So you're staying?" she prodded. "Edna made a chocolate pound cake," she said, enticing him.

"Damn!"

Her eyebrows arched over twinkling gray eyes.

"I can't leave when there's chocolate pound cake," he muttered. "Hit me right in my weak spot, why don't you?"

She just grinned.

BLAIR SAT AND watched television with Todd and Niki until late. There was a movie on pay-per-view that they all liked, a funny adventure one. She loved to hear Blair laugh. He did it with his whole heart. His eyes shimmered, that sexy broad mouth tugged up at both ends, his chest heaved. Niki wondered if he did everything that wholeheartedly. She loved to see him smile. Because he did it so rarely.

Her father got a phone call just then and went into his office, because it was from the other side of the world, he'd said.

Niki walked up with Blair to the guest room.

"You look well, despite the pollen," he mused.

She laughed. "I use my meds these days. I don't want to cost you or the company money by taking too many sick days."

He moved a step closer and tilted her chin up to his black eyes. "If you're sick, you stay home. I'll know if you don't. And I won't be happy about it."

"Now who's the worrywart?" she chided.

"You're fragile, young lady," he said, tracing a path down her cheek with one long finger. "I don't want you taking chances on my time."

That finger was erotic. It made her pulse dance. It

made her breathing come quick and jerky, as if she'd been running. She flushed and hid it in laughter.

"I won't take chances. I promise."

He drew in a long breath. His face was harder than she'd seen it in a long time.

"What's wrong?" she asked softly. "Can I help?"

His face contorted. "It's Elise," he said gruffly.

"Your ex-wife," she recalled.

He nodded. "She wants her alimony allowance raised again. She can't afford the right couture garments to suit her lifestyle, she says." He said it with utter disgust. He was recalling Niki's delight over an inexpensive bracelet, when Elise had never thanked him for a single thing he'd bought her.

Niki didn't know what to say. He looked…defeated.

He glanced down and her expression melted the hurt away. He drew in a breath and managed a smile for her. "I don't cope with it well," he said. "My attorneys handle the requests and forward the checks. I have no contact with her at all. That suits us both just fine."

She just stared up at him, her expression one almost of grief. "Why is money so important to some people?" she asked. "You really can't take it with you when you go. Why buy fancy clothes to impress other people who are wearing fancy clothes, trying to impress you?"

He chuckled softly. "What a way to phrase it," he mused.

"Fakers faking fakers," she said, pursing her lips. Her gray eyes twinkled. "It's like a con game with clothes."

He threw back his head and laughed.

"There. That's much better," she said, and she smiled.

He shook his head. "You chase the black clouds away, every time I see you. What a rare gift, Niki."

"Incurable optimism," she said with a grin. "It's contagious."

"It must be. I felt like ten miles of rough road when I walked in the door."

"Get a good night's sleep. Then you can have a day to get to California and a night to rest there before you jump back into negotiations again."

"Good idea."

"I hope you sleep well," she said.

"I always do here," he said. "Even the night sounds are soothing. No ambulances. No police sirens."

"You live in Billings," she recalled.

"Yes. It's close to the office."

She didn't say what she was thinking. It was too close. He spent far too much time on the job, too little time enjoying life.

"I have to fly to Cancun next week for trade talks." He hesitated. "Go with me."

Her lips parted on a sudden breath. "Me? Go with you?"

Her expression confused him. "Yes, with me."

She bit her lower lip. She wanted to go, desperately. But how would it look?

"Oh. I see." He pursed his lips. "Should I have added that your father is also involved with the trade talks, at the hotel we'll be staying in?"

It was like the sun coming out. "Really?"

"Really. I look out for you, Miss Ashton, old-fashioned ideals and all. I'm sure your father will approve," he added with a glimmer of amusement, "of the care I take of his daughter's reputation."

"Don't tease," she said softly, flushing.

"Honey, I like you just the way you are," he said softly. He bent and brushed his mouth over her soft cheek. "Sleep tight."

"You, too… Oh, gosh, Blair, I can't go. I have my job!" she exclaimed, suddenly remembering her commitments.

"Jacobs won't be in the office Friday and Monday, so we'll leave Thursday and come home Monday. You won't need to be at work when he isn't. Just to make sure, I'll have a talk with him."

She grimaced. "He'll think I asked you!"

"No, he won't." He drew her close for a few seconds, savoring the touch of her soft, young body. "Stop worrying." He bent again. His mouth hovered over her lips for a few aching seconds before it lifted to press a tender kiss on her forehead. He let her go abruptly and went into his room, closing the door between them.

Niki went down the hall to hers, almost floating. He wanted to take her to Cancun. But more exciting than that was the way he'd held her. He'd wanted to kiss her, and not chastely. She saw it in his face.

She was so excited that she didn't sleep a wink all night. When she got up, far too early, her eyes were bloodshot, and she was moving like a zombie.

Edna met her at the kitchen door. "Good Lord, what happened to you?" she exclaimed.

"Didn't sleep a wink," she confessed, laughing.

"Oh, dear. Are you all right?"

"Yes, yes, my lungs are fine," Niki corrected.

"Then why didn't you sleep?"

"I'll tell you all about it later," she said, because until her father agreed that she could go, she wasn't leaving the country with Blair, regardless of her feelings for him. A chaperone would be just the thing, to keep her from throwing herself at him.

THEY WERE HALFWAY through breakfast the next day before her father glanced at her with a raised eyebrow. "I hear we're going to Cancun next week," he mused.

She laughed and glanced at Blair, whose eyes were glimmering with amused pleasure.

"That's what I hear, too," she said.

"We both think you need a holiday," Blair told her. "The trade talks will only take a day or so. We'll have time left to explore. I could use a vacation myself, and I know Todd could. The Yucatán Peninsula is fascinating. There are Mayan ruins, and our hotel is right on the Gulf of Mexico. There's a long, beautiful beach."

"It sounds lovely!" she replied. Although his reason for asking her to go away with him dulled her spirits just a little. He made it sound as if he was giving a child a treat. She was sure he probably meant it that way, too. He was determined to keep space between them. Because of his marriage, she supposed, because he'd been in love and that vicious woman had savaged his heart. Now he didn't trust his emotions, and he wasn't going to let another woman close. Not even Niki.

But then, she reminded herself, Rome wasn't built in a day. So she smiled and listened to travel plans, as if she hadn't a care in the world.

CHAPTER FIVE

NIKI DIDN'T TELL anybody at work about the planned holiday in Cancun. Mr. Jacobs was going to be out of town on Friday and Monday, so Niki wasn't expected to work. She and her father and Blair would fly to Cancun Thursday and leave Monday. It would be a long trip, but Niki was excited and looking forward to it. Cancun, from what she'd read, was a mix of old and new. She'd looked it up on the internet and she was growing more excited by the day.

Her coworker, Dan Brady, mentioned an outing he was taking with a hiking club.

"We're going up to Jackson Hole and hiking some of the forest trails," he said. "You should come with us," he added. "Your father protects you too much, Nicolette. You'll never toughen up if you don't get out of that cocoon he's weaving around you."

She tried not to be offended. He didn't know anything about her family, really. "He's the only family I have," she said noncommittally.

"Of course, and he loves you. But parents can do damage when they don't let kids stand on their own feet. And your lungs would toughen up if you'd just use them more. Don't let allergies stop you from enjoying the outdoors! There are all sorts of new herbal mixtures to combat that. The right diet, the right herbs, and you'll be a new woman!"

She didn't want to hurt his feelings. He was a nice man. So she smiled and nodded, agreeing with everything he said. But inside she was grimacing. Asthma couldn't be cured by just a mixture of herbs and a rigid diet. She knew that even if he didn't. But sometimes you just couldn't argue with people in that sort of mind-set. So she didn't try.

"Want to come with us this weekend?" he prodded.

She smiled. He was nice-looking. Tall and tanned and blond, with pale blue eyes. He had a nice smile, too. "Not this weekend," she said. "Dad has plans, and I'm going with him. We're going to be out of town."

"There's another one next month. Come on. Say you'll go."

She laughed. "Okay. I'll go."

"That's the spirit! I'll print out an allergy-fighting diet plan for you and a list of herbal remedies to start taking to boost your immune system and protect you against allergens!"

She wanted to ask where he got his medical degree, but that wouldn't have helped. So she nodded and agreed.

He walked her back to Mr. Jacobs's office and paused at the door. "You really are pretty, you know," he said suddenly, his eyes twinkling. "Why don't you date anybody?"

"I've been… I just haven't been interested. I had a bad experience with a guy in college," she said.

"Oh, I see," he mused. "Broken heart, lost love, all that jazz?" he asked, getting the wrong idea. "Don't let it bug you. I've had bad relationships myself. You get over them and move on. So how about lunch to-morrow? I'll take you out for seafood."

"Seafood?"

He nodded. "They have a lovely crab salad at Buster's," he said, naming a local café. "Blue plate special. No dairy." He grinned. "What do you say?"

"That would be nice, Dan," she said.

"I'm glad you think so, Nicolette," he replied. "It's a beautiful name. Who were you named for?"

"It was my mother's middle name."

"Do you look like her?"

"Dad says I do. I don't remember her well. She died when I was very young," she added.

"Tough luck."

"Yes. I have Edna, though. She's our housekeeper."

"Can't you do your own housework?" he chided.

"Dad likes a certain routine in the house. We've had Edna since my mother died. She's like family," she said.

"Well, if you say so. I do all my own housework, wash clothes, even cook."

She just nodded.

"I'd better get back to work. See you later." He grinned and jogged off toward his own office.

She glared after him. He was a nice man until he opened his mouth. She wondered if any other woman had wanted to see him at the end of a pitchfork.

The thought amused her, and she had to hide a smile when she walked into Mr. Jacobs's office and sat down at her desk.

"Miss Ashton?" he called through the open door. "Can you take a letter, please?"

"Of course, sir," she said politely, and got her notepad.

He dictated at an even, slow pace so that she never had to ask him to stop or repeat a sentence. The terms, and their spelling, were familiar to her, since she'd helped her father with his paperwork for years now.

"That will need to go out today," he added when he finished.

"Yes, sir. I'll have it ready."

"You've been a surprise, Miss Ashton," he said unexpectedly.

She turned. "Sir?"

He shrugged. "Blair Coleman handed you to me without any explanation except that I was to give you the position. Forgive me, but I thought perhaps there was some personal reason for that."

She lifted her chin. "There was. My father asked him to."

He nodded, then smiled. "I figured that out on my own. You're quite young for a man his age," he added on a chuckle. "You've surprised and delighted me. You're efficient, courteous, and you can spell. I'm pleased with your job performance. Quite pleased."

"Thank you, sir."

"I understand that you're going to be away until Monday," he said.

"Well, yes, if you don't mind. My father has trade talks in Cancun and he wanted me to go with him…" She flushed. She was too insecure to mention Blair's name, as well.

"I like your father," he said unexpectedly. "He's an empire builder, like our own Mr. Coleman. Certainly, you don't have to be here if I'm not, but we'll both have to make up our time, you know. It might mean some overtime later on next week."

"I don't mind in the least," she assured him with a smile.

"You do know your geology," he said. "You have a degree in it, don't you?"

"Yes, sir."

"Wouldn't the field position we have open have been a better fit for you?" he asked, but kindly.

She sighed. "Yes, sir, it would, but I'm plagued by asthma. A position that required great amounts of time outdoors, especially in spring and autumn, would be a health risk."

"Health." He rolled his eyes. "My daughter, God bless her, has rheumatoid arthritis. She's only ten. Mr. Brady actually said that he could prescribe a helpful diet and list of herbal medicines that would cure her overnight. As if two generations of researchers haven't been knocking themselves out trying to find even a temporary relief for the pain and inflammation!"

"He said he could cure my asthma with a new diet and herbal remedies, too," she said. Sensing a kindred spirit, she smiled. "I just agreed with him and walked away."

"I should have done that," he chuckled. The smile faded. "The discussion got rather heated. I imagine asthma is difficult. But RA…" His face tautened. "Sometimes I hear her crying at night. She doesn't want me to know how bad it gets. Herbal medicine. Diet…"

"We could have someone rope Mr. Brady to a chair

and fill him full of fried chicken and hash brown potatoes," she suggested helpfully.

He threw back his head and roared. "I'll just smile
and walk away myself, next time." He smiled, and
meant it. "Thanks, Miss Ashton. You're a tonic."

"Thank you, Mr. Jacobs."

"Get that letter typed, then. I've got to make some
calls."

She nodded, smiled again and went out the door.
One new disaster averted, she thought to herself. At
least Mr. Jacobs didn't think Blair had designs on her.
That was probably true. Blair might like the way she
looked, might even have a purely physical attraction
to her. But his mind was still locked up in Elise and
their past together. He was too bitter to think roman-
tically about any woman right now, let alone Niki.

Well, Blair had said there might be gossip. She
hadn't anticipated how it might look, when he insisted
on letting her have this job. On the other hand, it hurt
her that Mr. Jacobs thought Blair was too old for her.

Who was she kidding? she thought miserably. Blair
thought she was too young for him. He'd said it many
times. Why should it surprise her when other people
agreed?

She gave a thought to Mr. Jacobs's poor daughter,
in so much pain. Someday there would be a cure for
that terrible disease, even one for asthma. Meanwhile,
she used her medicines and tried to mitigate the damage by avoiding triggers.

She sat down at her computer and started to work.

DAN WAS WAITING for her at the exit when she'd clocked
out and was on her way to her car in the parking lot.

"Feel like going jogging with me?" he asked with a grin. "I'm just going to do three or four miles, nothing heavy."

That was nothing heavy? She thought fast. "I promised Dad I'd get some letters out for him tonight. They're important."

"Oh. I see."

"Thanks anyway," she said, smiling.

"Okay. Your loss," he mused, sticking his hands in his pockets. "You really don't like physical activity, do you? That's going to be hard for you later in life."

"I'll see you tomorrow, Dan," she said pleasantly, with her social smile pasted on her face.

She walked away from him, got into her car and drove off.

BUT THE MINUTE Niki walked in the door, her father's eyebrows started climbing.

"Tidbit, what in the world is the matter with you?" he burst out.

She stared at him. "Excuse me?"

"I don't think I've ever seen you in a real temper before." He scowled. "Did somebody say something about how you got that job?"

Mr. Jacobs had, but she wasn't about to tell her father and have Blair heave him out a window. That would really mess things up. Besides, she liked Mr. Jacobs a lot better now that she knew more about him. He really was nice.

She put her purse down and took off the lightweight sweater she was wearing over her beige dress. "No. It was one of my coworkers, Dan Brady. He thinks I coddle myself too much. He was irritated because I turned down a four-mile jog with him tonight."

"Four miles?" he exclaimed.

"He said it was just a little light exercise." She drew in a breath. It was hard just to do that, with all the pollen in the air, and she hadn't even been outside long. Actually, though, getting the air back out was easier than getting it inside in the first place. "Honestly, the man is a nut!"

He shook his head. "It takes all kinds," he said.

"Yes, it does, and I find them like pennies on the sidewalk," she muttered.

"Want me to talk to him for you?" her father asked, his blond eyebrows meeting in the middle of his forehead.

"No, thanks," she said, having heard stories of her father's "talks" before from Edna.

He pursed his lips. "Come on. I probably wouldn't hit him. Hard."

She laughed softly. Then hugged him shyly. "You're the best dad in the world and I love you very much. But I can manage one annoying coworker. Honest."

"All right." He hesitated. "Better not tell Blair what he said," he added suddenly.

She glanced at him, eyebrows raised.

He shrugged. "He's pretty protective of you," he said.

She smiled. "He's my friend."

He cocked his head. He was still smiling. "Just friends?"

She nodded, hiding what she really felt. "Just friends, Dad."

There was an odd expression on his face. But he just shrugged again and turned away.

BLAIR HAD A small Learjet waiting for them at the airport in Billings, complete with pilot and copilot and a flight attendant.

"What's the use in having money if you don't ever use it?" Blair chuckled as Todd and Niki buckled up beside him. "I told you. I hate flying commercial."

"So do I," Todd commented drily, "but some of us don't have the option."

Blair just grinned. "Doesn't matter, if you have friends who do. And we're off!" he added as the jet taxied down the runway.

CANCUN WAS INCREDIBLE. Their hotel was one of many on a long strip of beach separated from the mainland of the peninsula. They ranged from fancy to luxurious. Blair apparently owned one of the more opulent ones, right on the beach, with a five-star restaurant downstairs. He'd booked a suite for himself, and one for Todd and Niki, so that they both had enormous bedrooms right off an elegant sitting room.

"This is too much, Blair," Todd protested.

"I own the hotel," Blair reminded him with a smile. "It's not an extravagance."

"All right, then. Thanks," Todd said, returning the smile.

"I have ulterior motives," Blair confessed. "The Mexican industry leaders we're seeing are staying here, as well. No travel time involved in the meetings."

Todd's eyebrows arched. "I see. And are they getting the full treatment? Lovely beach, excellent food, all the amenities?"

He grinned. "Of course. And," he added, tongue in cheek, "a group of world-class models are filming a commercial here. Eye candy." He glanced at Niki, who was glowering. "Pretend you didn't hear that," he instructed.

She grimaced.

"You're much prettier than any of them," Blair teased. But his eyes weren't teasing. They were intent on her face, very dark and quiet.

She flushed, to her embarrassment. "I think I'll go get unpacked," she said. "You men can talk about… swimsuits and stuff," she added with a wicked grin as she left.

SWIMSUITS, INDEED. SHE COULD just picture darkly handsome Blair surrounded by svelte models with gorgeous faces and bodies while poor Niki in her boring black one-piece bathing suit lounged on a towel nearby.

No. That wasn't going to happen.

There was a nice boutique downstairs. She went shopping. She did settle for a one-piece after all, but it was golden and stretchy with bare flesh displayed tastefully inside golden rings that outlined it at both sides of her waist and just above her breasts. It had a built-in bra so that she looked a lot more endowed than she really was.

She bought it, and a lacy cocktail dress, in black, that she could pair with strappy black high heels and her evening bag. She left the shop feeling extravagant, although it was her own money she'd spent, inherited from her late mother, who had been an heiress.

On the way out the door, she spotted Blair. She almost went to him, to show off her purchases, when he was joined by a woman. This one wasn't a model. She was only a few years younger than Blair, from the look of her, dark-haired and elegantly dressed with long hair in a complicated bun and a fancy manicure, her fingers trailing lovingly across his shirt as she spoke to him.

Blair wasn't protesting her touch. In fact, he was smiling.

They knew each other. Niki knew it without a word being spoken. And from the look of things, it hadn't been a platonic sort of thing. There was a familiarity in the way they stood, in the way they looked at each other. A former lover, probably, she thought miserably. Just when Niki had hoped against hope that she might do something, anything, to make Blair see her as older, more sophisticated, desirable...

She turned away, almost colliding with her father. "Watch where you're going, there, Tidbit! What have you been doing?"

"Just shopping," she said, trying to smile and failing miserably.

He looked over her head. "Well, I'll be. That's Janet Hardman over there with Blair."

"You know her?" she asked, trying not to sound interested.

"Yes. She and Blair were an item years ago, before he married that wild woman and got taken for the ride of his life. She's an executive with a film company. Apparently, they're involved with the commercial he was talking about. Lovely, isn't she?" he added, with a calculating look at Niki that she missed.

"Lovely." She hesitated. "He likes brunettes, doesn't he?" she added, recalling a photo of Blair and Elise that she'd seen in a tabloid just before they'd married.

"They remind him of his mother. He loved her very much. She had a raw deal with his stepfather. He was nobody's idea of the perfect husband, and he was brutal with Blair. His mother liked Janet, if I recall correctly."

The comment about Blair's stepfather went right over her head. She was miserable. Her heart was breaking. She would never be the same. She wished she'd stayed home. She wished…

"I'm going to the beach for a while," she said.

"Okay, but watch the flags on the beach before you go into the water out there. If they're red, don't even tip your toe in."

She frowned. "Flags?"

"They tell you the condition of the ocean," her father said patiently. "Red means danger. Riptides."

"Oh. Okay. There's a pool, anyway, if I want to swim," she added. She smiled. "I don't like sand in my bathing suit."

He chuckled. "Neither do I. Go on, Tidbit. Have fun. We'll see you for dinner later."

"Of course," she agreed. But she was thinking it likely that Blair wouldn't be joining them. Or, worse, that he might invite his old flame to eat with them. In which case, Niki was already planning on a vicious headache that would appear at the very best time.

"I won't be out long," she added, touching her forehead. "My head feels achy."

"You shouldn't lie in the sun," her father said, concerned.

"Just for a little while. I can't help it. I love beaches!"

"I know. Don't stay out too long, then."

"I won't." She tossed him a smile and walked away. Out of the corner of her eye, she saw Blair joining her father and looking after her with an odd expression. She ignored both of them and went on her way.

NIKI'S SWIMSUIT HAD an odd effect on her looks. With her platinum-blond hair long, waving around her shoulders and reaching almost to her waist in back, with designer sunglasses perched on her straight nose, it made her look older, sophisticated, very worldly. She loved it. The way it clung to her figure gave away secrets that didn't normally show. That she had long, tanned, lovely legs. That her breasts were high and firm. That she had a tiny waist and curvy hips. That she was almost perfect physically. Usually, she didn't like those things to show. She dressed conservatively. But today she felt reckless, as if she had nothing to lose. Blair had found a woman from his past, who was obviously still interested in him, and she was apparently staying at the hotel. Niki felt the sting of competition for the first time in her life.

She walked down to the beach without even a cover-up, picking up a towel from the steward at the beginning of the beach. She smiled at him, trying to ignore his very appreciative stare.

She picked a spot near an elderly couple, spread her towel and stretched out. The sun was very hot, but she loved the feel of it on her skin. She slid her sun-glasses over her nose and settled into the soft sand.

Overhead she heard birds. Seagulls, by the sound of them, dancing in the air as they fluttered by. She smiled to herself. Her father had mentioned that there was a day trip out to the Mayan ruins at Chichen Itza. She thought she might go tomorrow, even if her companions didn't have time to spare. It would be the trip of a lifetime.

She arched her back to ease the stiffness she'd felt from the long trip here, relaxed, then dozed lightly, trying not to remember the way Blair had looked at the dark-haired woman in the hotel. Why had she been born blonde? Why wasn't she older and more sophisticated? Why, why, why?

When she'd had dinner with Dan Brady at the seafood restaurant, he'd lectured her nonstop on her lifestyle, her lack of physical stamina and her diet, especially when she'd ordered the fried fish plate. She liked him, in a way. But he was a shadow of Blair. They both cared about her well-being, but she was definitely attracted to Blair much more than Dan.

Well, wishing wouldn't do her any good. Blair was determined to keep her at arm's length, and she couldn't change his mind. Somehow, she had to accept that and deal with it and move on. Somehow, in the middle of her misery, she fell asleep.

A TINY SPRAY of water hitting her face woke her. Blair was standing over her, glowering. He was wearing swimming trunks, white and clinging, and the rest of him was bare. He was absolutely glorious. Niki ached just looking at him. He was broad-shouldered, narrow-hipped, with legs like tree trunks, tanned and muscular. His chest had a wedge of curling black hair that ran down into the waistband of the trunks. His feet, like hers, were bare. He was staring at her. Not only staring. She'd rolled over to her side in her sleep, so that the deep cut of the suit showed her breasts to their very best advantage. His eyes were on them, and she felt his look all the way to her toes.

His eyes zoomed in pointedly to her breasts and she knew, now, what he was seeing. The tips went hard when she looked at him. She wanted him. And he knew it.

Self-conscious, she sat up and brought up her knees, hiding her breasts from view. She laughed, trying to make light of her embarrassment. "I wasn't going in," she said, anticipating the reason for the scowl. "Dad told me about red flags." She indicated them, flapping madly in the breeze, a few feet away. She felt the hunger in him in a way she never had before.

His trunks were wet, like his hair. Even the hair on his massive chest glittered with water. He was trying desperately to reason with his aching body. In that bathing suit, Niki was the most beautiful, seductive woman he'd ever seen. She was years too young for what he wanted from her. But he couldn't drag his eyes away. And very quickly, he had a physical reaction to her that he couldn't hide.

He bent over and picked her up in his arms, shifting her as he turned toward the ocean.

"Blair, there are red…flags," she faltered.

He looked down at her and brought her close, so

that she could feel the thick hair on his chest against the strip of bare skin that showed in her bathing suit.

His eyes were on her mouth as he walked, oblivious to the whole damned world. "Why did you have to put on that damned bathing suit?" he said harshly.

He waded into the water, until it was up to his rib cage.

Niki's heart was beating like mad. She could feel his heart against her, under the warm, hard muscles of his chest, a drumbeat that gained rhythm by the second.

His black eyes dropped to her mouth. He bent, very slowly, and touched his lips to hers in a soft whisper of contact.

Her nails bit into his shoulders. It was like flying. She'd dreamed of having him kiss her for so long, wanted it, wondered how it would feel. She didn't hear the cries of the seagulls flying overhead, the laughter of children way down the beach. She didn't hear the slap of the ocean against the sand. All she felt was the shaky beat of her own heart.

Blair's warm, firm lips parted against hers, teasing the upper lip away from the lower one, sliding over her soft mouth with pure seduction. At her back, his arm contracted, moving her breasts against him, feeling the tips harden as they pressed into the warm muscle of his chest.

"Blair," she moaned huskily.

He nipped her upper lip. "Open your mouth."

"What?" she whispered, dazed by the contact.

"Open it for me, baby," he whispered. "Let me inside."

The husky words shocked her into doing as he said.

She felt the slow, velvety stab of his tongue into the warm darkness, felt the seductive movement work on every cell in her body. She shivered with her first taste of real desire.

He felt that, felt her eager, shy response. He felt her fingers in the thick hair at his nape, biting in, caressing. Her body was trembling, like his legs.

He eased her down into the water and pulled her very slowly into the thrust of his body, letting her feel the power and heat of the arousal.

She gasped.

He lifted his head, just a little, just enough to see the shock in her slitted eyes. They glittered like silver in sunlight. "I want to peel you out of that bathing suit and lay you down on the beach," he whispered as his mouth teased hers. "I want to go into you, hard and slow and deep, and feel you curl into me, possess me, while I take you…"

His mouth crushed down onto hers, and she shuddered as his big hands went to her hips and ground them into his. He wasn't thinking anymore. He was living, breathing, only through the contact with Niki's exquisite body. He wanted her to the point of madness. It had never been this bad, not even with Elise, when he thought he'd die if he couldn't have her.

Niki tried to protest, even if weakly. But the warm, slow crush of his mouth on hers was like a drug. She couldn't get close enough to him. She couldn't get enough of him. She wrapped her arms around his neck and held on for dear life, tears stinging her eyes as the incredible pleasure, borne on excruciating tension, felt as if it might tear her apart. She wanted…something.

Something more. She ached all over. It was as deep as pain. She sobbed helplessly under his hard mouth.

His hands tightened on her hips as he drew back to look into her eyes. She was totally yielding, helpless. He could have her. He could take her back to the hotel, to his room, and have her on the king-size bed with sunlight streaming in through the blinds. He could give her paradise. She wanted him as badly as he wanted her.

And then, as the cold water began to soothe the heat in his tormented body, he felt the tremors running through her, saw the shock in her flushed face. This was Niki. He was treating her like a sophisticated woman, but he had to remember she was a virgin. She'd never had a man before.

That excited him even more. He closed his eyes on a shudder. He pulled her close and held her tightly, but without passion.

"Blair," she sobbed at his throat.

"Just hold on until it passes," he ground out. "Be still, Niki. Be still, honey."

She had some vague memory of warnings from older women about hungry men and how it hurt them. He might deny it, but he'd wanted her desperately. She'd felt it. She closed her eyes and let herself dream as they clung to each other in the cold, restless ocean. Surely he couldn't walk away from her after this and pretend nothing had happened.

But apparently, he could. He drew back a minute later, his face hard and quiet.

"We need to get out of here. We're too close to the current, and the riptides are dangerous," he said. He picked her up and carried her back to the beach, hating himself for what he'd done, for letting her tempt him.

"You'd been swimming already," she said breathlessly.

"I know what to do in a riptide. I've been in them before." He put her down on the sand.

She looked up at him with her heart in her eyes, waiting, hoping, self-conscious.

He didn't look down at her. "I have some phone calls to make back at the hotel. I'll see you later, Niki."

Then he just walked away. Just walked away, as if nothing had happened, as if he hadn't held her and kissed her and said…incredibly intimate things to her. He didn't look back. It was as if he'd never touched her.

She went back to her towel, spread it back out, put on her sunglasses and lay down, trying to stop her racing heart. She noticed that Blair had already taken his towel and sunglasses with him when he left. Now what? she wondered. For her, the world had shifted two degrees. But for Blair it obviously hadn't. Was it because Janet was here, and he was feeling a rekindling of their old romance?

Her heart fell. Was that why he'd kissed her so hungrily, because he'd been thinking of Janet, and Niki in her seductive bathing suit had tempted him? She had to fight tears. At least she was wearing sunglasses. The few people on the beach wouldn't see them.

BLAIR WAS DYING inside as he strode back into the hotel, away from the temptation on the beach. He'd been cold to her, when that was the last thing, the very last thing, he felt. Niki was in his heart. She had been for a very long time. But he wanted more for her than an old, used-up oilman who lived for his business. He couldn't afford to let her fixate on him.

He thought back over the past two years: Niki lying in his arms after her disastrous blind date; Niki taking care of him when he'd had bronchitis; Niki with the children at Christmas, laughing, her face as bright as the season itself; Niki, when he was drowning in anguish after the divorce, leading him out of a drunken stupor and taking him home with her and her father, to take care of him. There had never been a woman in his entire life who'd nurtured him so much, yet made him so hungry for her. But for her own good, he was going to have to smother those feelings. He couldn't give in to temptation and ruin her life. He wanted her desperately. But she was the one woman on earth he absolutely could not have. Ever!

A FEW MINUTES LATER, Niki got up from the sand, picked up her towel and walked slowly back to the hotel. All her dreams of love, of Blair, had seemed about to come true. But he didn't want to be close to her. He was angry, although he'd tried to hide it from her. Maybe he was disgusted with her, as well. She'd behaved like a wanton. She flushed with embarrassment.

He'd given her heaven, but all she had given him was an ache that she couldn't satisfy. He'd turned away from her as if the whole thing was her fault. Which, of course, it was. She'd bought a revealing bathing suit that showed too much of her body, and she'd tempted him. She'd known that he wanted her. He'd hidden it away, but something inside her had instinctively known, had understood his hunger for her. She'd worn the suit deliberately, to seduce him into acting on his feelings for her.

But nothing had gone the way she'd hoped it would. Her dreams of a shared future had gone up in smoke. He wanted her. He'd kissed her. He'd enjoyed it as much as she had. But it had only been physical, and she realized that with a start. He didn't want her in any permanent way. He felt that she was too young, had told her over and over again, and that opinion hadn't changed, even after the heated encounter in the ocean.

Tempting him had only dragged a physical response out of him, not an emotional one. He'd enjoyed her, as he'd enjoyed other women. As he'd probably enjoyed that woman, Janet, that he'd been talking to earlier in the hotel.

She recalled with pain the look that had always been on his face before when he spoke to her. His expression had been gentle, soft, happy. He was tender with Niki, but only when he was pretending that she was a child. After their physical interlude, he'd acted as if he found the whole thing distasteful.

From hope, she passed quickly to shame and embarrassment. There had been emotion growing between them, something deep and soft and gentle. She'd felt it. But with her stupid impatience, with her desire to tempt him out of his reticence, she'd ruined it.

She'd finally had what she'd wanted. She'd had him in her arms, kissing her, wanting her. But it was not to be. She remembered the old adage "Be careful what you wish for; you just might get it." After this afternoon's fiasco, it was only too true.

CHAPTER SIX

BLAIR HAD TOLD Todd that he wasn't having supper with them. Niki knew why, and it devastated her, but she couldn't let it show.

"Niki, you aren't eating enough to keep a bird alive," her father chided her at dinner. "This is excellent steak. Almost as good as what we raise ourselves. And you're just picking at it."

"Sorry," she said with a wan smile. "I really do have a headache. I shouldn't have stayed in the sun so long."

He laid down his fork and sipped red wine, giving her a long look. "He and Janet are friends. Just friends."

She looked up, feigning surprise. "Janet?"

He scowled. "I thought you were brooding because Blair wasn't eating with us."

"No, that's not it," she denied, then had to rush to find an explanation. "Mr. Jacobs had wondered why I got my job without going through the usual interview process." She held up a hand when he started to speak, angrily. "I told him that you'd asked Blair to have him hire me. He just wondered, that's all. He's a very nice man. Did you know that his daughter has rheumatoid arthritis?"

He shook his head. "No. No, I didn't."

"Dan was giving him all sorts of 'helpful' advice like he's given me. Herbal compounds and diets that can actually heal what's wrong with Mr. Jacobs's daughter and me, no doctors necessary," she added with a laugh.

"Good God!"

"He's nice, otherwise." She hesitated. "He wants me to go on a hike with his nature group. I said I would." She looked up. He was grimacing. "Dad, I'll take all my meds with me, and I'll be careful. Dan's right about one thing. I do pamper myself too much sometimes."

"No, you don't," he said, and the worry showed on his face. "Your lungs are fragile. Nothing is going to cure them. Not with current medical technology. Your friend Dan sounds like a health nut."

She laughed softly. "I suppose he does, at that. But he's kind, in his way. He thinks exercise will benefit me."

"I'm sure that you'd do just fine on a four-mile jog," he said, dripping sarcasm.

"Oh, Dad," she chided. "I won't let him drag me on one. I'd fold after the first five minutes. I know that, even if he doesn't."

"All right. But you make sure your cell's in your pocket. If you have a bad episode, we can follow GPS to find you and get you out of there."

"I will."

He drew in a long breath and sipped more wine. Things had seemed to be going so well between Blair and Niki. Now she was involved with this man who sounded like a complete lunatic, and Blair was cozying up to old flames. Sure, there was an age difference between Blair and Niki. But he knew, better than other people, how little it mattered when love was involved. He'd been almost eighteen years older than Niki's sweet mother, and they'd loved each other with an anguish of passion right up until her death, far too young, of lung cancer.

He shivered inside. Lung cancer. He'd seen her eaten up with it, undergoing surgery after surgery, chemo and radiation, and more chemo, for almost two years until she died. He'd stayed by her bedside every minute. When they'd diagnosed Niki with asthma, he'd been miserable. She had weak lungs, like her mother. He'd insisted on chest X-rays every other year, just to make sure her lungs were all right. Her next X-ray was a few weeks away. He held his breath when she had them, although her doctor found his obsession touching. He couldn't lose Niki. It would be like losing his sweet wife all over again. He couldn't bear that.

"You're very morose," Niki pointed out.

"Yes, sorry. It's almost roundup, on the ranch," he said, and looked at her with a suffering expression.

It was enough to bounce her out of her own misery. She grinned. "Let Tex take point this year," she said, referring to the cowboy who was their range manager, a man who was only ever known by an abbreviation of the state he came from.

"He's already taking point. But decisions have to be made that only I can make," he pointed out.

"I suppose so. All the more reason to enjoy this vacation while you can," she added, lifting her glass of sparkling water. "Cheers!"

He chuckled and touched his wineglass to hers.
"Cheers!" he replied, and drained it.

NIKI HAD LONG since gone to bed when Blair passed by
their suite. All the lights were out, so he didn't stop
to chat with her father. He was exhausted. Janet had
chatted with him for several hours about her film ca-
reer behind the cameras and her responsibilities and
her miserable, lonely life.

He'd smiled and pretended interest. Inside he was
agonizing over the way he'd treated Niki. He should
never have let himself be tempted. That damned bathing suit had undermined all his inward protests about
their differences.

But the worst thing had been the way he'd ignored
her afterward. How hurt she must have been, to have
him push her away without even a word about what
had happened, what he was feeling. He hadn't wanted
to. He'd been hurting, overwhelmed and in anguish
by his headlong response to her. He'd wanted to tell
her how exquisite their passion had felt to him, how
sweet and heady it was to love her like that, to feel
her first response to physical delight. It had been her
first real taste of intimacy, and he'd made it into a
shameful memory.

Her soft young body in that bathing suit would
have tempted a saint. He hadn't been able to resist her.
It was his lack of control that had made him angry, not
Niki's shy attempts to gain his interest. She'd given
him everything he asked for, and he'd turned away
from her with anger.

She hadn't even questioned his behavior. Apparently, she'd thought that she'd disappointed him, and

she'd gone quiet. No fuss, no argument. No woman in his life had ever been as gentle with him as Niki was. He was used to temperamental, fiery women who never even thanked him for gifts, who took his interest as their due. It had never bothered him before. But Niki was a new experience in many ways. He'd treated her shabbily. Now all he wanted was to make amends. But he didn't know how.

She was still too young for him. None of his arguments could change that. But he couldn't afford to backtrack, to let her think that he wanted more than a few minutes of passion with her. That he wanted… forever.

He clamped down hard on his hunger. He would find a way, a kinder way, to ease her out of his life.

With another woman, he'd have sent a diamond necklace, a fur, the keys to an exotic car. None of those were likely to please a woman who fell in love with a tiny strip of buckskin attached to a piece of deer antler. Her lack of avarice puzzled him. Losing her would just about destroy him. As he sat down on the sofa in his suite, he put his head in his hands and poured himself another whiskey. If he drank enough of it, he might get through the night.

THE NEXT MORNING, Niki went back down to the beach in her new bathing suit. She knew Blair wasn't going to come near her, but she did want to enjoy the surf and the sunshine and try to get over yesterday.

She had hardly slept the night before. She felt Blair's mouth on hers, his body hard and close, wanting her. She could hear his voice at her ear, husky with feeling, whispering things that made her blush.

She hadn't known what physical passion was. Now that she did, it caused an ache, a hunger that was almost painful. She wished that he'd never touched her, because he'd awakened her to a whole new world of pleasure, then dropped her like a hot horseshoe. She was certain that she'd never understand men as long as she lived.

When she got to the beach, understanding men was suddenly a real issue.

"Ooooh, baby, look at you!" a shabbily dressed young man catcalled, staring at her and walking around her as if she were on sale. "Why don't you come back to my room with me and we'll see if we can break the box springs?"

She just gaped at him. In her life, no man had ever made such crude remarks to her.

"I don't know you," she blurted out.

"Well, of course you don't, you've got too many clothes on! You look like one hot little piece of tail, honey," he chuckled. "Come on." He grabbed her hand.

She shook it off and backed away, the towel held in front of her like a shield.

His face contorted. His eyes were bloodred and he looked...something. Drunk, maybe. "Too good for the locals, huh?" he snarled. "What do you think you're doing, walking around like that?" He gestured toward her bathing suit. "No woman wears a bathing suit like that unless she's looking to get laid!"

Niki was shivering. Was that what Blair had thought, too? That she was offering herself up with no strings?

She didn't know what to do. She had no self-defense

training. There was nobody around that she could look to for help, although any of the hotel's employees would come running if she screamed. She was about to, when suddenly, a miracle happened.

"Oh, go away, you festering little fly," a harsh female voice said from behind her. A woman moved into view, in a one-piece bathing suit with a long, gauzy coverup over it. "Shoo! Go inflict yourself on someone else!"

The young man hesitated, as if he was shocked to be spoken to in such a manner.

Janet raised a hand toward a hotel steward and motioned him to the beach. She smiled at the worried young man. "How do you like jail, sweetie?" she purred. "I'm sure they've got a nice cell, but I'll bet you're already on parole, aren't you?"

"Damned woman!" The man took off running, going fast enough to almost overturn the steward on his way off the grounds.

"That man, he was bothering you, señorita?" he asked Janet.

"Not me. Her." Janet indicated her flushed companion. "Do you know who he is?"

"Yes, I know," the employee said coldly. "He comes here to sell drugs to the tourists. We know, and when we see him, we run him off. He has been most offensive to our female guests. I am very sorry. I will speak to the police."

"That would be a good idea," Janet said. "Thank you."

"Yes," Niki added. "Thanks very much." She was almost shivering with the upset. She turned to Janet as the hotel man left. "Thank you. I…I've never been spoken to like that by a man. I didn't know what to do."

"You're very young," Janet said gently, and she was thinking that this poor child had been sheltered overmuch by her father. Blair had said as much the night before. "You don't know much about the world, do you, honey?"

Niki grimaced. "I know a lot more this morning than I ever did before. You took a terrible chance," she added worriedly. "He might have hurt you."

She shrugged. "Tae Kwon Do. Brown belt." Her eyes twinkled. "If he'd touched me, he'd be on his back, unconscious. You might benefit from a self-defense class or two."

"I might. But…I'm not sure…it would help…" All of a sudden, Niki couldn't breathe. She looked in her small fanny pack for her inhaler, took it out and used it. Her breath came back, but very slowly.

"Asthma?" Janet asked worriedly.

Niki nodded. She waited a minute and used the inhaler again. "I'm on preventative meds, and I always carry my rescue inhaler." She smiled weakly. "I'm not in good health."

"I can see that." Janet had a very different picture of Niki than she got this morning. She wondered if Blair really knew much about her.

The medicine finally worked. Niki picked up her towel, which she'd dropped in the sand during the episode with the man.

"Don't go," Janet said. "Don't let that fungus spoil the day for you. Come lie down and talk to me. I don't know a soul at the hotel, except Blair." Her smile was full of sweet memory. Niki tried her best to hide the pain it gave her.

"My father's here for a business meeting," she said, without mentioning Blair. "Are you part of that, too?"

"Oh, no. I'm in film. Well, in filmmaking," she laughed. "I'm down here with my company making a commercial for a soft drink company. We've got five world-class models and an A-list actor doing it for us. I worry that the cameraman will forget to put film in the camera. He actually drools when the girls are lining up."

Niki laughed in spite of herself. "It must be a very good job."

"It is. I'd hoped to marry and have children, but Blair wasn't ready in those days. I never thought he'd marry at all. And then he found Elise." She ground her teeth together. "She should be hanged for what she did to him."

Niki knew more about that than Janet probably did. "He loved her," was all she said. "Or at least, that's what Dad said," she added, to make sure she wasn't telling Janet too much.

"He thought he did. She cured him of that illusion pretty quickly. You know that old saying 'what you see is what you get'? Well, that certainly wasn't the case. He had no idea what he was getting until it was too late. Now she holds him up for more money while she carouses around the world, mixing with the jet set. Her father was a plumber, and her mother cooked for a restaurant." She hesitated. "I guess I sound like a snob." She smiled at Niki. "I'm not. My dad was a cop. My mother worked in social services. I didn't move in the fast lane, either."

"How did you meet Blair?" Niki asked, trying to sound only mildly interested.

"I met his mother," she corrected, laughing, "in a Starbucks. We talked and she must have liked me, because she sent Blair down to the photography studio where I was working to have a portrait done. We dated for a few wonderful weeks."

"He didn't want to get married, you said."

"No," Janet replied wearily. "I ran out of ways to try to convince him. He was very stubborn. Business was all he lived for. That, and his mother, whom he loved dearly. He spent the rest of her life trying to make up to her what her husband did to Blair."

"His father, you mean?"

"Harrison wasn't his father," she said coldly. "His father died even before he was born. Harrison was rich and had oil wells. He fell in love with Blair's mother, who was pregnant, exquisitely beautiful and cultured, and moved in the same social circles as him. He charmed her into marriage. Then, when she had Blair, his true colors began to show. He hated having to raise another man's child, especially when he learned that he was sterile and couldn't have children of his own. He made Blair, and his mother, pay for that." She hesitated. "He punished Bernice by hitting Blair when she did something he didn't like. At least, until the day Blair grew big enough to turn the tables and use the belt on him. After that, things were quieter at home. They were better off when Harrison died while trying to show one of his workers the right way to set up a rig. Sadly, or not so sadly, he did it while dead drunk and oblivious to the fact that he didn't have the foggiest idea what he was doing."

"What a life he must have had," Niki said, wincing inside.

"Blair's never seen a good marriage, I guess," Janet said. "Even so, any man can be tricked into it by an unscrupulous woman. Every time I saw Blair and Elise together, she was wrapped around him like ivy, playing on his senses and pulling away when he tried to get her into bed." She shrugged. "I guess it finally worked. But she made him as miserable as his stepfather made his mother."

"She's still around, too, isn't she?" Niki asked absently.

"At every benefit he ever attends, trying to get him back," came the shocking reply. Niki's expression spoke for itself. "You didn't know?" Janet asked with an amused smile. "I guess not. But your father's his best friend. I expect he knows."

"I hope he has sense enough not to be taken in twice," Niki said heavily.

"Me, too. But then, I have some ideas about that," she added with a smile. "I thought you might invite me to have dinner tonight with you and your father, if you don't mind," she added coyly. "And if Blair just happens to show up, too…well, better me than Elise." She sighed and lay back on her towel, oblivious to Niki's pained expression. "At least she showed me one foolproof way to get him to the altar. This time, maybe I'll have better luck!"

NIKI DID INVITE Janet to dinner. Then she phoned the airport, got a seat on a commercial jet, packed her bags, left a note for her father and went home. She left the gold swimsuit in the trash can in her room. She knew that she'd never have the nerve, or the stomach, to wear it again.

TODD AND BLAIR came back to their rooms after a long day of discussions about drilling for oil in the Yucatán. It had been favorable, because Blair's reputation in the oil industry was well-known. He wasn't a polluter. Todd ran a business that supplied equipment to oil corporations, so he was in talks for the same reason. Mexico had its own oil interests, and Todd was hoping to branch out into a bigger market.

"That went well," Todd said with a weary smile. "Now maybe we can enjoy the rest of our vacation without business intervening."

"I hope so," Blair said. He was dreading seeing Niki. Neither of them was going to be able to hide their discomfort from her father, and that would lead to questions he didn't want to answer.

They stopped by Blair's suite when they reached their floor. They were sipping whiskey and discussing dinner venues when there was a knock at the door.

"That's probably Niki, looking for me," Todd said with a laugh. "The meetings did run late."

"Yes, they did." He steeled himself not to react when he opened the door.

But it wasn't Niki. It was Janet, in a slinky silver cocktail dress, looking very expensive and pretty.

"Am I late?" she asked.

"Late for what?" Blair asked.

"Dinner, of course. Niki invited me to eat with all of you," Janet said and smiled.

Blair's heart skipped a beat. "Where did you speak to her?"

"On the beach, this morning. There was a little unpleasantness," she added. "One of the local drug dealers made an obscene play for her on the beach. I made him leave her alone, and I called one of the hotel stewards to run him off. Poor thing," she added softly. "She was shocked. It brought on an asthma attack. Thank God she had her rescue inhaler on her."

"Who was it?" Blair asked, barely able to contain the utter fury he felt.

Janet saw the expression on his face, and all her hopes died. He was livid. In all their time together, he'd never been like that when Janet was badly treated by anyone, although he'd been supportive. This wasn't supportive. It was homicidal.

"The hotel steward knew him," she said uneasily. "He's a local drug dealer."

Blair jerked out his cell phone and started punching in numbers. His eyes were blazing like black coals.

"Thank you, for what you did for my daughter," Todd said with a smile. He was reeling from Blair's reaction to what had happened. It told him things Blair never would.

"I like her," Janet said. "She's very fragile, isn't she?" she added gently. "Like thin porcelain. Just as brittle, just as beautiful."

"Her mother was like that," Todd said, the pain of loss still in his eyes after so many years. "I lost her when Niki was very young."

"You never thought of remarrying?" Janet asked.

He shook his head, smiling softly. "Never. I have

memories that will last me until the day I die. And her name will be the last thing on my lips, even then."

Janet tamped down hard on her feelings. She couldn't imagine an emotion that deep, that lasting. Even with Blair, whom she'd loved, there had never been such intensity. She glanced at him covertly. He was giving somebody hell on the telephone, in perfect Spanish. He finished the call, hung up and made another.

"I almost feel sorry for the drug dealer," Janet said, tongue in cheek.

"So do I. Blair's like a train going down a mountain when he wants something badly enough. I should probably be making those calls. But my Spanish isn't half as good as his." He grimaced. "My poor Niki. She's so unworldly…"

"That's not a bad thing, in this day and age," Janet told him.

"I suppose not. But I've sheltered her. Maybe too much. She's twenty-two, but her experiences with men have been pretty daunting. Blair saved her from a very bad experience some years ago and sent the perpetrator running. I had my attorneys run him out of the state." He leaned toward her, laughing softly. "I thought Blair might hurt him if I didn't. He didn't let Niki see, but he was furious. He knocked the guy around a bit before he threw him out the front door. When I got home, Niki was curled up in his lap in an armchair. That was when he was just engaged to Elise and looking forward to a happy marriage." He made a face. "Some happiness she gave him!"

"I know. His mother would have hated Elise," she added.

"He was staying with us and got sick just before Christmas one year, while they were married. Niki made me call Elise and tell her how bad he was. She said she had a party to go to and sick people disgusted her."

"True to her nature," Janet said coldly.

"So Niki nursed him, risking pneumonia, just to take care of him. The doctor and I protested, but it did no good at all."

Janet was getting a clear picture of the relationship between Niki and Blair, and it did nothing for her ego or her plans for the future. There was something powerful between the two of them. Apparently, Blair was fighting his own feelings tooth and nail. Niki had pretended not to care when Janet told her about her plans to seduce Blair. It must have hurt her.

Blair was off the phone. He put it back into the holder on his belt. His eyes were still blazing. "I've got the police looking for him. He's on parole for assault. He'll go back. I promise you he will, no matter what it takes! Nobody treats Niki like that!"

Todd moved close to him and put a hand on his shoulder. "Calm down," he said gently. "They'll find him and he'll be dealt with. But we need to talk to Niki. I'm sorry now that I suggested this trip," he added sadly. "I only wanted to give her a holiday."

Blair felt the guilt all the way to his toes. He had hurt Niki, probably more than the drug dealer had. He dreaded facing her.

"I suggested some martial arts training when I ran the drug dealer off," Janet said as they left Blair's room and walked toward Todd's suite. "I'm a brown belt in Tae Kwon Do. It might help build up her self-confidence, toughen her up just a little."

"You ran him off?" Blair asked.

She nodded. "Poor little thing, she was too shocked by the things he said to her. It was painful to watch."

"Thank you for helping her," Blair said quietly. He could hardly bear the pain he felt at letting Niki out of his sight. The way he'd behaved had hurt her, he knew. Now this only added to her pain. He had to find some way to apologize, to explain, to smooth over what he'd done to her. He never should have touched her in the first place. He'd blamed her, blamed the bathing suit that showed so much of her creamy skin. But in the end the only blame was his own. He had nothing to offer her, and he'd let his body dictate to his brain. It had been, in many ways, the sweetest interlude of his life. But Niki couldn't know that. He had to find a kind way to keep her at arm's length, to protect her. To protect her from himself.

"Niki?" Todd called when he walked into the suite. There was no answer. The door to her room was closed. "She said she had a headache. She might have gone to lie down. I'll check."

He opened the door. Blair was right behind him. But the room was empty. Blair's eyes looked around it and landed on the chest of drawers. There was a note. Beside the chest, in the trash can, was the gold bathing suit she'd worn to the beach. Blair's teeth ground together.

Todd had spotted the note, too. He read it with a grimace. "She's gone home," he said heavily. "I guess it was too much for her, what happened this morning."

He walked back into the sitting room. "I'm going to call and make sure she's getting home okay."

Blair was staring at the trash can, his face hard and lined.

Janet moved beside him. "I told her that we'd been an item once," she confessed in a dull, quiet tone. She looked up at him, her keen eyes not missing the expression that drifted across his face. "Do you know how she feels about you, Blair?"

"She's a child. The daughter of my best friend. That's all she is." He managed a cool smile. "She's infatuated with me. Last year it was a singer in a pop band. After that the actor in a lawman series on TV." He chuckled, making a joke of it. "There will be somebody new by Christmas."

"Oh. I see." She brightened. "Well…"

Todd came back into the room. "She's landing in Billings now. I sent Tex there to pick her up."

Blair's eyes narrowed. "Tex is sweet on her."

"Yes, he is," Todd laughed. "For all the good it will ever do him. He doesn't get out much, and Niki's usually around, especially during roundup. She actually goes out with the men to watch the branding." He grimaced. "Dust everywhere, and I can't stop her. At least I convinced her into wearing a surgical mask."

Blair turned away. He glanced at the bathing suit and sighed.

"Well, we might as well go to dinner," Todd said. "Janet, you coming?"

"Yes, if you don't mind," she said.

"We're happy to have you."

Blair took a breath. "You two go ahead. I've got another phone call to make."

"We'll wait to order until you get there," Todd said.

"Just order me a steak and salad. Rare, mind you," Blair said. "No dessert."

"Okay. Will do. Janet?" Todd took her arm and led her out into the hall.

Once they were gone, Blair picked up the gold bathing suit out of the trash. He looked at it, remembering how Niki had looked in it, how sweet it had been to touch her, to hold her, to kiss her. He touched the suit tenderly with his lips. Then took it back to his own suite and stuck it in his suitcase.

DINNER WAS QUIET. Very quiet. Blair was brooding. Todd was worried about Niki and couldn't hide it. He was worried about Blair, as well. Before he made the phone call, he'd gone back to ask him what sort of dressing he wanted on his salad. Blair had been standing by the dresser, with Niki's discarded bathing suit in his big hands. As he watched, the younger man touched his lips to it with a tenderness he'd rarely ever seen in him.

Todd went back out quickly, before his friend even knew he was there. The look on his face, unguarded, had told him everything. He was in love with Niki. Desperately in love. And fighting it with his whole heart.

Janet tried to brighten things up at dinner with party talk and jokes. He was still upset about Niki's encounter with the drug dealer. But he didn't want the girl forever. He'd made that clear. Janet still had a chance, and she was going to take it.

After dinner, while they walked on the beach, she told him about the conversation with Niki, adding that

the younger girl had said she was going to make a play
for Blair and see if she could lure him into marriage.
That was why she'd worn the seductive bathing suit.

Blair didn't say a word. He took her hand in his and
asked how the commercial she was making was going.

Janet felt a twinge of guilt. Niki was frail and
couldn't really hide how she felt about Blair. But this
was war. Janet had seen him first, so to speak, and
she wasn't giving him up without a fight.

NIKI LOOKED AROUND for Tex at the Billings airport, on
the Rimrocks. It was a small airport, but very modern, very nice. She had a suitcase with wheels, easy
to roll. She was feeling miserable and just wanted to
go home.

Tex came around the corner, smiling from ear to
ear when he saw her. "Well, hello, kid," he teased,
using his pet name for her. "Glad to be home in civilized surroundings again?"

"*Civilized* and *cowboys* aren't words that go easily together," she said on a laugh. "Thanks for coming to meet me."

"Your dad was worried. Weren't you supposed to
fly home with him and Mr. Coleman on Monday?"

"I had a bad experience on the beach," she said,
averting her eyes as they walked. "It spoiled the trip
for me."

He put the suitcase in the back of the big, black
Ford truck he drove and turned to her, pushing his
Stetson back over thick black hair. "What sort of bad
experience?" he asked, his pale blue eyes flashing in
his tanned face.

"A drug dealer on the beach made some...vulgar

remarks to me and tried to get me to go to his room with him," she said.

"Damn! I hope your father has the police lock him up for the rest of his miserable life!" he said harshly.

She smiled gently. Tex was only a few years older than she was, but mature and kind and patient. She liked him a lot. "Thanks, Tex. So do I."

"Odd that Mr. Coleman didn't punch him," he mused when they were in the truck headed home. "The way he did that stupid football player a while back," he added on a chuckle.

"He was busy at the time," Niki said, making sure her voice sounded normal. "He and Dad were in a business meeting with some Mexican officials. I went to the beach alone. But Blair's old girlfriend showed up and made the man leave, with some help from one of the hotel stewards. She's nice. I guess if Blair married her, it wouldn't be so bad. At least she's far and away a better match for him than that vicious ex-wife of his who left him sick and refused to give up a party to come see about him!"

"You get hot about him, don't you?" he mused as he drove. "He's a good man. One of my friends works for him. He's a drill rigger. He said that Mr. Coleman would shed his fancy suit jacket and get right out there to work with the men when there was a problem with one of the rigs. He's fair and honest, and he treats his workers well."

"That's what Dad says, too," she agreed. The casual remark that she got hot about him was true, but she didn't want to talk about it.

Tex drew in a breath when he glanced at her and saw her expression. "Harry has a sister who works at the restaurant downtown," he said. "She mentioned that she saw you and Dan Brady there."

"Yes," she sighed. "I ordered fried fish, and the battle began." She glanced at him. "You know, anything that tastes good is especially bad for you. We should all be eating alfalfa sprouts and taking herbal supplements."

He scowled. "You got a fever or something?"

She chuckled. "That was Dan's attitude. I have asthma because I don't exercise enough or eat the right foods." She glanced at him from under her eyelashes.

"A man who wants to change you doesn't love you," he replied.

She smiled gently. "You're very perceptive, Tex."

"I'm a student of human nature," he replied. "Plus, I did a few courses in psychology when I went to college, after the military."

"Gosh, you never mentioned that you were in the military."

"Never talk about it," he said. "I was in Iraq."

"I see."

He glanced at her. "The fighting was pretty brutal. Some things get to you."

She studied his lean, handsome face. There were more lines in it than she'd realized. He wasn't as young as she'd first thought. "I thought you were only a couple of years older than me. But you aren't, are you?"

He shook his head. "I'm pushing thirty-four."

She grinned. "Old and ancient, aren't you? Do your poor old bones creak when you move?" she teased.

He laughed. "They do. I was in an armored vehicle when the lead vehicle in our convoy was hit by an IED." His breath let out slowly. "We all caught some shrapnel. I got mine in the hip. So I can tell you really accurately when it's going to rain," he added. "Bone injuries lead to arthritis in the joints."

"I'm sorry. I didn't mean…"

"Stop that," he chuckled. He looked at her with warm, soft eyes. "Everybody has scars, kid. Some are deep." The smile faded. "Heart deep," he added, as if he knew how she felt about Blair.

She turned her purse in her hands and stared at it instead of him. "Yes," she confessed. "Some are… very deep."

She turned her eyes to the pasture as they approached the turnoff to the ranch. They didn't speak again.

CHAPTER SEVEN

BLAIR AND TODD showed up at the Ashton ranch on Monday, but Niki was nowhere in sight.

Todd called Tex at once. "Where is she?" he asked.

"Went to work," he replied on a sigh. "Said even if her boss was gone, there was some work she needed to catch up on, so she wouldn't have so much overtime when he came back."

"Okay. Thanks, Tex."

"I hope they get that lowlife drug dealer," Tex said coldly. "And shut him up in jail for the rest of his miserable life."

"So do I, frankly. I'll talk to you later."

"Yes, sir."

"Got the purebred calves through the process?" he asked, because his breeding herd dropped calves in late spring.

"Almost," Tex replied. "We'll finish up by tomorrow. We've got a lot of calves to brand and vaccinate and tag," he added on a chuckle. "That's not a complaint! Nice to have the pastures full again, after that winter nightmare we had a couple of years back."

Ranchers had lost almost a hundred thousand head of cattle in the worst winter storm in years over the territory two years ago. Todd's ranch had suffered along with many others.

"I certainly agree," he told Tex. "If you need anything, pick it up at the hardware and charge it to my account."

Tex knew that, but he didn't say a word. Mr. Ashton was obviously worried about Niki and not thinking straight.

"Will do, boss." He hung up.

Blair's eyebrows were arched.

"She went to work," he told the other man. "I suppose she didn't want to sit around here and brood."

Blair drew in a long breath. "Then I should go home…"

"Stay the night," Todd replied. "We've had a long trip. Don't push it. You need rest."

Blair hesitated, but he gave in. He wanted to see Niki. Wanted a chance to explain, to make things right with her, if he could. Hurting her wasn't an option. He'd done enough of that already.

DAN BRADY COULD be good company, but today he was driving Niki to distraction.

"Listen, I appreciate your interest in my health," she told him finally after ten minutes of nonstop prompting about the herbal remedies he wanted her to take. "But I really am allergic to a number of herbs. Do you want to explain to my father why I went into anaphylactic shock because I took some herbs that my allergist didn't know about?"

He just stared at her. "How can herbs cause you to go into shock?" he asked, exasperated. "They're there to help you!"

"They won't help me if I'm allergic to them!"

He threw up his hands. "I give up. You won't even try!"

"Dan," she said, pretending a patience she really didn't feel, "you can't prescribe substances for anyone without risking a lawsuit, don't you know that? You don't have a medical degree, for God's sake!"

He started to reply when Mr. Jacobs came in from the parking lot, looking worn and disheveled. He overheard part of the conversation and gave Dan a cold look.

"I agree with Miss Ashton," he said at once. "Doctors prescribe, Brady. Doctors!"

Dan glared at both of them and walked off without another word.

"Sorry," Niki said when they were in Mr. Jacobs's office behind a closed door. "He was getting rather agressive."

"Don't you listen to him," he cautioned. "Herbs can be beneficial, I agree. But there are specialists if you want to go that route. I wouldn't risk my health or my daughter's on the say-so of some…quack who thinks he knows what he's doing!"

"Thanks, Mr. Jacobs," she said, and smiled. "He really cares about people, I think. He just goes overboard."

He cocked his head. "Do you want to know what sort of person he is, Miss Ashton? He's the sort who will let you drown in the river, and then be the first to come to your funeral and criticize the way you drowned."

She had to muffle a laugh. She turned it into a cough. "Sorry."

He chuckled. "Since you came in early, and I came

in early, we might as well get a little work done. How was Cancun?"

"Hot," was all she said.

He nodded. "Beautiful, though. Did you get to see the ruins?"

"I ran out of time," she replied, without explaining how.

"Well, perhaps another time."

"Perhaps," she agreed.

DAN HOVERED BY the front door when Niki was leaving the office. "Listen," he said, "I sort of hammer things to death, you know? I just want to help you. I don't mean to be pushy about it."

She smiled at him. "It's okay. It's not a bad thing to be passionate."

"Of course it isn't. You're coming on the hike week after next, right? You promise?"

She drew in a breath. "I'd like to."

"Great! We'll talk about specifics closer to time. You going straight home?"

"I have to," she said. "My father will be getting home."

He frowned. "I thought you went together."

She hoped the flush didn't show. "His meeting ran over, so he had to stay an extra day," she prevaricated.

"Oh, I see." He smiled. "Well, catch you tomorrow. Have a good evening."

"You, too, Dan."

SHE DROVE HOME SLOWLY. She dreaded having to talk to her father. She couldn't tell him what had really happened. That would have been too involved anyway. But she had to come up with some excuse that would placate him.

The story about the drug dealer on the beach would be enough. Surely Janet had gone to dinner with Blair and her father, after cajoling an invitation out of Niki, and she would have told them all about the incident.

She recalled leaving her bathing suit in the trash can. If her father had seen that, he'd know for himself that she'd been upset over the beach. With any luck, he'd never realize that her bad experience had more to do with Blair's coolness than her encounter with the drug dealer.

SHE PULLED INTO the garage at the ranch, parked her car and went slowly into the house. She was tired. The trip home had been uncomfortable enough, without going into work so early. And the pollen was already getting to her. It was so thick that the sidewalk leading to the front porch was yellow.

She started into the door and almost walked right into Blair Coleman.

A scarlet flush bloomed on her cheeks. She swallowed, clutching her purse. "Blair," she began, nodding as she tried to go past him.

It didn't work. His mouth made a thin line as he caught her arm and led her back outside to his rental car. He put her inside, got in himself and drove off.

Niki didn't say a word. She couldn't think of anything that wouldn't make a bad situation even worse.

He pulled up at a roadside park, cut off the engine, helped her out and walked down to the wide, shallow river with her. A stand of lodgepole pines sheltered the cleared area from the road. He stuck his hands in his pockets and stared out over the river.

"Janet told us what happened to you at the beach," he said, with his back to her. The eyes she couldn't see were stormy. "Your father and I sent the authorities after the drug dealer. He'll be caught and sent back to jail. No matter what it takes," he added bitterly.

She wasn't surprised that her father had wanted revenge on the man. But Blair's attitude was curious. She crossed her arms tightly around her chest and stood quietly beside him, watching the river flow by.

She said, "I bought that new bathing suit because it was so beautiful. It looked sophisticated and I thought…" She ground her teeth together. "It's a mistake I won't make twice. I'm…sorry, about wearing it out on the beach…" She couldn't go on.

He groaned, deep in his throat. His hands, in his pockets, were balled into fists. "No. It was my fault," he said curtly. "I should never have touched you."

So he regretted it. What had she expected, that he'd say he had no regrets? That was the stuff of romantic films, romantic books, not of life.

"I threw it away," she said, hoping to placate him.

He closed his eyes on a wave of pain. She'd looked so beautiful in it. He'd carry the picture of her like that for the rest of his life, and he couldn't, didn't, dare tell her. He'd crossed the line with Niki. Now he had to control himself. It wasn't going to be easy.

He drew in a long breath. "I'm not going to be around for a while," he said, without looking at her. "I have divisions I need to visit in person, conferences I need to have with my managers. I've let things slide in the business since the divorce."

"Janet is very nice," she said, averting her eyes. "I liked her a lot. She was kind to me. She gave the drug dealer what-for and ran him off."

"I know. She told us," he said absently. "I've known her for a long time."

"She said your mother liked her."

"Yes. She was fond of Janet."

She swallowed down bitterness. "She's a brunette, too," she said, trying to smile. "You're fond of brunettes."

"I always have been." It wasn't the complete truth. He had a passion for a beautiful young blonde woman who was an arm's length away but might as well have been on Mars.

The sound of the river flowing by, watery and soothing, was all they heard for a few minutes. Then Niki spoke.

"Janet said the two of you were very close."

"Is that why you invited her to dinner with us, then got on the first plane back home?" he asked with faint bitterness.

"I thought it would make you happy," Niki replied. "After all, you took her to dinner the previous night."

Yes, he had, trying to avoid Niki and what was going to be inevitable if he spent any time around her. Especially after the taste of her he'd had on that Mexican beach. Just the memory of it almost brought him to his knees.

Niki drew in a breath. "I'm really sorry...about what happened," she said through her teeth.

"Not your fault," he returned. "You can't help it if idiots make stupid comments about your choice of bathing suits. He'll be found, and dealt with, no matter what it takes!"

She turned, hesitant. Her cheeks colored. Eyes the color of an August fog looked up into his black ones. "I meant, what happened in the ocean…"

He looked down at her. His broad face hardened. His eyes glittered. She was wearing a beige suit with a pale yellow blouse. It wasn't low-cut or even suggestive, but her breasts under it had hard little peaks. The sight of them hurt him. She was attracted to him, violently attracted. She couldn't hide it because she didn't have the experience. It flattered him, maddened him, because there was no way she could fake her reaction. He was years too old for her. He was going to have to make her believe he felt nothing…

"Oh, God," he groaned. He drew her against him, swallowing her up in his hard arms, her head in the crook of his elbow, his eyes stabbing down into hers. She was already having trouble breathing. He could feel her heart hammering against him. His eyes fell to her soft mouth. "I tried…" He whispered huskily as he bent his head to hers.

She felt the hunger in him even before his warm, hard mouth slowly covered hers. He was a little rough, because desire was riding him. But he was slow and patient.

She didn't even protest when one big hand smoothed up her rib cage and swallowed her small breast.

He nipped her upper lip tenderly. "Help me," he ground out.

"Okay." Her arms lifted around his neck, and she stood on tiptoe to tempt him.

"That…is not…what I meant," he bit off against her eager mouth. Even as he said it, his body hardened blatantly against hers.

"Are you sure?" she whispered against his lips.

He lifted her closer, grinding her breasts into his broad chest as he deepened the kiss into levels of pleasure he'd never felt in his life with anyone.

Her hands tangled in his thick, wavy black hair, enjoying the coolness of it against her fingers, loving the hard, hungry crush of his mouth.

"I might as well be hung for a sheep as a lamb," he managed as he bent suddenly and lifted her clear off the ground in his arms. Still kissing her, he walked slowly back to the car.

He put her in on the passenger side, let her go long enough to get in beside her and reached for her again.

"This is not going to end well," he bit off against her mouth as his fingers searched for the buttons on her shirt and opened them.

"I don't care." She arched her back as he found the front clip of her bra and pushed it away.

His black eyes devoured her from the waist up, enjoying the creamy soft skin of her breasts and their hard pink crowns. He touched them almost reverently, teased the crowns until she gasped and lifted again.

"We all make mistakes," he said as his head bent. "This is the worst I've made in a decade."

"Pencils have erasers," she said helpfully.

"No eraser is going to help this," he said. His mouth opened and took one soft, silky breast right inside it. His tongue worked against it. The quick, high-pitched little moans she made went through him like silvery stabs of pleasure. He drew on the soft mound, a gentle suction that produced an unexpected, violent reaction.

She arched up to his lips and shuddered. Her nails bit into the back of his head. She undulated against his mouth as pleasure took her, arched her, convulsed her in a shock of fulfillment that delighted the man whose mouth had provoked it.

She collapsed against him, tears rolling down her cheeks.

He kissed them away, staggered by her capacity for passion, by the reaction she couldn't help. All his adult life, women had wanted him for what he had, for what he could give. Niki only wanted him, and it was so obvious that it was like a knife in his heart.

He wanted her, too. But he was too old for her. He was cheating her of a proper life, with some young man who'd cherish her, love her, give her children. Children!

He groaned inwardly. His big hand went to her belly and pressed there. He thought of Niki with someone else's baby in her arms, and the pain was like an ice pick in his heart.

He lifted his head and looked into drowned silvery eyes. She was still shivering in the aftermath of her climax, embarrassed, shocked…ashamed.

"Don't," he whispered, bending to kiss her tenderly. "Don't be embarrassed by it. In all my life, I've never had that reaction from a woman, any woman."

She swallowed. "Never?"

He shook his head. His eyes went to her bare breasts. The one he'd suckled had a faint red mark. He touched it tenderly, loving the way her body responded to him.

"Women want me for what I have, Niki," he said with faint bitterness. "Only for what I have, what I can give them."

Her soft hand touched his hard cheek, tracing down it to his faintly swollen, sexy wide mouth. "Not me."

"No," he whispered. "Not you."

He bent and kissed her tenderly.

Her fingers went to the buttons on his shirt.

"No," he protested.

But he wasn't protesting very hard. She opened his shirt and drew the edges aside. "I loved looking at you like this, when you were so sick."

He drew in an unsteady breath. "Did you?"

"Yes. But you were married," she recalled. She bent her head to his chest and kissed him there, pressing her mouth against thick hair and hard, warm muscle.

He caught her head. Hesitated. But the temptation was just too much. He drew her mouth to a hard male nipple and pressed it there.

"Like...you did to me?" she whispered.

"Yes," he bit off.

She opened her mouth and suckled him. He arched, shuddering, aching for her, loving the touch of her soft mouth on him, loved knowing that she was enjoying him as much as he was enjoying her.

Only this, he promised himself, just this one, last time, before he had to walk away for her own good and give her up to a more suitable man. Just...this...once!

He drew her up, across the console between the seats in his car, so that she sat on his lap, her young breasts pressed to his broad chest, and he bent to her mouth.

But he hesitated. His eyes met hers. "Never again, Niki," he said at her lips. "Do you understand?"

"No."

His mouth teased hers. "We're both curious. But this is as far as it goes. When I drive you home, I'm leaving, and I'm not coming back until this heat between us subsides."

"You want me," she whispered against his hard, warm mouth.

"Yes. I want you. But I never want to marry again. You're a marrying woman, Niki," he ground out. "You need a young man who can cherish you, give you children."

She hung at his lips. "Don't you want children, Blair?" she whispered.

He groaned. His mouth ground into hers. He drew her closer, dragging her soft breasts against him, drowning in pleasure. Yes, he wanted children. He wanted to give her a baby and watch her grow big with it. He wanted nothing more in life.

But those sixteen years were a burden she couldn't understand now. As he grew older and she stayed young, she wouldn't, couldn't, want him forever. He would die years before she would, or perhaps grow sick and have to be taken care of. She'd want a younger man then, perhaps, and he wouldn't be able to let go.

So it was painful now to walk away. But it would be more painful down the road, especially if he took her completely. He'd never get the memory out of his mind, his heart; he'd never be able to go on.

She was on fire for him. She moaned helplessly under the heavy, hard crush of his mouth, loving the feel of his skin against hers, his arms holding her, cradling her, cherishing her.

"Blair," she moaned huskily. "Couldn't we...?"

He lifted his head and looked into drowned gray eyes in a flushed face. Her mouth was swollen from the force of his kisses. Her nipples were dark pink, hard with the same desire that had him in its grip.

"No," he said after a minute. "We can't. You know that. You know why." He drew back from her, taking one long, last look at her bare breasts before he refastened her bra and her blouse. He moved away from her, his hands going blindly to the buttons on his own shirt.

She moved back over to the passenger seat in the car, stared at him with helpless longing and grimaced. He was encased in ice again, as far away as a star.

He drew in a steadying breath and got himself under control before he glanced at her. "I have to leave, Niki."

Her mouth hurt from the pressure of his. It was a sweet pain, like the faint discomfort in the breast he'd suckled so hard. "I don't want you to," she said honestly. "But I won't try to make you feel guilty."

"You're very young, honey," he said after a minute, and there was a world of sensual wisdom in his black eyes. "I was like you, once. On fire with curiosity and desire. But I satisfied it with a procession of worldly, experienced women. There's no mystery left for me, Niki," he said quietly. "I'm not curious anymore." He smiled with faint sarcasm. "I don't need a curious twenty-two-year-old virgin. So don't build daydreams on what just happened. We satisfied a mutual lust. Partially, at least. That's all it was, a little raw passion to top off a long day. Tomorrow I won't remember that it even happened. And I'll have other women to assuage the ache, if it comes back. Janet's still available," he added with a cold smile. "She wants me, too."

It was like a knife through her heart, but Niki wasn't going to let him see how badly his words hurt. She just smiled. "Yes, she does," she returned. "I'm sure she's ready and willing to start over where the two of you left off. And she's closer to your age."

"Much closer," he agreed.

He cranked the car and pulled out into the road. His movements were so controlled, so patient, that Niki knew he was telling the truth when he said he could take her or leave her. He wasn't dying of an unsatisfied lust for her. And lust was all it was.

Something inside her curled up like a wounded thing. She'd hoped that what he felt had something more than desire in it, that the tenderness he showed her meant that he cared, even if only a little.

But then, he'd always been tender with her. When he saved her from the football player, he'd cuddled her in his lap until she'd stopped shaking. For the most part, he treated her like a beloved child. This new hunger was just a fluke. She tempted him and he was a man. He reacted to her passion. But that was all it was. He didn't believe in marriage or love anymore. Certainly he didn't believe in it with Niki.

She stared at the landscape as they drove along the road that led back to the Ashton ranch. But she didn't really see it at all.

HE PULLED UP at the back door of the sprawling ranch house and cut the engine.

"Your father thinks you're upset about the drug dealer," he said after a minute. "Let him go on believing it."

"I had that in mind already."

He drew in an angry breath. She looked utterly defeated, dejected. He hated seeing the pain in her face and knowing that he'd caused it.

"It's just sex, Niki," he said coldly. "Once you've had it, you'll understand how it is. A man can want a woman without feeling anything else for her."

"Poor Janet. Does she know that?" she asked sarcastically.

His face froze. "Janet is my business. I won't discuss her with you."

She searched his black eyes. Her own were sad. "We were friends once."

He smiled. It was icy cold. "We were," he agreed. The smile faded. "Until you tried to seduce me. You won't get a second chance at it. I don't want you, Niki," he said coolly. "I never will, except in one way. And you know exactly which way I mean."

"Of course I do," she said, trying to hide the hurt.

"You're still living in fairy tales, happily-ever-after, romantic nonsense," he bit off. His eyes glittered. "It's a lie, Niki. It's just sex with frosting. That's all it ever is, for a man."

Her face drained of color. "I see."

"If you weren't so damned naive, you'd have known it from the beginning! You have a beautiful body and I wanted it. Any man would. But that's all it was."

Naive. She only nodded. She was that. Stupid about men and totally clueless.

She couldn't meet his eyes. "Goodbye, Blair."

His face betrayed nothing. "Goodbye, Niki."

She opened the car door and got out. She closed it gently, without looking at him. She went straight into the house without speaking to Edna or her father, up the stairs, to her room. She locked the door. Then she sat on her bed and let the tears fall, hot and silent as they rolled down her cheeks.

I will get over you, Blair Coleman, she promised herself. *I will. I will!*

DOWNSTAIRS, BLAIR WAS in such agony that he could hardly bear it. Edna got a look at his face as he turned it toward Niki's disappearing figure, and she turned away before he saw her expression.

Whatever he'd told Niki to send her up the staircase in such misery, it had caused him even more. She'd never seen such a look on a man's face except once— the day Niki's mother died. Her father had worn almost the same expression, one of such grief and loss that she'd never gotten it out of her mind.

Blair was wrong. He thought Niki was too young. Edna smiled sadly. Someone should have told him about Niki's mother and father. But it was too late now.

BLAIR TOLD HER father that Niki was still upset about the drug dealer. Whether or not he bought it was up for grabs.

Niki cried herself to sleep. Blair was adamant that he wanted no part of a future that included her, and his only interest in her had been physical.

She had to admit that she'd gone out of her way in Mexico to try to attract him in any way she could. In retrospect, she should never have put on that sexy bathing suit in the first place, much less tempted a man who didn't want her except physically.

A few times she'd been almost sure that he felt something else for her, something deep and tender and lasting. But he'd disabused her of that idea pretty quickly. He wanted a woman, that was all it was, and he had scores of them waiting. Janet was at the head of the pack, apparently. He didn't want to get married again because Elise had damaged his pride. But then, Janet had learned from the ex-wife's example just how to land that sexy man.

She laughed to herself. It had a hollow sound. She knew, as Blair certainly had, that if he'd put on the pressure, she'd have given in without a single protest, even without a hope of marriage. She wanted him so badly, with such passion, that it almost choked her, even in memory.

He knew it. But it wasn't enough. He'd had women. He said the mystery was all over for him, that it was only a purely physical response that he couldn't help. Yes, she'd tempted him. She'd meant to. It was a last-ditch effort to try to make him see that she was mature enough for him; that she was a woman, not a child; that the years between them didn't matter.

To Blair, the years mattered. That was the bottom line. She'd offered him anything he wanted, and it wasn't enough.

Janet had already told her that she was going after Blair with Elise's tactics. Make him crazy and lure him into marriage. It might work. But it seemed a shoddy way to treat a man. It was dishonest. It played on his senses, not his heart.

Yes, Janet might use desire to get a wedding band, but if Blair didn't love her as well as want her, he'd be no better off than he had been with Elise.

Niki stared at the wall with her heart breaking in her chest. She and Blair had been friends. He'd been her protector, her confidant, her companion. She'd thrown all that away for a few heated minutes in Mexico, and in his car, and she'd lost his respect. He was going to stay away until she came to her senses. That was what he'd been saying, after all.

What he didn't know was that she was never going to come to her senses. She loved him. That was no flare of desire that would be quickly satisfied. She loved him. She wanted children with him, a future with him. But he couldn't give her that. He wanted her. But he didn't love her. What an empty, cold life that would have been, if she'd crossed the line with him and he'd married her out of guilt, with a one-sided love and the possibility of a child he wouldn't want. At least now, both of them had been spared that.

She wiped away the tears and changed out of her office clothes, sliding into jeans and a T-shirt. But she couldn't manage to go downstairs and face Blair over the dinner table. That would require more composure than she could manage.

A FEW MINUTES later her father rapped at her door. "Niki, aren't you going to come down for supper?" he asked gently.

"Sorry, Dad," she replied, working hard to keep the hoarseness out of her voice. "I've got an awful headache. I had sort of a blowup with Dan today at work."

"What sort of blowup?" he asked.

She opened the door a crack. "He was on about the herbs and the diet again," she said with a soft sigh. "He's been a little aggressive with me and Mr. Jacobs about them."

Her father frowned. "Exactly what does he think they'll do for you?"

She pursed her lips and forced a smile. "Cure asthma and rheumatoid arthritis. You might say he's made allies of Mr. Jacobs and me."

He scowled. "The man needs to be talked to. I could tell Blair…"

"No!" She swallowed. "No. Please. It would just make things worse. Dan did realize that he'd gone too far. He apologized. He cares, a lot, about people," she added. "He wants to help. He doesn't quite realize that he's being obnoxious."

He drew in a breath and jingled the change in his pocket. "Okay. It's your call." He cocked his head. "Want Edna to bring you up a tray?"

"No, thanks, Dad. It's been a trying few days." She managed a laugh. "My head really is splitting. I think I'll have an early night. Tell Blair I said to have a safe trip and thank him for the vacation."

"Some vacation, with you being insulted by some pig of a drug dealer right on the hotel grounds," he said shortly. "That's being dealt with, by the way. We called the authorities."

She nodded. "Janet was very kind to me," she said. She smiled. "She's nice. Blair could do a lot worse."

He didn't say anything. He was remembering how homicidal Blair had been about Niki's encounter with the lewd young man on the beach. He remembered even better the sight of Blair with his lips to Niki's discarded bathing suit. He wanted to tell her. But he couldn't betray his friend. "I guess," he said after a minute.

"Well, good night, Dad."

"Good night, honey. Sleep well."

She reached up and kissed his cheek. "You're the nicest father in the whole world."

"I wish you'd had time to see the ruins at Chichen Itza. I know you were looking forward to it," he added suddenly.

"Maybe next time."

He nodded. "That's a deal. Next time, you and I will go. And we'll spend the day at the ruins. How's that?"

She smiled. "That sounds very nice."

He winked. "I'll see you in the morning, honey."

She nodded, smiled again, and closed the door.

BLAIR LOOKED UP expectantly as Todd came back into the dining room. He wasn't really surprised that Niki didn't come with him.

"Headache," Todd said easily, sitting down. "She has a few issues at the office with…" he said, cutting off the remark he'd almost let slip. "Some of the equipment is new to her, that's all," he added.

"I see."

Edna started bringing in food, and the men fell into a discussion of new oil exploration venues.

CHAPTER EIGHT

NIKI DRESSED FOR work before she went downstairs to breakfast. She'd expected that Blair would be long gone. But he was sitting at the table with a cup of black coffee; her father was nowhere in sight.

She stopped in the doorway, steeling herself not to do anything stupid.

"Good morning," she said formally.

He looked up. His face was heavily lined. His eyes were bloodshot. He looked as if he hadn't had a minute's sleep. He drew in a breath.

"My pilot got a late start," he said.

"I see. Well, have a good trip home."

"You're leaving without breakfast?" he asked curtly.

"I never eat breakfast," she lied. "Well, not anymore, at least. I get coffee at the office."

He didn't answer her. He just sipped coffee.

She stuck her head in the kitchen. "Edna, I'll see you tonight."

"You be careful out there," Edna fussed. "Lots of pollen."

"It's spring," Niki said with a faint grin.

She started toward the front door, pausing just to grab her purse and lightweight sweater from the rack in the corner.

Blair was behind her. She could feel the heat of his big body.

She couldn't bear to look at him. She opened the door and went out.

He followed, closing the door behind him.

She stopped and turned, resigned, miserable. She couldn't force her eyes any higher than his paisley tie. "Was there something else?"

His hands, in his pockets, were clenched. "Yes. I wanted to make a point. What you feel is infatuation, Niki. It's flattering. But it isn't real."

Her fingers curled into the soft leather of her purse. She knew her cheeks were flaming red. She couldn't find the words to rebut him.

His jaw tautened. "For God's sake, don't make some great romantic interlude out of a few hot kisses! It was just lust, if you want to label it. Lust! It's demeaning to try to construe it into romance."

Demeaning. She could feel the blood draining out of her face. Demeaning. The sweetest few minutes of her life. Demeaning.

"Damn naive women!" he ground out. "Damn juvenile infatuation. And damn you for playing me like a trout, with come-hither bathing suits and Elise's tactics!"

That shocked her into meeting his eyes. "Elise's...?"

"Didn't you realize?" he asked sarcastically. "She got me so hot I didn't know my name and then drew back, every damned time. She left me doubled over, hurting like a teenage boy. Eventually, I married her just to satisfy the hunger."

She didn't know what to say.

His black eyes narrowed. "Janet said that you planned

to use the same tactics on me," he added coldly, "to force me into marriage. Nice try. But it won't work. I've taken the cure."

Nice one, Janet, Niki thought furiously. It had been Janet's tactic, but she was blaming it on Niki. Afraid of the competition, maybe, and that was a joke.

She lifted her chin and stared him down. Her heart was breaking, but he'd never know.

"I'm meeting Janet in New York later in the week," he said. "I should have had better sense when I was younger. She's twice the woman Elise ever was."

At least Janet was going to come out on top. The backstabbing turncoat.

"Well, at least if anyone ever attacks you, Janet can Tae Kwon Do them for you," she said with a vacant smile.

His face tautened to steel.

She turned while he was absorbing that final blow and headed toward her car. The driveway was a little blurry as she pulled out, but she smiled in Blair's general direction and even waved.

DAN BRADY WAS concerned about Niki when they had coffee together at break time.

"You're not yourself today," he said.

"I had a really bad night," she replied. "On top of a really bad trip to Cancun. I'm glad to be home."

His eyes narrowed. "Coleman went with you and your father, didn't he?"

"Yes. He was meeting an old flame there in the hotel, during the trade talks. She's very nice," she said, lying through her teeth. "Apparently, they were almost engaged some years back. She's still crazy about him."

"I see."

His expression was unguarded, and she laughed. "Surely you don't think I have a secret yearning for him?" she teased. "My gosh, he's almost forty years old!"

The last worry Dan had left his handsome face. He grinned. "No, of course that's not what I thought!"

Now they were both lying. But she just smiled and changed the subject.

BLAIR WAS FINISHING his second whiskey highball on the corporate jet. He hadn't said a single word to the crew or the flight attendant. He refused food, buried himself in his computer and put Niki in the back of his mind.

He hadn't meant to hurt her. But it had been necessary. He couldn't let her sink into a relationship with him, give up hopes of a young and energetic husband who could give her a home and children.

He was more suited to brief affairs. After Elise, he was certain that he could never stomach the thought of marriage again. Certainly not with Niki.

She'd turn to that young man at work, the one Jacobs had told him about. Dan Brady. The health nut. His teeth clenched. Well, he and Niki seemed to get along very well, and the man was young and intelligent and ambitious. It would be a good match.

He stared at the laptop screen without really seeing it. He was reliving those last few painful minutes with Niki, lying to her about what he'd felt, taunting her for being infatuated with him, for trying Elise's

seductive tactics on him. Infatuation. That was all it
was. Of course. She was far too young to feel anything permanent for a man. He'd introduced her to
passion and now she was curious.

He flushed, remembering how it had felt to have
her in his arms, to feel her mouth so hungry and eager
under his own. He'd wanted her so desperately that
he'd have done anything to get her.

Janet had warned him that she might try that trick.
She'd been bragging about it on the beach, she'd said
at the dinner she'd shared with him and Todd in Cancun. According to Janet, Niki had told Janet that she
wanted Blair and she could get him. It would be easy
because he was older and already drawn to her physically. It would be fun to make a man like that, a
worldly, sophisticated man, fall at her feet. It would
amuse her to try. He was vulnerable, and she wanted
to see how fast she could make him fall for her.

Odd, it didn't really sound like Niki. She was shy
and withdrawn with most people. Even with him, at
first. But the more he thought about it, the more he
believed it. She'd bought the bathing suit on purpose,
to tempt him. She'd as much as admitted it.

He hated the way he behaved when she was close
to him. He hated being vulnerable. Niki was fickle,
like all young women. She was only testing her femi-
nine powers, and he was handy. Probably she hadn't
thought that Janet would tell him what she'd said.

He grieved for the way things had been with Niki.
For almost two years, she'd been his confidante, his
friend, comforting him, nurturing him, making him
laugh. In so many ways, she'd helped make up for the
hell Elise had made of his life.

And what had he given her in return? Shame, for responding to his ardor, for wanting him, for caring about him.

He emptied the whiskey glass and groaned inwardly. That beautiful bathing suit, in the trash where she'd thrown it because he'd made her ashamed of wearing it for him. She was untried, innocent, kind, and he'd lacerated her emotions, her pride.

He wanted her more than he'd ever wanted anyone in his life. He wanted to take care of her, cherish her, have children with her, comfort her...

He laughed to himself. Janet had said that Niki wanted to tempt him into marriage. But he knew that wasn't Niki. She was too honest. He'd known that, at some level. He'd used Janet's insinuations to justify pushing Niki away before she got any closer, before he caved in to his own need and pushed hers aside.

She needed a kind, gentle young man who'd love her and make her happy. Blair was going to make sure she had the chance to find one, by removing himself from the equation. She'd been hiding from the world, from men, by clinging to Blair. But that had blinded her to their differences. They had no chance of happiness together. He hoped he'd made her see that.

He thought about the health nut that she was having meals with, and his heart ached. He was a hard worker, Jacobs had said, curious at the questions Blair had asked about the employee. It was for Niki's father, he'd lied. Todd had been concerned about some things Brady had said to her.

Jacobs had confessed that Brady was aggressive with both him and Niki about the ability of herbs and exercise and diet to cure any disease.

If only life were that simple, Blair thought angrily. He just hoped that Niki wouldn't rush into a relationship just to make Blair think she wasn't missing him. Of course, how could she miss him, after the things he'd said to her? He wished he could take back some of the things he'd said, especially what he'd told her about their interludes being nothing but lustful and demeaning. He'd seen the pain in her young face. But he'd told her he'd be seeing Janet, and he might have to do that for just a little while, just to make her believe he was turning away.

Janet. He laughed to himself. She was a self-contained, ambitious woman who loved the high life and would do almost anything to land herself a millionaire. It had been that way years ago. He'd known it even before his mother had come to her senses and realized that Janet was less desirable as a daughter-in-law than she'd first thought.

But he could handle Janet. He didn't love her, but she would make a good cover for him while he tried to get over slicing and dicing Niki's poor heart. He'd make sure Janet had some diamonds to comfort her when he broke it off.

That brought back the unwanted memory of Niki's utter delight with a rawhide and deer antler bracelet. He lifted his empty glass and had the flight attendant bring him another drink.

Two weeks later he was almost crazy as he tried to adjust to a life that didn't contain Niki in it. He'd phoned her often just to talk. He'd sent her text messages. There had been constant contact.

Now there was nothing. It was more painful than

he'd dreamed it would be. All he had was the memory of her in his arms, holding him, wanting him. He knew her now as he hadn't before, knew the surge of joy it gave him to feel her soft mouth opening under the crush of his lips, to feel her body lifting, pleading, for his arms to hold her even closer.

His good intentions were making him miserable. He groaned out loud as he recalled that sweet interlude in the rental car with her. Niki in his arms, dying for him. Then he'd pushed her away and told her it was only lust.

He'd taken Janet out a time or two, but she'd realized that he was only doing it for show. In fact, he deliberately maneuvered her in front of a tabloid photographer and put an arm around her.

Janet still had hopes that she could hold his interest. She felt a twinge of regret at the lie she'd told about Niki planning to trap him, and she was fairly certain that he felt more than he'd admit for Niki. She held on doggedly, phoning him when she didn't hear from him, leaving him text messages, pursuing him as hard as she could. He responded, but only in a pleasant way. He felt nothing for her. He never had. She'd been someone to eat with occasionally, an ear to listen, nothing more than that. He hadn't even slept with her. Perhaps, he thought, that was why she couldn't give him up. She was trying to recapture the past. She was, after all, still a struggling filmmaker, and he was filthy rich.

He'd bought her a dinner ring at their last meeting, just a trinket to make her happy. But while she enthused over the most expensive one in the jewelry case, he remembered again Niki rapt with joy over a

rawhide bracelet with a medallion made of deer antler. The comparison was actually painful.

NIKI'S BIRTHDAY CAME, and he couldn't consider ignoring it, despite all the pain he'd caused her. He sent her
a huge bouquet of roses in all sorts of colors, laced
with orchids. He enclosed a card, just greetings and
his name.

He phoned Edna a few days later to see if the bouquet had arrived, because he hadn't gotten even a text
message of thanks. He hadn't expected one. The tabloid had hit the stands the same day he sent the bouquet, with a caption noting Blair's attentions to the
up-and-coming filmmaker from his past.

"Oh, hello, Mr. Coleman," Edna said pleasantly.
"Mr. Ashton isn't here right now…"

"She gave the flowers to the church, and tore the
card into a dozen pieces and threw it into the trash,
didn't she?" he asked with a sigh of resignation.

Edna was too shocked even to reply. Just before
the bouquet arrived, Niki had tossed the tabloid onto
the kitchen counter and pointed out that Blair was
making sure Niki knew he was off-limits for good.

He laughed softly, but it had a hollow sound. "I
thought as much."

"She said you'd posed for that picture in the magazine on purpose," she blurted out.

He hesitated. "I suppose Niki and I know each
other very well, don't we, Edna?"

"I suppose you do," she confessed.

"I hope it was a happy birthday for her, just the
same."

"Her father took her to a movie," she told him.

He was relieved. At least she wasn't going out with other men. Which shouldn't have made him feel so smug.

"And that Mr. Brady at work took her out to a club in Billings to celebrate her birthday," she added a few seconds later.

Thunderclouds rolled over him. He felt the words like a knife in his heart.

"He told me she needs to do her own housework, and that me and Mr. Ashton need to stop pampering her," she said icily. "What a piece of work that young man is!"

He held on to his temper. Barely. "It's her life, Edna."

"Some life she'll have with him," she replied quietly. "Well, it's none of my business."

"Nor mine. Tell Todd I called."

"Yes, sir."

He hung up. He had no right to interfere. But Niki was making a mistake. The younger man would bring her nothing except heartache. Then he recalled that he'd pushed her into Brady's arms, and put the phone down.

He got on a plane for Frankfurt and didn't remember the plane ride there. He'd never been so miserable in his whole life.

NIKI HAD ACCEPTED the hiking invitation from Dan Brady with reservations.

"We're not going to gallop along in a race, Niki," Dan laughed as she checked her shoelaces at the beginning of the hiking trail. "And we all have cell phones. We won't abandon you to die on the side of the road!"

She made a face at him.

"All right, everyone, make sure you have plenty of bottled water, and let's not get separated on the path. Look out for snakes."

It wasn't snakes that Niki was worried about. It was something more. Something that she'd only just learned.

"You're very quiet," Dan commented.

She managed a wan smile. "Didn't sleep much last night," she said.

"Oh, you should try herbal tea," Dan told her. "Chamomile, with just a drop of honey, before bedtime. It works like a charm!"

It wouldn't work if they'd found a spot on his lung X-ray, she thought bitterly. Especially with her family history. Her mother's cancer had started just like that. A spot on her lung on an X-ray. Two years later, gasping and cyanotic, lying on the couch with only twenty percent lung capacity, just trying to suck in enough air to breathe, her mother's heart had finally given out.

Niki had been there. She'd seen it. Her father had tried to kill himself afterward. It had been Edna and one of the older cowboys who'd found him in time and stopped him. Todd had watched his beloved wife go through surgery, followed by treatment, only to have the spot return four months later and the process start all over again. Twice they'd operated. Twice they'd assured him that they got it all, that she'd be fine. And the third time it had spread to both lungs and they'd abandoned hope.

She knew what it was like to have lung cancer. Despite Doctor Fred's assertions that it might not be anything to worry about, that a CT scan could easily rule out cancer, Niki wouldn't be moved. She knew what would happen if it was cancer.

All her life, she'd dreamed of having a child of her own. She browsed baby boutiques. She loved holidays because the ranch hands would bring their children up to the big house for all the celebrations.

Now there would be no children. She'd thought, once, that Blair might turn to her after his divorce. She knew he wanted a child, too. She'd hoped that he might want one with her. But that dream was dead. Dead, like the future, like Niki's future.

She would never hold her child in her arms. She would never have a husband, a home, a life beyond what she had right now.

So it didn't matter what happened to her. The hiking trail led right through one of the biggest orchards in the valley, and the late-blooming fruit trees were putting out pollen by the bucketload.

It was a cowardly thing to do. But Niki didn't care anymore. She'd lost Blair. Life had nothing left for her. She only wanted it over. She'd left her rescue inhaler at home. She felt a moment's panic when she thought how it felt when she had an attack. She could only get a little air in and no air out. It was like suffocating. But hopefully it would be quick. And they were far enough out that time would be in her favor. It was unlikely that they'd be able to get a rescue team out here before her life drained away. Her asthma was severe. An attack without her rescue inhaler could quickly be fatal.

It didn't even matter. She moved ahead like a sleepwalker with her fanny pack around her waist, her feet in expensive boots that peeked out from under her jeans. She had on a tank top and no sweater, which was bad because it was a cool morning. That didn't matter, either. She heard Blair's voice telling her that it was only lust, that he didn't care, that he and Janet were getting back together. He must have meant it, because that tabloid photo of the two of them was very informative. Janet had been pressed close to Blair's chest, looking up at him with pure worship. Blair had his arm around her, smiling down at her, the way he'd smiled at her in the hotel in Cancun when Niki had come upon them unexpectedly.

At least Janet had a future worth looking toward. Maybe she'd make Blair happy, at least.

"Earth to Niki, are you there?" Dan teased.

She snapped out of her reveries and smiled. "I'm here."

"Great! Let's go!"

IT IRRITATED BLAIR that Janet had shown up in Frankfurt. It irritated him more that she had a room right next to his suite.

"I'm making a film here, darling. Isn't it nice that we're here at the same time?" she teased.

"I've got meetings most of the day and half the night," he said quietly. "No time to party. Sorry."

"Oh, that's all right. Maybe I'll see you at breakfast," she added, her eyes bright with hope.

"Maybe."

He walked away, sick at heart. It should have been Niki here with him, right here, in the hotel, in his room, in his bed, in his arms. He almost groaned aloud. He missed her more than he'd dreamed he ever could.

Now he had Janet stalking him the way Elise had done, trying to tempt him into indiscretion.

She couldn't know that it would never work. He felt nothing for her. In fact, he felt nothing for any woman except Niki, especially after the taste of her he'd had that haunted his dreams, made him hungry, tortured him in the wee hours of the morning.

He'd been reckless enough to send her a text message, asking how she was. There had been no reply. Well, there had been one. An emoji with the mouth pulled to one side. Expressive. A visual "who cares?"

It disturbed him enough to phone Todd, on the excuse of business, from his hotel room.

"How's that equipment sale to Mexico coming along?" he asked on his way down the street from yet another meeting with a European distributor.

"Slowly," Todd chuckled, "like any business we do south of the border. They're a lot more cautious than they used to be."

"Mexico has had her problems with outside interests, and it goes back a long, long way."

"Yes." He hesitated. "How are you and Janet doing? I heard she was making a commercial in Frankfurt."

There was a long pause. "She's fine, I suppose. I've been too busy to see much of her." He hesitated. "How's Niki?"

"Quiet."

He frowned. "That's not like her."

"I know." Todd's voice was laced with concern. "She'd just come from her physical. She didn't say there was anything wrong, and I can't intimidate

Doctor Fred enough to make him talk to me. Maybe some female problem she didn't want to discuss with her dad," he chuckled. But he was worried. Even the humor didn't hide that.

"It's spring," Blair pointed out. "She always has trouble with her lungs in the spring."

"I know. Just like her mother," he added involuntarily.

"You never talk about Martha," Blair replied quietly.

"Hurts too much," the older man confided. "I went off the deep end when I lost her. It was the last thing on earth I expected. She was so much younger than I was. I always thought I'd be the one to go first."

"Younger?"

Todd took a deep breath. "Eighteen years younger," he said. "I had all these worries about the age difference, what people would think, what if I ended up in a nursing home while she was still young enough to date…that sort of thing."

Blair's heart was pounding. "But you married her anyway."

"Against my better judgment. Of the two things in my whole damned life I got right, Martha was one of them. Niki's the other. We only had eight years, but they were the best, most beautiful years of my life. I'd give anything, anything, to have her back!"

"What happened?"

Todd swallowed. "Lung cancer. She was frail, like Niki. Pollen bothered her, and she had asthma, too. I spent many a night in emergency rooms with her when the attacks got too bad. She hated that," he laughed softly. "She felt like she was a burden.

I told her that she was the sweetest burden any man ever had, and why couldn't she consider it a date? We were touring emergency rooms and getting familiar with new equipment and meeting people. That always made her laugh."

Blair felt the other man's pain to his bones. Niki was fragile like that. He thought about losing her, and his whole body clenched. He could only imagine what it had been like for his friend.

"I went crazy when she died," Todd recalled. "Stayed drunk for two weeks and tried to get myself killed any way I could. But Edna had just come to work for me, and she reminded me that Niki only had one parent, and why wasn't I thinking about her instead of myself. So I came to my senses."

"You never remarried."

"No," Todd said softly. "And I never will. I had the most wonderful marriage any man ever dreamed of, lived with the sweetest, kindest woman on earth for eight beautiful years. Why the hell would I want to trade that memory for some woman who wants minks and a Cadillac?"

Blair took a long breath. "I'm sorry. I didn't know you then."

"It was a long time ago."

Blair was thinking. Quiet. "Is Niki there?" he asked, because it was very early on a Saturday morning. Perhaps they could talk and make peace.

"No," came the reply, and there was concern in it. "She went hiking."

"Hiking?" Blair asked, frowning. "Isn't that tricky, when the pollen count is so high?"

"Our Mr. Brady thinks it will be good for her not

to pamper herself," Todd said coolly. "She took plenty of water along."

"And her rescue inhaler?"

"I'm sure she did," Todd replied. "She knows better than to leave home without it this time of year."

Blair hesitated. "I might come down for a few days next week. If it's all right."

"It's all right with me," Todd said. "On the other hand, you might want to make sure it's okay with Niki. She's been rather vocal about you lately, and not in a good way."

He grimaced. "I've made some mistakes with her. Some bad ones."

"You might want to patch them up before she ends up married to the California health nut," Todd said curtly. "She spends too much time with him, and he has an influence on her that I don't like. Asthma isn't just in the mind. A man like that could push her over the edge. She had an attack once that almost killed her when she couldn't get to her inhaler, and she was even at home at the time. Tex, God bless him, was quick on his feet or we'd have lost her. Got her the inhaler, had the ambulance there in a heartbeat."

"He's fond of her," Blair said, and couldn't manage to keep the edge out of his voice.

"He's crazy about her," her father corrected. "But Niki likes him the way she likes most men. He's just a friend."

That was a relief. But the California man worried him. A lot. "She doesn't need some insensitive nut taking her places she shouldn't be going in the first place. Hiking, for God's sake!" he burst out.

"Well, I can't stop it," Todd replied heavily. "Believe me, I tried. He's convinced her that she's just pampering herself, that she's not frail, that exercise and fresh air will turn her into an Amazon."

"Not likely." Blair's tone was ice-cold.

"You and I know that. Niki doesn't. She's been different since we came home from Mexico," he added quietly. "She's grown old in front of my eyes. I miss the daughter who was sparkling like a jewel, always smiling no matter how bad things got."

Blair closed his eyes and shuddered mentally, because he knew why Niki was that way. He knew who'd turned her old overnight.

"It might do you good to come down here for a while," Todd added. "Just, uh, don't bring Janet with you, okay?"

"I'd like to leave her in Frankfurt forever," the other man said shortly. "I know how deer feel in hunting season."

"She really has the hots for you."

"She has the hots for my money," Blair said. "That's the only thing she wants."

"I wouldn't say that, Blair," Todd replied. "You're a good man. She'd be lucky to have you."

He drew in a breath. "I knew her years ago. We were just friends. But she wanted to settle down. I didn't. At least, I didn't until Elise charmed me to a wedding chapel in Vegas."

"That ended badly."

"Yes, and now Janet's taking over where Elise left off," he laughed humorlessly. "It's not working. I can't stand the sight of her now. I had my attorney tell her that if she showed up in one more place I was, I'd have the police arrest her for stalking. I could make the charge stick, too."

"That would hit her right in the pocketbook."

"It's the only vulnerable thing about her," Blair sighed. He looked around the lonely hotel room in Germany and thought absently that he spent his whole life in hotels. He had a house that he never saw. He hated it, because it was empty. Like he was empty. Like his life was empty.

"Maybe I need a break from business," he added.

"It might help."

"Don't let her marry the health nut, Todd," Blair said quietly.

"I can't stop her from doing anything she wants to," came the wry reply. "You know that." He paused. "If you want to stop her, get down here and do it yourself."

Blair pursed his lips. "I might just do that. Of course, people would talk."

"People always talk. So what?"

He smiled. "I'll phone you the night before I come down."

"That works. Be careful over there."

"I'm always careful. See you."

"See you."

If he'd wondered how his best friend would feel about him and Niki, he had the answer. He felt as if a weight had been lifted from him. Maybe he was wrong. Maybe it could work between them. He remembered the feverish hunger Niki had for him, the love shining out of her bright eyes, the response she couldn't even hide when he held her.

He ground his teeth together. First order of business was to get home and see Niki.

"Niki, you're falling behind," Dan muttered, coming back to see about her. "You have to keep up."

"I'm…trying…" she panted. It was hard to even draw a breath. Her harebrained scheme felt more and more ridiculous as she tried to get air into her lungs. The problem was that she couldn't get it out in the first place. Air came in and stayed.

She felt dizzy. She looked at Dan with eyes that barely saw him through the discomfort.

"I…can't…breathe," she whispered.

"You have to just work your lungs," he said curtly. "Come on, Niki, just breathe!"

If she'd had the strength, she'd have smacked him in the head with all her strength. She didn't even have enough wind to answer him.

An older woman in the party, Nancy, came back to see about her, frowning.

"Niki, do you have your inhaler?" the woman asked gently.

Niki managed to shake her head. "Forgot…it…"

The woman lifted Niki's hand and stared at her fingernails, then at her lips. "Call 911," she told Dan. "Do it right now!"

"But we're almost halfway through the hike," Dan said, not comprehending. "She can make it. She just needs to rest a minute or two and concentrate on her breathing."

"You lamebrained idiot!" the woman snapped at him. "She's cyanotic, can't you see?" She held Niki's blue fingernails up to him. "She'll go into anaphylactic shock and die if you don't get help for her right now!"

"Oh, that's ridiculous," Dan started to argue.

Niki started wheezing violently and fell to the ground.

"I'm a nurse. I know a medical emergency when I see one!" She pulled out her cell phone and dialed 911.

CHAPTER NINE

NIKI WAS AIRLIFTED out of the area by helicopter. She didn't remember much of the trip. She was given an injection and oxygen, and the nurse on the hike who'd called 911, Nancy, went with them, helping the EMT with the saline drip.

"Of all the stupid men I've ever seen in my life," the nurse was raging. "The fool wanted to wait and make her hike the rest of the way!"

The EMT shook his head. "I've seen people die like this. It doesn't take long, either. Good thing you were there and knew what to do."

"Good thing I always carry strong black coffee in a thermos wherever I go," the nurse said with a smile. She'd fed coffee to Niki while they waited for the helicopter. "How are you doing, sweetheart?" she asked Niki, touching her hand lightly.

Niki managed to nod and gave the woman a weary smile. Her own stupid idea had led to all this trouble, and she couldn't admit to these kind people that she'd been hoping not to be saved in time. Looking back, it was a terrible way to die. She could still hardly get her breath.

"Not a lot of people know about strong coffee stopping asthma attacks," the EMT chuckled. "I used it on a coworker who didn't even know he was asthmatic until he started coughing around a flower bed and couldn't stop. Some people cough instead of wheeze. He went to a doctor and was diagnosed."

"How did you know about it?" the nurse asked, curious.

He smiled. "I'm asthmatic myself."

She smiled back. "I'll bet you don't go on hiking trails with brain-dead idiots."

"Not like the one leading your group, and that's a fact," he said flatly. "He went on to the end with the rest of them, I gather?"

"Oh, yes, couldn't be bothered to make sure Niki was all right." She leaned forward. "He thought she was faking it for attention!"

Niki blocked out the conversation around her and closed her eyes. The coffee had tasted nice, and it had helped the spasms. She'd have to remember to do something nice for the kind lady who'd helped her. But she was still left with the terror ahead, and didn't know how she was going to cope. It would be horrible for her father, who'd already gone through it once.

But he didn't know yet, and she'd made Doctor Fred promise not to tell him. It was her burden. It was her decision. When she finally decided what she was going to do, she'd tell him then.

DOCTOR FRED CHECKED her out in the emergency room, where he was on duty that morning. He gave her a very angry glare when he discovered that she didn't have a rescue inhaler with her.

"Dan says I'm pampering myself too much," she said hoarsely. "He says I don't need inhalers or preven-

tatives, I just need—" she paused for breath "—herbs
and vitamins and fresh...air."

"The fresh air damned near killed you. You tell
him that!" he said irritably. "I can't believe your father lets you date such a fool!"

"I just turned...twenty-three," she pointed out.

"Age and maturity are two separate things," he said
curtly. He finished his examination. "You're better,
but I'm keeping you overnight."

"I won't have the test, so don't start," she told him.

He ground his teeth together. "It could be nothing," he pointed out. "It could be a lot of things besides what you're afraid of."

She lay back down and winced. "My chest hurts."

"You've got bad bronchitis. We'll treat that while
you're here. Antibiotics and rest. And no more
damned hiking expeditions!"

She shrugged. "He said it would help me."

He didn't reply. He wanted to slug the man who'd
taken her on that hike. When her father found out, it
was going to take some muscle to save Dan Brady.
And if Blair Coleman found out, the young man had
better be on his way out of the country.

"Did you call your father?" Doctor Fred asked.

She winced.

"You don't have your cell phone with you, either,
do you?" He glowered at her.

"No."

"I guess Dan thought that would be bad for you,
too," he muttered as he left her to the nurse. "Get her
into a room, please," he called over his shoulder. "I'll
call her father."

"Yes, Doctor," the nurse replied, smiling at Niki.

THEY GAVE HER something for the discomfort, along with antibiotics and the ever-present IV. She fell asleep, exhausted from the day's trauma.

Hours later she felt a hand on her hair.

She opened her eyes and looked up and smiled wearily. "Hi, Daddy."

"Gave us a scare, Tidbit," he said, trying to hide the terror he'd felt when Doctor Fred called and told him what had happened. "Left your phone and your inhaler at home. Bad girl."

"I was excited about the trip," she lied. "I remembered it when we got to the hiking trail."

"Some help it was, then."

"I guess."

"I owe that nurse a dinner," he added. "The EMT told Fred Morris about her. She had strong coffee in a thermos and fed it to you while they waited for the rescue chopper. Saved your life, most likely."

"She did. She was so kind." She grimaced. "She gave Dan the devil."

"I'm waiting for him to show up so I can give him a little evidence of my displeasure," he said, his blue eyes flashing like ice crystals. "He actually finished the hike without you!"

"He thought I was pretending," she said.

"My God."

She studied him. "You haven't…talked to Blair?" she asked quickly.

He frowned. "I should call him…"

"No!"

He scowled. "Niki, I know you two had an argument, but…"

"No!"

"Honey, he cares about you," he began.

"He cares about Janet," she said harshly. "Didn't you see the magazine? She told me she was going to get him." She closed her eyes, blind to his shocked expression. "He told me that Janet was worth a dozen of Elise and he wished he'd never broken it off. So no, don't call him. This isn't his business. It's ours."

He bit his lower lip almost through. "Niki…"

"I mean it."

He gave in, as he always did when she was insistent. "If that's what you really want."

She closed her eyes. "It is. He'd come out of misplaced loyalty to you, but that's the only reason he'd come. He told me how it was. I'm infatuated with him. It's demeaning, is how he put it."

Todd's face contorted. Blair had dug himself a very deep hole there, and it was going to take a lot more than words to fill it back up again. He knew the man was conflicted, and he knew how he felt about Niki. But he'd apparently done some major damage to her pride and she was running.

Better a man years her senior than a stupid young man who'd almost killed her.

"You're not leaving the house with Dan Brady ever again," Todd said curtly. "I mean that. If you push me, I'll have Blair fire him, and I'll tell him exactly why he needs to fire him."

"Daddy!"

His face was as hard as she'd ever seen it. "He needs to go back to where he came from and start a health-food store. Then he can spend all his time advising people with illnesses how to overcome them with methods every researcher on earth never knew!"

Niki had to smother a grin. Her father was eloquent when he got going.

He shrugged. "Hey. You're my daughter. I love you."

She did smile then. "I love you, too, Dad." She drew in a breath, amazed that she could. "Thanks."

He smoothed back her disheveled blond hair. "For what?"

"For being my dad."

He fought tears. "Go to sleep, honey. I'll be right here."

"I'm sorry."

"You don't have a thing to be sorry about."

SHE FELT EVEN more guilt when she saw how upset her father had been about her misadventure on the hiking trail. It had been a selfish act, what she'd done. She'd thought only of herself, not of her father.

He didn't know, and she couldn't tell him, about the stupid decision she'd made out of panic. But she was afraid. She couldn't share that fear, not after what he'd endured when her mother had gone through the treatment. If he was upset now, he'd be ten times more upset to know what was really going on. She just couldn't tell him.

She tormented herself with the fear. If it was more than just a spot in her lung, and they did radiation, she could never get pregnant. She'd researched it on the internet. She knew that people had tried to get pregnant afterward, but most attempts ended in miscarriage. If she'd been barren, perhaps it wouldn't matter so much. But she was certain that she wasn't.

She couldn't bear the thought. Her mind went back

to the Yellowstone trip with Blair, back in the days when they were happy together. When he smiled at her and liked her and spoiled her. It hurt to recall the last time they'd spoken. It hurt too much for her to want to see him again. He had Janet now. He'd marry her and be happy. It was what she should want for him, if she truly loved him—for him to be happy. It was selfish to want him for herself, especially under the circumstances. She might not even have a future. She turned her head on the pillow, so that her father wouldn't see the tears.

DAN BRADY SHOWED up at the hospital that night. Her father had gone downstairs to the cafeteria to get a bite to eat.

Niki stared at Dan with pure fury. She didn't dare get upset. It would only bring the spasms back, despite the medicine they were giving her. She just glared.

He came into the room and looked around. His hands were in his pockets and he looked oddly hesitant.

"I guess you weren't faking it after all," he said slowly.

Niki glared even more.

He moved a step closer. "The others said to tell you they hope you'll be better soon."

She didn't speak.

"Oh, come on, Niki," he muttered. "This is what happens when you're overprotected! You can't even cope with the outdoors at all! If you'd spent more time outside, and if you'd been eating right and boosting your immune system, you wouldn't even have a breathing issue!"

Niki stared at him and wondered if she could get up just long enough to push him out the window.

BLAIR HAD JUST made it home from his trip to Frankfurt. He was bone tired and still irritated at Janet's persistence. He'd cut one of his meetings short mainly to get her off his back. She'd have no reason to trail him back to Montana. If she did, he'd have her arrested for stalking, he promised himself.

He couldn't stop thinking about Niki. It had hurt her, the things he'd said in the heat of the moment. He'd been doing it for her own good, but that didn't make it any easier. She was such a gentle soul, so kind and compassionate. A woman like that came along once in a man's lifetime.

Janet had tried to convince him that Niki had plotted to seduce him, but that had been a lie. He knew better. Niki was no seductress. She hadn't even known how to kiss properly until he taught her.

He groaned inwardly, remembering all the things he'd taught her, first in Mexico, and then in the forest near the Ashton home outside Catelow. She'd never even tried to resist him. She wanted him as badly as he wanted her. But he'd made her ashamed. He'd told her that what they'd shared was demeaning. He closed his eyes on an inward shudder of guilt. To make a tender, kind woman like that ashamed of passion, oh, that was the mark of a man, all right. He felt the guilt right down to his feet.

Well, he needed to see the Ashtons and find a way to apologize. She might never forgive him, but he had to try. He thought of her new boyfriend, the health-food fanatic, and worried that it might already be too late to make amends. If only he hadn't been so stupid!

He picked up his cell phone and dialed Todd's number, but it was cut off. He tried the house phone instead. It rang three times. He was about to hang up when a tired voice came on the line.

"Ashton residence."

"Edna?"

"Oh. Hello, Mr. Coleman."

"Is Todd there? I can't get him on his cell phone."

She hesitated. She swallowed, hard. She wasn't supposed to say anything about Niki. "He's not here right now."

"Is Niki there, then?" he persisted.

"No…" Her voice broke.

He felt his stomach clench as if he'd been struck. "Edna, what's going on?" he asked curtly.

"I'm not supposed to tell you," she said, but her voice was so wobbly that he could barely understand her.

"My God," he whispered, terrified. "Something's happened to Niki! Tell me! God, Edna, please tell me!"

The desperation in his tone melted her resolve. "Mr. Ashton's at the hospital, Mr. Coleman," she said, swallowing tears. "They had to airlift her. That stupid man took her hiking, and she didn't have her inhaler…"

"Is she all right?" he asked, and his voice sounded as tormented as Edna was certain her own did.

"They stabilized her, but her lungs are messed up again, so they've kept her. Mr. Ashton is there, hoping that stupid man shows up so he can beat the living hell out of him. Sorry, sir," she faltered.

"I'm coming down. Don't tell them."

"Yes, sir." Ten minutes later, Blair was on his way to Catelow in his executive jet. He prayed every step of the way. If he hadn't behaved like a fool, Niki would never have let that maniac take her hiking. She'd have been at home, or at work, or with him. He closed his eyes on a wave of guilt. He'd been running. Somehow, he was going to make amends. It was time to stand and fight. For the woman he loved.

"I KNOW YOU don't think exercise is the answer," Dan was droning on, "but it makes your body strong. It's good for your lungs, too. You have to stop babying yourself and letting your father be overprotective…"

Niki's eyes had grown wide while he was speaking. But he didn't realize why until he was snapped around and his jaw connected with a big, angry fist.

He ended up out in the hall on his butt, and a man the size of a steamroller went after him, his black eyes glittering like a poisonous snake, his big fists clenched at his sides.

"Get up," the man said in a voice like thunder.

Dan was on the floor gaping at Blair when Todd Ashton rounded the corner and took in the scene.

"Well, hell, couldn't you have saved a piece of him for me?" he asked with pure malice.

Blair didn't answer. He was consumed with rage. He pulled out his cell phone and dialed. "Ed? I want this California maniac out of the office and on a plane back to San Francisco first thing in the morning. That's right. He can have a shot at saving his job

by accepting. If he refuses—" he looked right at Dan
Brady "—terminate him!" He hung up, gave Brady
one last flaming glare and went into Niki's room.

"He can't fire me. Who does he think he is?" Dan
asked as he dragged himself to his feet and touched
his aching jaw.

"That's Blair Coleman," Todd told him. "And your
job isn't all you're likely to lose if you don't take that
offer."

"Blair Coleman?" Brady faltered, red-faced. "*The*
Blair Coleman?"

"There's only one." He jerked his head toward the
stairs. "If I were you, I'd think carefully about giving
him any reason to come back out here."

"I was only trying to help," Dan said irritably.

"You almost helped my daughter into the morgue,"
Todd said flatly. "Out."

Dan didn't hesitate. Todd Ashton looked almost
as formidable as Coleman had. He moved toward the
stairs. "Niki's never going to get better unless you all
stop pampering her," he began.

Todd took an angry step toward him. Dan ran for
the staircase.

A nurse at the desk gave him an amused glance
and went back to her computer.

NIKI WATCHED BLAIR knock Dan Brady out of her room
and into the hallway with total shock. She hadn't
known he was back in Montana. She'd never really
seen Blair lose his temper that badly, not even when
she was assaulted by the football player and he res-
cued her three years ago.

He talked to someone on the phone, then came

back into the room, right about the time her father showed up in the hall and talked to Dan.

Blair's eyes were still glittering with anger when he paused by her bed. "How are you?" he asked.

She averted her eyes to the blanket. "I've been better." She was still hoarse. "Nobody was supposed… to tell you."

"Nobody did," he lied convincingly. "I stopped by to see your father. He wasn't there and Edna was almost in hysterics. It didn't take much guesswork to know why."

"Oh."

He stuck his hands in his pockets and did his best to get his temper back under control. He felt as if he were still vibrating. "I told Ed Jacobs to get Brady on the next flight to San Francisco."

She bit her lip. "He didn't make me go on the hike," she said weakly.

"No. I did that, didn't I?" he asked. "I pushed you right into his arms."

She couldn't meet his eyes. "It was my decision. My fault. All of it." She closed her eyes and tried to get a deep breath. It was still difficult.

"He means well. He really does," she added weakly.

He felt as breathless as Niki sounded, but he was still choking on rage. He turned his eyes toward the window. The sun was just going down.

Her father came back in the room, breaking the awkward silence. "I told Brady to get out or else," he said. His face was as hard as Blair's was. "Did she tell you what he did?" he raged.

"Dad, don't…" she began.

"He left her! She went almost into shock. If there

hadn't been a nurse on the hike who knew what to do and called 911, she'd be dead!"

"Dad, you're shouting," Niki protested weakly.

Blair's face had gone pale. "What?"

"He thought she was faking," Todd said icily. "The nurse gave her coffee from her thermos to help with her breathing and called for an airlift to get Niki to the hospital. Brady thought she was faking and took off with the other hikers to get to the end of the trail! The nurse stayed with the paramedics and flew in with Niki so that she could tell the emergency room physician what had happened."

Blair didn't speak. He couldn't. He'd never felt such rage in his entire life. If Brady had been close by, he'd have killed him.

"I know," her father said gently, patting the other man's shoulder as they both stared at Niki. "I was thinking the same thing. But Niki would have to come and visit us in prison if we kill Brady. Besides, we both look bad in orange."

Blair took deep breaths. So this was what he'd condemned Niki to, with his coldness, his fear. But for the grace of God, she would have been dead today. He'd thought because of the age difference she'd be stuck with an older man and have to watch him die. How naive and stupid he'd been. Her health was so uncertain that keeping her alive would be the challenge. She needed someone to take care of her, to nurture her. To love her. That idiot health-food fanatic had almost killed her by telling her she was pampering herself, that her father was overprotective! The longer he thought about it, the more the rage grew inside him.

"Blair, if you don't relax, your muscles are going

to atrophy in that position. How about some coffee?"
Todd said after a minute.

Blair swallowed. "I could use a cup."

"So could I. I'll be back in a minute." He smiled
at Niki and left them alone again.

Niki was left with Blair's guilt and her own. She
picked at the coverlet. "I did a stupid thing. Several stupid things. I won't do them ever again." She
glanced up at his set features and back down again.
"You probably should come back another day, when
things are less hectic for Dad so that you can talk
business."

"I didn't come to talk to your father."

He moved closer to the bed, his hands still in his
slacks pockets. "Can't you look at me?" he asked quietly.

She tried to smile. "Not really." She swallowed.
"I'm tired, Blair." She closed her eyes. "I don't want
to talk, okay?"

He stared down at her wan, drawn face. He was
remembering a happy woman with the sun shining
out of her face, teasing and smiling and always upbeat. What a contrast it was now.

"I've made so damned many mistakes with you,"
he said solemnly. "I don't know how to begin to apologize for any of them."

"It doesn't matter. Not anymore."

His teeth ground together. "Niki…"

She turned her head away, trying to hide the tears
that were seeping out of the corners of her eyes. But
she wasn't quick enough.

She heard the quick intake of his breath, smelled
the cologne he wore, the faint clean scent of his cot-

ton shirt. Then she felt his mouth moving over her closed eyelids, sipping away the tears. One big hand rested on the pillow at her head.

"Don't," he whispered roughly. "I already want to put a gun to my temple."

"Not…your fault."

"Everything is my fault," he said gruffly. His mouth moved to her cheeks, her temples, and back to her drenched eyes. "I'm sorry, honey. I'm so sorry!"

Which did nothing to stop the tears.

He drew her face into his throat and smoothed her disheveled hair. His face was drawn into such torment that the nurse who'd come in to check on Niki walked right out again.

He held her while she wept. When she calmed, he drew out a spotless handkerchief and mopped up her face.

"I'll buy you a deer antler necklace to match your bracelet if you'll stop crying, Niki," he said softly.

She looked up into sad eyes in a drawn, but smiling broad face. She dragged her gaze back down to his chest before he could see the loving anguish in her face. It was too late. And just as well. He didn't need to be involved in her life, in what was coming. He was carrying enough guilt already, and it was unnecessary. It wasn't his fault that he couldn't love her back.

She lay back on the pillows. "Sorry," she managed. "It all caught up with me."

He stood up, wincing as he saw the result of the tears and pain and fear on her face. Odd, though, how the fear was still there. She was safe now. Why would she be afraid now? And of what?

HE DROPPED INTO a chair beside the bed.

"You should go…" she began again.

"I'm not leaving Catelow until your bean sprout–eating friend is on that plane and gone," he said flatly, the residue of the rage he still felt in his black eyes as they met hers.

"I'm okay," she said.

He drew in a long, steadying breath and locked her fingers into his on the edge of the bed. "No, baby, you're not okay. Something's wrong. Something more than this."

Her head turned on the pillow. Her eyes were huge and frightened.

He was right. There was more. His fingers became caressing around hers. "Niki, I didn't get where I am by missing details," he said softly. His black eyes moved over her face like an artist's brush, sketching every soft line. "You didn't take your rescue inhaler or a cell phone with you, did you? I might buy that you could forget one at home. But not both."

Her face flushed. She tried to draw her fingers back, but he held them tight.

"You're afraid of something. You won't tell your father." His eyes narrowed. "Come on. What is it?"

She swallowed. "Not your business, Blair," she said, and managed a wan smile.

"Not my business." He looked at her small hand in his, at the nails only colored by a transparent layer of polish, short and pretty. He smoothed his fingers over them. "It used to be. We were friends."

"Yes, until Cancun…"

He drew her palm to his lips and pressed it hungrily there. "Dear God, of all the mistakes I've ever made in my whole damned life, that was absolutely the worst!" he ground out.

"We were friends until then," she said huskily. "I'm so sorry!"

"Baby, don't," he pleaded, and his voice was tormented. His heavy brows drew together as his mouth ground into her soft palm. "You didn't do anything wrong. The fault was mine. I lost my head and I was so ashamed that I just walked away, without a word."

"You said it was demeaning…"

"God!" He bent his head over her hand, gripping it so tightly that it was almost painful.

She couldn't understand his behavior. She drew in a breath. "It's okay, Blair," she said gently. "Really. I know it was just…infatuation." She smiled, but her face was almost white.

He lifted his head and looked into her pale, wounded eyes. "I said that, didn't I? That, and a lot more." His broad face was sad, still. His chest rose and fell heavily, and his black eyes fell back to her hand. "I thought I was doing what was best for you," he said in a soft, husky tone. He brought her fingers to his mouth and kissed them tenderly. "I wanted you to be happy, Niki."

"That's what I wanted for you, too," she said. Her eyes searched over him like seeking hands, loving hands. She averted her gaze when his eyes lifted. "Janet is kind, and you've known her for a very long time." She swallowed. "She'll take care of you."

His black eyes narrowed on her face. "You never told her that you were planning to seduce me, did you?" he asked pointedly.

She wouldn't meet his eyes.

His fingers wrapped around hers. "She's followed me all around the world for the past several weeks," he said. "I haven't encouraged her. I left Frankfurt a day early to avoid her. She's persistent. Just as she used to be." He stood up, so that she had to look up to see him. "Didn't it occur to you that if I'd wanted to marry her, I'd have done it when we were dating?"

She bit her lower lip. "Sometimes people don't see what's right under their noses," she said noncommittally.

"And sometimes they do, just in time," he replied gently. "I've still got your bathing suit," he said in a casual tone.

"What?"

"Your bathing suit. I brought it home in my suitcase. I put it in my closet."

Her face was flaming. "What? Why?" she stammered. "You said—"

"Baby, I said a lot of things," he interrupted. "I'd do anything to take them back, but it's too late. Now we have to go forward."

She was confused, and it was evident.

He smiled tenderly. "First things first." His eyes narrowed. "What's wrong, Niki? What sent you out into the wilds with Brady without an inhaler or your cell phone?"

She was scrambling for a lie that would cover the situation when the door swung open and her father walked in with two cups of coffee.

"Latte for me, cappuccino for you," he said, handing a cup to Blair. "Sorry, honey, but they'll string me up if I share it."

"Let them string me up." Blair raised the head of

the bed, uncapped his coffee and held it to Niki's lips. "You always order cappuccino everywhere we go," he said simply.

She took a sip, her eyes locked on to his, her heart pounding like a wild thing in her chest. He only smiled.

Her father pursed his lips and tried not to notice the interaction between them.

"Thanks," Niki whispered unsteadily.

His eyes were on her mouth so intently that she knew exactly what he was thinking. She flushed a little as he stood back up, with that smug, wicked smile on his lips.

He sipped from the cup exactly where Niki's lips had touched it, and he did it deliberately and let her see before he turned away.

"I'll be right back," Blair said. "I want to talk to Ed Jacobs."

"He doesn't know any hit men," her father pointed out.

"Damn our luck." Blair grinned, glanced at Niki and walked out.

"Your erstwhile hiking companion is going to have one hell of a black eye tomorrow," her father said smugly as he dropped into the chair beside Niki's bed.

"Blair is scary when he loses his temper," Niki said.

"He never loses it. Not like that. If I hadn't shown up, it might have ended in a homicide charge. Edna's sorry, by the way," he added. "She was so upset that Blair knew something was wrong and wormed it out of her."

"It's all right," Niki said quietly. She stared toward

the doorway with her heart in her eyes. "But it will make things harder."

"What things?" her father asked grimly.

She searched for an answer. "Janet."

"Oh. Her." He shook his head. "Blair's been trying to get rid of her for two weeks. Hopefully, she'll get the idea now."

"He's rich and she wants to be. But they were close when his mother was still alive."

He leaned forward. "Because his mother wanted them to be, and he did everything he could to make her happy." He sat up straight. "If Bernice had still been alive, however, Elise would have been out on her ear before she could have gotten her claws into him." His face hardened. "She's after him again, too." He shook his head. "Life is hard."

"Then you die," she said, and laughed. It was a tag line from Dempsey and Makepeace, an old television show that her father had loved. They watched episodes of it together on YouTube.

"Can I tell you something?" he asked.

"Sure. What?"

"Men don't get that angry at men like Brady without some violent emotions being present."

"He's my friend," Niki began.

"No, Niki. Blair's not just your friend," Todd said softly. "And you know it."

Blair came back into the room just in time to save her from responding.

"You're smiling," Todd said. "Did Ed know a hit man?"

"He just saw Brady off at the airport." He pursed his lips as he looked at Niki. "Apparently, he felt he was going to be safer a few states away from me."

CHAPTER TEN

BLAIR REFUSED TO leave the hospital room. One older, belligerent nurse tried to evict him when visiting hours ended, before the other nurses could warn her. He simply picked up his cell phone, called the administrator of the hospital at home and handed the phone to the nurse.

Flustered and apologetic, she finished her duties and went out again, her face very flushed.

"You're very intimidating," Niki pointed out.

He shrugged. "I'm not leaving you." His eyes said that, and more, as they locked on her face. "'I'm with you to the end of the line,'" he added huskily.

She smiled as he repeated the line she'd loved from *Captain America: The Winter Soldier*. She'd seen it with Blair several months ago.

He nodded and smiled back. "It was a great movie. A true friendship, undaunted by time or circumstance."

"I wasn't really impressed with Captain America until I saw the *Avengers* movie. I loved him in that, so I went with you to see Cap in his own movie. He's awesome, like the actor who plays him."

"Yes, he is." He cocked his head at her. "When are you going to trust me enough to share secrets with me?"

The smile faded. "Some secrets should be kept, Blair," she said quietly. "Besides, you have enough women in your life right now, don't you?" she added with a forced laugh.

"Everyone except the right one," he replied. "I pushed her out of my life for her own good. See where that got us?"

She stared at the coverlet, not responding.

"I can afford to fly the most expensive, famous specialists in the world to Billings to consult on your case," he said out of the blue. "I won't even tell your father if you don't want me to."

She bit her lower lip because it was trembling.

He stood up, leaned over the bed and kissed her cheek. "We'll talk about it later, when you're out of here." He stood up. "I know I've given you no reason to trust me lately. But I'll earn that trust back, if you give me the chance. I've never been as miserable in my life as I have since we came back from Mexico, Niki."

More tears made a path down her face.

"If friendship is all you want," he said huskily, "I'll try to manage just that. It isn't what I want. But I can settle for anything that will get you back into my life, in any way."

She looked up at him from drowned pale gray eyes, almost silver with the glitter of her tears. "You pushed me away! Said what I felt for you was...demeaning!" she said, repeating what he'd said that hurt most.

His eyes closed on a wave of guilt. "I lied. God forgive me, I lied to you. Niki, I'm almost thirty-nine years old," he ground out.

"What does that have to do with anything?" she asked softly, and seemed really not to know.

"I'm sixteen years older than you. It will matter one day," he bit off.

"To whom?" she asked reasonably. "Not to me."

"You're very young." He felt torn. "Brady wasn't the one, but there are nice men your age, Niki. You could still find one who'd love and cherish you, take care of you."

"Dan said I'd had too much of that already, that I needed to take care of myself," she said. "Maybe he was right. I do avoid exercise, and I don't always eat right."

"May I quote Ed Jacobs on that theory?" he asked her. "I might get thrown out of the hospital for language if I repeat exactly what he said. The gist of it is that while exercise and diet and supplements can help, they won't cure a cureless disease. Least of all his poor daughter's rheumatoid arthritis or your asthma."

She shifted in the bed, not knowing what to say. Blair's black eyes flashed like lightning. "I wish I'd hit him harder."

"Oh, Blair." She looked at him with soft, sparkling eyes. It was the first time since she'd been airlifted to the hospital that she'd really felt happy.

He caught his breath at the picture she made. Even with her pale blond hair unwashed and disheveled, her face pale from her experience, she was like sunshine.

"*Maste,*" he said, pronouncing it *mah-shday*.

"What?" she asked softly.

"It's a Lakota word," he said. "One of my security people is Lakota, from South Dakota. He taught me a little of the language. It means 'sunshine.' It's what I always think of when I think of you."

Her eyes brightened. She felt warm from the inside out. She searched over his broad, hard face. "You look so tired."

"I've been traveling for a long time," he replied. "Too long, maybe. I went to meetings when I could have delegated. I guess I was trying to outrun my conscience." He sighed. "Useless, but it gave me something to do while I was tormenting myself."

"About what?"

"You know about what," he returned. His eyes narrowed as they slid down her body and back up again. "Yes, you know, Niki. One sweet, long taste of you wasn't enough."

She closed her eyes on a silent moan. Then opened them and spoke.

"Janet told you that was what I was trying to do, with the bathing suit, trying to trick you into a relationship you didn't want, didn't she?"

"She lied. You won't admit it, but we both know it's true."

Her eyes opened into his and searched them hungrily. "I could never do something so dishonest," she said simply. "I thought… I thought you knew me better than that."

He went to the window, looking out it with anguish in his eyes that he didn't want her to see. "I told you that I believed her because I needed to." He touched the blinds. There was a very thin layer of dust. "It gave me a reason to run, to get away from you before I did something I couldn't take back."

She didn't understand what he was saying. She watched him quietly, curiously.

He turned back to her. "We'll save that discussion for another time, though," he said. "They should be bringing you something to eat soon."

"You should go down to the cafeteria and get something for yourself," she said. "You don't have to stay here all the time."

He moved closer. "I can't leave you." The words were simple. What his eyes were saying was far more complex. "I'll have no peace anywhere else in the world."

Tears threatened again. She was a watering pot, probably as a result of her recent trauma. But before she could answer, an aide came in bearing a tray. She pulled the one-armed table over Niki and put the tray down.

"JELL-O and soup, right?" Niki asked with resignation.

"Oh, no. Something much nicer." She lifted the metal lid.

"Beef stew? It's my favorite!" Niki enthused. "And strawberry ice cream?"

The aide exchanged a mischievous smile with Blair. "Well, the administrator thought it would be good for you. Since it's your favorite food and all," she teased. "Enjoy." She left, and Niki's eyes went to Blair's face.

"You wicked man," she teased.

The fatigue and worry went out of him at once when he saw that look on her face. He smiled and couldn't stop smiling. "I just donated a new MRI machine," he said. "It helps me get a few doctor-approved meal additions."

The mention of the machine made her uneasy. The smile faded.

"Come on, now, don't let that hard-won meal get cold." Blair told her gently. Whatever was wrong, he'd find some way to fix it later. No matter what.

She looked up at him worriedly. "It's just…"

He picked up a fork and captured a potato wedge. "Open up," he whispered, smiling.

She opened her mouth, and he ladled the food into it. She watched him, fascinated, while she ate. He fed her every bite, right down to the small cup of strawberry ice cream they gave her for dessert. She didn't take her eyes off him the entire time.

After an aide picked up the tray and she was given her last meds for the day, he covered her gently with the blanket.

"Try to sleep, honey. I'll be right here."

"You can't sleep in a chair," she argued.

"It's no use, don't you know?" he whispered, bending to brush a soft, tantalizing kiss across her mouth. "I won't leave you. Ever."

He kissed the hot tears off her cheeks, sat back down in the chair and linked her fingers with his. He stayed like that until long after she was asleep.

WHEN SHE WOKE the next morning to the sound of bustling noises in the hall, Blair was fast asleep in the chair. A fine growth of beard made his face a little darker. He wasn't even snoring. When he heard her move, he came awake instantly.

"I wish you'd go to the house and sleep in a bed," she said gently, wincing.

"I'll go home when you do," he replied. He got to his feet and stretched. He touched his chin and grinned. "Well, I might go to the house and beg a shave and a bath. But I'll be back by the time they get through with your bath and breakfast," he promised. He leaned over and kissed her forehead. "Don't try to escape."

"Okay." She was looking at him with soft, wondering eyes.

He was barely able to make himself walk out the door. In spite of everything he'd done, all the mistakes he'd made, she was forgiving him, loving him all over again. He thanked God for miracles and drove back to the Ashton house.

TODD WAS JUST having breakfast. "How is she?" he asked.

"Better," Blair said. "They were getting ready to bathe and feed her, so I thought I'd take advantage of that to have a quick shower and shave."

"You can have coffee and breakfast, too," Todd chuckled. "Listen, I talked to Fred Morris. He said they can put a rollaway bed in Niki's room for you."

He shook his head. "I'm punishing myself, didn't you know?" he asked gently. "I've made her miserable. Now it's payback time."

Todd shook his head. "Okay. But a bed is better than a chair for sleeping."

"She'll be home soon anyway." He paused. "There's something she's hiding, Todd. Something that worries her. I can't get it out of her. But I thought, when she's recovered a bit, I might take her home with me for a few days. Jameson will spoil her, and I'll try to get her to talk."

Todd drew in a breath. "I know. I can't get her to tell me anything, either. Doctor Fred looks guilty all the time but when I ask him why, he clams up. He knows something. I just can't intimidate him enough to get it out of him."

"I'll get it out of Niki. I'll do it in a nice way," he added. He pursed his lips. "What does she like, Lindt chocolates and French pastry? I can have the first shipped in, and Jameson can make the latter. We have a cappuccino machine, as well."

Todd chuckled. "All the comforts of home and more, eh?"

Suddenly, his cell phone rang. He checked the caller ID, glared at it and answered. "Yes?"

Janet purred, "Hi, Blair, I was wondering if you would mind a houseguest for a few days?"

"Sorry, I'm expecting other company."

"Oh." She hesitated. "Perhaps some other time?"

"Perhaps," he bit off, "you'd better find some other man to pursue or you're going to be facing stalking charges. I thought my attorney told you that. I also know the owner of the film company you work for. Keep that in mind."

There was a shocked pause. "I… I thought… I mean, you took me out in New York and bought me diamonds," she began.

"The diamonds were a nice way of saying go away," he added harshly. "I'm sorry that I have to use threats to get you to understand that I meant it."

She hesitated. "I see. It's Niki, I guess," she added

heavily. "Look, I'm sorry. I got things backward. I was caught up in the memories of how close we were and hoping we'd be that way again. I just lost my way a little. I'm sorry."

He was, too.

Janet laughed nervously. "I'm sorry I didn't get the message. I won't bother you again. Honest."

"I'd appreciate it."

"Goodbye, Blair. I really hope you'll be happy."

He didn't reply. He just hung up.

"Janet again, I guess?" Todd asked.

"Some women won't give up."

"Not a problem I've ever had," he chuckled. "But you could buy and sell me, buddy. Women like trinkets."

"I bought Niki a bracelet at Yellowstone," Blair recalled with a smile. "Rawhide with a medallion made of a deer antler. She thought it was the most beautiful thing in the store." His smile faded. "When I took Elise there, on our honeymoon, she wanted the most expensive turquoise jewelry in the case and never once said thank you."

"Have the lawyers hashed out that situation yet?" Todd asked.

Blair shrugged. "I hired a private detective," he said surprisingly. "You might know him, Dane Lassiter out of Houston."

"No, but I've heard of him."

"There's something about Elise, something I can't quite figure out," he continued. "She has more than enough alimony to keep her comfortable, but she keeps wanting more and more. I thought it was greed at first, but I'm wondering if someone isn't trying to blackmail her."

Todd's eyebrows arched. "Blackmail her about what? She doesn't have a job, does she?"

"In fact, she does. She's an actress. The producer of the play she's currently starring in has given her a cut of the profits. If it's a success, she'll be rich in her own right, without having to depend on what I give her." He pursed his lips. "Apparently, acting is what she wants most in life, and this is her big chance."

"She is beautiful," Todd replied with grudging praise.

"Not like Niki," the other man said quietly. "Elise's beauty is only on the outside," Blair said. "Niki's beauty shines out of her like the sun itself."

Todd sipped coffee and pretended not to notice the rapt expression on his friend's face.

"I left my bag in the car. If you don't mind a house-guest for a few days…?" Blair asked.

"Don't be absurd," Todd chuckled. "You do need a shave," he added with pursed lips. "You look like a grizzly bear."

"What ever happened to that cowboy who was buying metal construction toys for his little girl and complaining that she was female?" Blair asked suddenly, remembering a Christmas he'd spent here.

"Oh, Roy Blake's little girl." Todd's eyes twinkled. "Her mother just had a little boy. So for her birthday, Daisy got her first real doll."

"Good for her."

"Niki loves children," Todd said. "When she was younger, every time I'd take her out, she'd find her way into a baby shop or the children's section of a department store."

Blair's heart soared. He wanted children, too. Niki would look sweet with a baby in her arms.

"I'll clean up and come back for breakfast. Thanks," he added.

Todd just grinned.

NIKI WAS SITTING up in bed in the hospital, reading a book on her iPad. It was a sweeping romance, set in Paris, with a hero who curled her toes. She looked up when Blair walked back in, wearing tan slacks and a yellow knit designer shirt. He looked elegant and very handsome.

"You look rested," she said.

"So do you, honey." He bent and brushed his mouth gently over her soft lips. "Feeling better?"

The brief caress had shaken her, and she tried to hide it. "Yes. Much better, thanks. Doctor Fred may let me go home tomorrow."

He sat down in the chair beside the bed. "Suppose you come home with me for a few days?" he asked.

She hesitated.

"Jameson isn't invasive, but he's usually around," Blair said with a teasing smile. "I can even have a dead bolt put on your bedroom door and tell any visitors that you're a relative."

She flushed. "Stop."

He chuckled. "Nothing will happen," he said softly. "I'll drive you over to Hardin and we'll look at the battlefield. We won't walk far. And I'll carry your inhaler and your cell phone. Just to make sure you don't forget them," he added, tongue in cheek.

"Blair, I don't know," she faltered.

He took her fingers in his and linked them. "You won't tell your father. But you'll tell me," he added quietly, holding her eyes. "Whatever it is, whatever's wrong, I'll fix it. I promise."

She winced. "What if you can't fix it?" she asked.

He felt, for the first time, a skirl of real fear. "What is it, Niki?"

She averted her eyes. "I can't talk about it. Not yet."

His fingers contracted. "Will you? If I promise not to tell your father?"

She didn't speak for a minute. But finally, she nodded. Blair wasn't really involved with her. He didn't want her for anything except a friend, so it wouldn't hurt him to know. She had to tell someone. It was killing her, holding the fear inside.

"That's a promise, then," he said.

"Yes, Blair," she agreed. "It's a promise."

THE NURSE WHO'D saved Niki on the hike stopped by to see how she was. She worked in the hospital in Billings, but she was visiting a friend in Catelow.

"You look much better," she said, smiling at Niki. She glanced curiously at Blair sitting in the chair by the bed, holding Niki's hand. He stood up. Old-world courtesy still occupied a place in him. He smiled at her.

"This is Blair." Niki introduced them. "This is Nancy, the nice lady who stayed with me and fed me coffee until the rescue helicopter got to us."

"Her father and I owe you a tremendous debt," Blair said, shaking her hand.

"I was happy to help," she replied. Her face hardened. "I would, however, like to shake that young man who thought she was pretending."

"I knocked him out into the hall," Blair said complacently.

"Good for you!" the nurse chuckled.

"Thank God you knew what to do," Blair continued. "And that you had GPS on your cell phone."

"It comes in handy. I've always liked hiking. Fresh air really is good for you." She stared at Niki. "Unless you have asthma, and pollen counts are through the roof," she added pointedly.

Niki flushed and laughed softly. "I let Dan convince me that I was overreacting to the great outdoors."

"Dan is an idiot. One day he'll prescribe some herbal supplement and involve himself in a lawsuit or a homicide complaint," Nancy said. She shook her head. "I believe some of that is beneficial. But fanaticism is dangerous in more ways than one."

"I agree," Blair said.

The nurse was staring at him. "Odd, but I think I know you."

Blair's eyes narrowed. "I have the same feeling."

She thought for a minute. Then she laughed. "You're Blair Coleman. Of course! I did private duty with your mother when I was just out of nursing school. She had gall bladder surgery and I cared for her at home for a few days." Her expression softened. "She was a unique woman. Compassionate and kind. She was worried that I'd strain myself lifting her." She shook her head. "Such a rare person. Especially in this day and time."

"She thought a lot of you, Nancy."

The nurse, who was in her fifties and blonde, grinned. "That's me. I'm in charge of a ward at the hospital in Billings, so I don't do private nursing anymore." She glanced at Niki. "I'm so glad you're mending. I was worried that the helicopter might not be in time. You should always carry a thermos of strong black coffee with you on outings, just in case."

"I'll remember," Niki promised.

Nancy smiled. "I'm going home today, but I wanted to check in on you. Take care of yourself."

"I will. Thank you again. I won't ever forget you."

"I won't forget you, either. Mr. Coleman," she added, nodding, as she left them alone.

"Dad and I should do something for her," Niki said a minute later.

"Dad and you and I should do something for her," Blair amended, glancing at her warmly.

DOCTOR FRED CAME by that evening on his rounds. He was amused to see Blair still sitting by Niki's bed in the uncomfortable chair.

"You're mending nicely," he told Niki. He paused by the bedside. "You can go home in the morning, but I want you to use the respirator. You've got albuterol for it?"

"Yes, sir," she replied.

"Twice a day. Continue on the antibiotics and that pulse of steroids I also prescribed. And stay out of the outdoors unless you wear a mask!"

"Yes, sir," she sighed.

He glanced at Blair. "Don't let that tofu-eating idiot do this to her again."

"He left town," Blair replied.

Fred pursed his lips. "I understand there was an altercation and Mr. Brady left here with a few bruises?"

"I only hit him once," Blair said. "And not as hard as I wished I had, when I learned exactly what happened."

Doctor Fred studied Niki. "Won't you change your mind about what we discussed?"

"No," she said stiffly.

Blair looked at the doctor. "She's going home with me," he told the other man. "I'm going to bribe her with Lindt chocolates and cappuccino and make her tell me what's going on. I promised I wouldn't tell her father."

"Thank God," the doctor said heavily. "I delivered her, you know," he told Blair. "She's making a mistake and she won't listen to me."

"She'll listen to me," Blair said gently. He smiled at her. "Won't you, baby?"

She flushed and couldn't answer.

Doctor Fred just grinned. "Okay, then, I'll give the order to release you first thing tomorrow. The nurse will have your prescriptions ready. You call my office for an appointment in a week. I want to check you out, to make sure there are no complications. You know the drill, right?" he said to Blair. "Any congestion that brings up colored sputum, any fever…?"

"I know it very well," he replied. He looked at Niki with an expression the doctor recognized. "I'll take good care of her," he added huskily.

Niki didn't say anything. She was lost in the black tenderness of his eyes.

BLAIR AND HER FATHER came to get her at the hospital
the next morning.

"Both of you?" she laughed, sitting in the chair in
her room, dressed in jeans and a pullover white knit
blouse. Her blond hair was loose, a little dingy but
still beautiful.

"I'm driving," her father said with a grin. "Blair's
riding shotgun, in case your friend Brady tries to
sneak back into the county."

"Oh, my goodness, my job!" Niki exclaimed. "I
didn't think to tell Mr. Jacobs...!"

"Jacobs hired a temp," Blair said, "and you're on
official sick leave for two weeks. Don't fuss," he
added when she opened her mouth, smiling down at
her. "He's so happy to have Brady out of the state that
he's willing to go along with anything."

"His poor daughter," Niki said softly. "Imagine,
to be so young and have that kind of illness, with
constant pain."

"One day there will be a cure," her father said.
"For her and for you."

Niki averted her eyes. "That would be nice," she
agreed, but she wasn't thinking of asthma. Her heart
was like lead in her chest. She felt the fear all over
again, and despite her best efforts to hide it, Blair
recognized it.

They drove her home. She was still coughing a little, but Doctor Fred had said that her lungs were clear.
He was less enthusiastic about her getting on a private
jet to go to Billings, so several days later Blair had a
limousine sent to Catelow to bring him and Niki up
to his home in Billings.

"I made you a cake," Edna told Blair and Niki,

handing them a lemon cake in a carrier. "It's your favorite—both of you." She beamed at Blair. "I would have made you stroganoff if you'd been here longer, from scratch. It was so kind of you."

"What was, Edna?" Blair asked.

"Beating the hell out of Mr. Brady," the housekeeper said curtly. "I would love to have kicked him myself," she added thoughtfully. Then she flushed. "Sorry."

"Don't be sorry," Niki said. "I considered the kicking part, too." Niki kissed Edna's cheek. "I won't be away long. We're going to see the Little Bighorn battlefield!"

"With a rescue inhaler, a cell phone and a surgical mask," Blair said darkly.

Her father chuckled. He hugged his daughter. "Have fun. We'll see you when you get home."

"Love you, Dad," she said at his ear.

"Me, too, Tidbit," he replied as he kissed her cheek. "Have a safe trip."

"We will." Blair handed her suitcase to the driver, who put it in the trunk with Blair's. He opened the back door for them. Niki got in, and Blair slid in beside her. And they were off.

THE ONLY PARTS of Blair's home that Niki had ever seen were the living room and the door of his study, when she and her father had gone to Billings to bring him to their house after his divorce was final.

So the rest of the house was something of an adventure. He had a huge indoor pool with potted plants all round it, and a miniature conservatory with exotic plants like orchids.

"It's amazing," Niki breathed, drinking it all in.

"I had the conservatory and the swimming pool added year before last," he said.

"Oh. For Elise."

He studied her. "No. For you." He smiled at her surprise. "Elise never even spent a night here, Niki. She hated Billings. She wanted Paris or Rome or New York."

"You don't like big cities," she said absently.

"I like Billings," he said. "In fact, I like Catelow just as much. Montana and Wyoming have a lot in common, the least of which is enough wide open space to keep a man from feeling crowded. And no, I don't like big cities."

She smiled at him shyly as she touched one of the orchids, a yellow one on a tall stem, gently, with just the tips of her fingers. "I've always loved orchids."

"You remind me of one," he replied quietly. "You did from the first time I saw you."

She turned. "That brooch you gave me, it wasn't off the shelf," she said knowingly.

He shrugged, smiling. "No. I had it commissioned especially for you. You're like that orchid, Niki," he added, and the smile faded. "You need careful handling."

She bit her lower lip. She averted her eyes and moved on to the ficus trees in their huge pots.

"I didn't mean that in a critical way," he said from behind her. He moved closer, taking her small waist in his hands and pulling her back to him, so that she could feel the power and heat of his body behind her. "I meant that you need nurturing. That's all."

Her fingers rested on top of his, idly caressing. "My lungs have always been weak," she agreed.

He felt a chill go through his body.

She drew in a long, shivering breath. She leaned her head back against him. "It's such a mess," she said quietly. "I don't know what to do. I'm so scared, Blair."

He turned her gently, framing her face in his big, warm hands. "Tell me."

She searched his worried black eyes. "Do you know how my mother died?"

"Yes. Your father told me."

"They found a little spot on her lung. Just a tiny dot. They said it would be easy. They'd take it out, do radiation and chemo, she'd be fine. They said that two times, Blair. She died, finally, in agony, struggling to breathe." She took a breath. "I was holding her hand when she died. I was only seven years old."

He drew her into his arms and held her, rocked her, against him. "I didn't know that."

"Dad doesn't talk about it. He gets so upset. He loved her more than anything in the world."

He was feeling the fear that ran through her. "What you don't want him to know, does it have something to do with that checkup you had, before the hike and the asthma attack?" he asked in a quiet, deep tone.

"I suppose so. I was being selfish, cowardly." She closed her eyes and rested her cheek against his chest. His heartbeat was very heavy and fast. "I thought how it had been for Mama, and about putting Daddy through all that again. I thought…it would be quick… but it wasn't, and I put a lot of people to so much trouble. Scared Dad to death, too. All for nothing."

He swallowed. His arms tightened. "Niki, what are you trying to tell me?"

She didn't know how to say it. She hadn't thought it would affect him, but she could feel a faint tremor in the big arms holding her.

He lifted his head and looked down into her wide, sad gray eyes. They were the color of fog rising off the river in late autumn, he thought.

"Come on. Tell me."

She drew in a breath. "Blair, they found a spot on my lung in the X-ray."

CHAPTER ELEVEN

BLAIR DIDN'T MOVE for a minute while he tried to deal with what she'd just told him. He thought of all the time he'd wasted running from her, and now there might not be any time left. What a fool he'd been!

He drew back. "What does Doctor Fred want you to do?"

"He wants to do a CT scan," she said heavily. "I don't see the use. I won't go through what Mama did, Blair, I won't put Daddy through it!"

"Listen to me," he said curtly. "I can get specialists, the best in the world, on your case. We can find a way to stop it!"

"And if we did? Blair, once I have radiation treatments, I can never have a baby. Never." Tears stung her eyes as she looked up at him. "What sort of life is that? I dreamed of having children, all my life…" Her voice broke. She pulled away from him and wrapped her arms around her waist. "They'll cut and treat and cut and treat until I'm a shadow of the person I was, and I'll still die."

"You won't," he said through his teeth. "No matter what it takes!"

She turned, and the look in her eyes was ancient. "Blair, you can't stop cancer. I know."

His face was pale, his eyes frightening to look into.

"Now do you understand?" she asked. "I was trying to spare my father. I know it was stupid, what I
did, letting Dan talk me into the hike, leaving my
medicine behind." She closed her eyes and shivered.
"I didn't realize until the attack started how horrible it would be, to die like that. I felt so stupid. All
those people trying to save me, Dad worried out of
his mind. I must have been crazy!"

"No. You were just afraid. I don't blame you. But
life is still life, Niki, for however long you might have
it."

"I…"

"You don't have to decide today," he said after a
minute. "Jameson had the cook prepare something
very special for supper. We'll eat and watch TV, then
you'll get a good night's sleep. Tomorrow we'll talk
about it again. Deal?"

"I won't change my mind," she told him.

He studied her wan face. "How big was the spot?"

"I didn't ask."

His eyes narrowed. "And Doctor Fred is certain
that it was cancer?"

She hesitated. "Well, no. He did say that it could
be a lot of other things. But with Mama's history…"

"I understand." He moved closer, drawing her into
his arms. "If it's very small," he said very gently,
"they might be able to remove it and give you time to
have a baby before it became dangerous."

She stared up at him. "You think so?"

"We can find out. A college friend of mine is an
oncologist. I can have him down here in a day to
confer."

She brightened. "There are fertility clinics," she began.

He put a big finger over her soft lips. "We'll talk about that when the time comes," he said huskily.

Her face was agonized. "I don't know what to do," she said. "Even if I had a child, I'd be gone. Daddy would have to raise it…"

His face was hard. "Decisions can wait until we know what we're up against. Okay?"

She grimaced. "That's the problem. I'm not sure I want to know what I'm up against." She closed her eyes and shivered. "Once they actually say the words…"

He drew her close and buried his face in her soft throat.

He was thinking about her father, about the horrible loss he'd faced. But he'd had Niki, a living symbol of the love he'd lost, a reason to stay alive.

Niki wanted a child more than anything. So did he. But he wanted Niki more. He couldn't bear to think of the long, lonely years ahead without her.

He forced the thought to the back of his mind. Whatever happened, whatever it cost, he wasn't going to lose Niki. No matter what it took, he'd find a way!

He let her go slowly. His face was hard. His black eyes were glittery with strong feelings. "One day at a time, Niki. Okay?"

She searched his black eyes slowly. Her whole body seemed to vibrate with the strength he was radiating.

"Yes?" he asked softly.

She hesitated, but he was so determined that she felt hope begin to rise in her. She nodded.

"And you'll stop worrying until we know something for sure," he said firmly.

She reached up and drew her fingers slowly down
his hard cheek. "You're my best friend, Blair," she
said huskily. "Thank you. For everything…"

"I'll call my friend Trevor tonight and speak with
him. If he has some free time, I'll get him down here
tomorrow to consult. He and Doctor Fred can arrange
the CT scan at the hospital here. I'll go with you."

She ground her teeth together. "So soon?" she
asked in anguish.

"Niki, the sooner, the better," he said, his voice
deep and troubled. "Knowing is always better than
guessing. You can't fight unless you know what you're
going to have to fight against."

She drew in a breath. "All right, Blair."

He pressed his lips to her forehead. "Optimism
doesn't cost anything, you know."

She laughed. "No. You're right." She moved closer
to him. "I love your house, by the way."

He smiled as he threw a big arm around her thin
shoulders. "I'm glad you like it, honey." He bent and
brushed his mouth tenderly against hers. He lifted
his head and searched her soft eyes. He felt as if he
were flying. "Let's see what the cook fixed us to eat."

She smiled. "Okay."

AFTER SUPPER, WHICH included all Niki's favorite
foods, Blair had two neat whiskeys while he and Niki
watched a movie on TV. His mind wouldn't stop worrying about the future.

Niki noticed that his glass was staying full. She
gave him a concerned look.

"It relaxes me when I've got things on my mind," he said. He drew in a breath. "I had half a bottle the day you and your father came up here." He grimaced. "Your college graduation day, too. What a hell of a day for you."

"It was a nice day. I graduated, then I kept my best friend from doing something desperate." She smiled at him tenderly. "I'm sorry things didn't work out for you. I remember when you were engaged to Elise, how happy you were."

"She reminded me of my mother," he said quietly. "She resembled her. But it was only skin-deep, as I found to my horror after it was too late and I'd married her."

"Dad said she wanted more alimony," she said without looking at him while the commercial blared out of the television.

"She likes living high." He finished his second whiskey. "But I think there's more to it. I really think she's being blackmailed."

"Would she tell you, if you asked her?"

"Depends," he said, dropping down beside her on the sofa. "If it gave me a reason to stop paying her alimony, perhaps not."

"Why does she need alimony?" she asked.

He stared at her with amusement. "Because she likes being able to buy a new fur each season and drive a Ferrari, Niki."

She stared at him as if he were speaking a foreign language.

"You only wanted a rawhide bracelet with an antler medallion," he recalled. His teeth ground together.

"You could have had anything in the store, Niki! Elise always wanted diamonds and furs and cars."

"I've never wanted any of that," she replied.

"Rare little hothouse orchid," he said under his breath. He drew her closer and looked down into her soft, gray eyes. "I wish I'd knocked Brady down a flight of stairs."

She put her fingers across his broad, sexy mouth. "We've already agreed that it was my decision to go on the hike. Dan didn't force me."

He kissed her fingertips and then cradled them against his hard cheek. "I can't remember the last time anything scared me that much, and I'd never heard Edna in tears before."

"You said you went to the house…"

He shrugged. "I lied. I phoned. I felt guilty for what I'd said to you," he confessed. "I wanted to make things right between us." His face hardened. "Amazing, how things become crystal clear when you think you might not have time to do it."

"I did a stupid thing…"

"You wore a bathing suit. It was very sexy. I loved the way you looked in it. I just couldn't quite control what I felt when I saw you in it."

She stared at him blankly.

"You aren't worldly at all," he mused as he drew her slowly across his lap, so that her head fell back against his broad shoulder. He searched her soft eyes for a long time. "I lost control with you, out in the ocean. You didn't realize, did you?"

She shook her head, fascinated.

His big hand traced her cheek, the curve of her throat. His fingers worked their way down her body to the softness of her breast and pressed there tenderly. "That was what set me off, that I couldn't stop. If we'd been alone, Niki, it might have been a lot more serious than what happened."

She blushed furiously.

His black eyes narrowed. "People can do it standing up, honey, and we were far enough out in the water that nobody would have noticed."

"Standing up?"

Her wide-eyed fascination amused him. "Yes, honey, standing up."

Her eyes fell to his hard mouth. She reached up hesitantly and traced it with her fingertips. "I felt so ashamed afterward," she said.

"I felt so guilty about what I'd done that I couldn't face you over a dinner table," he confessed. "So I asked Janet out, to make you think I didn't care. It was a lie, like so many other lies I've told you." He drew in a long breath. "You're sixteen years my junior. It mattered."

"Why?"

"Because one day you'd want someone younger, honey," he replied matter-of-factly.

"You really think so?"

"You haven't lived, Niki," he said. "You've only dated two men. One was a drunken idiot and the other was certifiable. There are nice young men in the world."

She toyed with his bottom lip. "And you think a younger man would be what I wanted?"

He brushed his mouth softly over hers. "It might be, one day."

Her hands slid up into his thick, wavy black hair.

There were just a very few threads of silver just at his temples. "If you were twenty years younger or twenty years older, it really wouldn't make a lot of difference. It's the man you are that I care about."

"I'm the only man you've ever been intimate with," he pointed out.

She pressed her cheek against his broad chest and listened to his heartbeat. "Not that intimate."

"The night is young," he mused, and laughed.

Her fingers worked at his buttons.

"Not wise," he said, catching her hands.

"Really?" She felt dangerous, reckless. She might have very little time left in the world, and this was one thing she'd always wanted. She wanted Blair. "Couldn't we mess around, just a little?"

"Mess around?" he teased. "And what do you suppose messing around consists of?" he added.

"What we did in Mexico," she said.

"I was sober then."

She cocked her head and looked up at him, smiling. "What's the difference?"

"Inebriated men have even less control than I had that day," he said.

"So…you might not be able to stop?"

"I might not."

Her fingers teased around a button. "Suppose I didn't mind?"

His heart was hammering. "First, you have a CT scan and we talk to an oncologist."

"If we do that, you might decide to be noble and refuse to sleep with me."

"I want you to live, honey."

She looked up at him. "And I want a baby, Blair."

She lifted her mouth and slid it softly, teasingly against his hard mouth. "I want one so much."

The hand smoothing over her breast became caressing. His mouth opened over hers, pressing her lips apart. He could barely breathe, his heart was beating so heavily. He'd wanted her so much, for so long, that he couldn't stop. If she thought she was pregnant, it might give her hope. At least, that was what his not-quite-sober brain was telling him. He wanted her to the point of madness. He thought it unlikely that she'd get pregnant after just one night. Men his age weren't as fertile as younger men. There was also the fact that Elise had never become pregnant. He might be sterile. But Niki didn't know that, and it was one way to get her to listen to reason. If she thought she'd conceived, she might fight, and fight hard, to live.

"Please?" she whispered into his mouth.

He couldn't resist her. There were a dozen reasons why he should, but the liquor was working on him as much as the feel of her soft, warm, young body in his arms.

She lifted against him. "Please?" she whispered again.

He shivered. "All right," he ground out against her mouth. "But you let me lead, this once," he said as he stood, holding her in his arms. His eyes were glittering with feeling. "I don't want your first experience to be something you'd rather forget. Do you understand?"

"I do," she said softly. She stared up at him with soft, loving eyes, watching him watch her as he paused to click off the television and started down the hall with her in his arms.

"Jameson…" she said suddenly.

"Sleeps on the other side of the house," he said against her soft mouth. "And he sleeps like a log." He bit at her lips. "You can scream if you want to," he teased huskily as he carried her down the long hall to his room and opened the door, balancing her on one broad thigh.

"Scream?" she asked curiously. "But you said it wouldn't hurt…"

"God, Niki," he ground out. "You don't have a clue!"

While she was trying to understand what he meant, he shouldered the door closed and put her down long enough to lock it behind them, just before his open mouth went down on her breast.

She shivered. It had been a long time, a very long time, since he'd touched her like this. She lifted up to his warm, hard mouth, loving the feel of it on her even through a layer of cloth.

He picked her up and carried her to the bed, pausing just long enough to pull back the sheet and comforter before he put her down in the middle of it.

It was still light outside, and she was shy. He didn't seem to notice. He stepped out of his shoes and stripped down to black silk boxers before he tossed Niki's shoes over the side of the bed and started removing her slacks and blouse.

She was flushed by the time he got to her underthings.

He chuckled wickedly as she caught his hand when he found the catch of her bra behind her.

"I hate to break it to you, honey, but we can't make

love fully clothed," he whispered as his mouth hovered over hers.

"Blair!"

He laughed. His lips teased hers, working over them softly, tenderly, while he slowly peeled the bra away and tossed it aside. His eyes slid over her pretty, firm little breasts, their dusky crowns already hard with desire.

He traced them with his fingertips, his breath coming rapidly. He brushed his lips over the hard peaks, tasting them with his tongue. She arched and shivered.

"It was like this when we got back from Mexico, in the car," he whispered. He lifted his head and looked down into soft, curious gray eyes. "I've never wanted a woman so badly in my life. I was cruel. I didn't want to be."

"You think I'm too young," she whispered back.

"No, I know you're too young," he corrected. His big hand slid over her breast again. His face was hard. "But it doesn't matter anymore. I'm not going to lose you, Niki."

Her fingers touched his hard mouth, traced it lovingly. Her face was sad. "I thought I could never have you," she said huskily. "I went out with Dan Brady because it didn't matter anymore. Nothing mattered. You were gone, and I had nothing left…"

His mouth covered hers. He groaned as he kissed her hungrily. He levered his broad chest over hers. She felt the warmth of his body sliding against hers. The sensations she felt made her shiver with feeling.

"Do you like it? It gets better," he whispered roughly.

"Can…it?" she gasped, her mouth following his.

"Wait and see."

She slid her arms up around his neck. "Is it going to hurt?" she asked worriedly.

He laughed softly. "I'm going to remind you that you asked me that, in a couple of hours. But for now..."

He touched her in a way he never had. The shock lifted her off the bed, and she tried to grab his forearm to stop him. But very soon, the skilled motion of his big hand left her no breath for complaints. She cried out softly as stars exploded in her mind.

"And just think, baby, we've barely started," he whispered as his mouth swallowed a warm breast.

SHE WENT WITH him every step of the way. He felt her body ripple as he touched and tasted it, his mouth on her breasts, her flat stomach, the soft inner flesh of her thighs. She lifted up to him, her nails digging in as the pleasure went from plateau to plateau. She hadn't even read about some of the ways he touched her, in her most passionate romance novels.

"They never told us...in health class...that it felt like this!" she gasped.

He laughed softly. "They wouldn't dare."

She shivered again as his big hands slid under her bare hips, lifting her to his mouth.

She felt his body against hers without any fabric in the way. She didn't remember when he'd removed the rest of his clothing. She didn't care that light was still coming in the windows as the sun went down. She looked up into his glittery black eyes with wonder, as desire rode her hard.

"Gently," he whispered as his hips moved slowly

in between her soft legs. "Gently, baby. It's all right. I'm not going to hurt you. You're ready for me."

She didn't understand what he meant until she felt the slow, soft possession of her body while he looked right down into her wide, shocked eyes. She gasped. Even in her most erotic dreams of him, it hadn't felt like this.

He moved from side to side, intensifying the exquisite stabs of pleasure. She felt him tense, just a little, and he pushed down.

There was a flash of pain. She bit her lip and turned her head to the side.

"No," he whispered, his body shuddering. "Don't look away. Let me see. I've never been anyone's first. Not in my life. I want to remember this as long as I live."

She turned her shocked face back to his and let him see her eyes. Her short nails dug into his back as he moved again.

"Only a little more," he whispered, his hips moving very gently. "Yes." His face clenched. "Yes!"

She felt him possess her completely. Felt the shock of it all the way down her body to her toes. She lay watching him, feeling the crush of his big body lift and fall as he moved deeper inside her.

"How does it feel to have me inside you?" he whispered.

She shivered. "Blair!" she cried, lifting her hips suddenly toward his to coax him even deeper. She shivered again. "Oh, gosh!"

"Yes," he ground out. "Do that again. Yes. Yes!"

She moved with him, incited him, lifted up and demanded, as the heat of possession washed over her like molten joy. She caught her breath. She couldn't breathe, couldn't think, couldn't exist without the rhythm he was teaching her. She shuddered with each hard thrust, so enthralled with the sensation that she only lived through him.

He'd never dreamed he could feel something so intense. Never in his life had a sexual experience produced the exquisite pleasure he was feeling. He moved with her until he saw the same explosive passion in her face that he was experiencing.

"Hard and fast now," he bit off as the sensations became a tension that tore him apart. "Hard, Niki, hard, hard, hard…!"

She opened her legs as widely as she could, her nails biting into his back, as the tension grew and grew and finally snapped in such a maelstrom of pleasure that she screamed out in a voice she'd never heard her throat make. She bit his shoulder, hard, as she felt the first climax of her life.

Blair went with her every step of the way. His big body shuddered over and over again as she satisfied him. He groaned harshly, his hips arched down into hers, his chest lifted, his head thrown back as he shot up into the sky like a rocket.

Niki watched him, fascinated. She was barely able to catch her breath, her body relaxed now in the aftermath of fulfillment as he finally collapsed on her damp body. He was breathing like a distance runner, his big body trembling with the force of their pleasure.

"Wow," she whispered.

He laughed. He couldn't help it. He could feel her delight in what they'd shared. He tried to feel guilty, but all he could manage was pride. She'd been a virgin, and he'd given her complete fulfillment her first time.

Finally, he lifted his head and looked down at her flushed, rapt face.

"Wow?" he mused.

She stretched under him, the pleasure echoing in the soft movement of her hips. "Wow," she whispered. She smiled up at him with her whole heart.

He rested on his elbows and brushed his mouth over her eyes, closing them. "For a first time, it was pretty cataclysmic."

"Yes, it was."

He rolled over onto his back and pulled her beside him as he lay trying to catch his breath. She sat up, a little shy as she looked at him, filled her eyes with the incredible masculinity of his big body, his broad chest covered with thick, curling hair, his broad thighs feathered with it. He was glorious to look at.

"Anatomy 101?" he mused.

She grinned.

He laughed and drew her back down into his arms.

She nestled close. He hadn't used any birth control. She hoped with all her heart that there would be a baby, no matter what the future held. She drew in a long breath. Of course, she'd done something she'd sworn she never would—sleep with a man she hadn't married. But she loved Blair with all her heart. There could never be another man for her, not like this. So perhaps God would make allowances. Under the circumstances, it might never happen again. She might not live long enough.

"You're brooding again," he murmured.

"Sorry."

He got up, went to the small refrigerator in the room, pulled out a beer and opened it on his way back to the bed. He sipped it and handed it to her.

"I know you hate beer. But it's cold."

"Yuck," she muttered. But she drank several swallows.

He had a few sips himself. He put the can on the bedside table and turned back to her, his eyes dark and quiet.

"There is no tomorrow," he said as he drew her back into his arms. "Only us. Only tonight."

She reached up to him. "Yes," she said softly. "Only tonight."

He kissed her and rolled her gently onto her back.

VERY EARLY THE next morning, he drew her into the shower with him and bathed her as if he'd been doing it all his life. She found the new intimacy fascinating. She hadn't realized what it would be like to be intimate with a man. She looked at him in a new way, felt differently with him than she had before. She looked at him with love in her eyes.

They hadn't spoken of love. She knew he wanted her. But he didn't say what he felt. And she didn't insist. There was no more time for that. Today would bring answers that they might not want.

Wrapped in towels, he blow-dried her long blond hair and let her do the same for his thick, wavy black hair. All the while, he watched her, as if he could never get enough of just looking at her.

"Do I have warts?" she teased when she was putting away the dryer.

He smoothed back her long hair. "You're beautiful," he corrected. "I never tire of watching you."

She smiled. "Thanks."

He drew in a long breath. "I'm sorry."

"Sorry?"

"About last night," he said curtly. "I had too much to drink and I couldn't stop. I didn't mean for things to happen like that."

"Oh."

He tilted her face up to his. "Don't pretend that it isn't worrying you, too."

She swallowed. "This is a time out of time," she tried to explain. "I don't know what's coming. I... thank you, for getting me through the night."

Was that all it had meant to her? She'd enjoyed him. She cared for him. But he'd hoped there was more. He berated himself mentally. He'd had the one sweet taste of her he'd wanted for years, and now it was time to put his selfish needs aside and tend to hers.

"I phoned Trevor before you woke up," he said. "He and Morris are arranging the CT scan for this afternoon."

"I see."

He brushed his mouth over her forehead. "We have to face it, Niki. Then we'll do whatever we have to do. All right?"

She bit her lip. "All right."

"Let's get dressed."

She looked haunted.

"What is it?"

"The bed," she said, flushing as she remembered the tiny smear of blood on the sheets. "Jameson..."

He brushed his thumb over her soft mouth and felt guilty. "Jameson and the maids are paid to be discreet. Nobody is going to talk about it."

"Okay. If you're sure."

He drew her close and rocked her in his arms. "We'll find out what we're up against with your health, then we'll make plans. All right?"

"All right." She swallowed. "Blair, what if there's a baby?" she added hesitantly. "Would you hate me…?"

"Hate you? My God!" His broad chest rose and fell heavily. His arms tightened, his eyes closed as his face buried itself in her soft throat. "It would be like Christmas," he whispered.

Her heart jumped. He didn't sound as if he was reluctant to have it happen. "Really?"

His mouth smoothed over the soft skin tenderly. "I'd want it with all my heart, Niki. It's just…"

She swallowed. "Just what?"

He lifted his head and sighed as he met her eyes. "Honey, men lose some fertility as they age." He grimaced. "And I've never tried to make a woman pregnant." Actually, he'd tried to make Elise pregnant, and he hadn't been able to. He couldn't tell her that yet.

She bit her lip.

"Don't look at me like that," he said huskily, enveloping her hungrily against him. "We can try. God knows I want it as much as you do!"

The tight knot in her stomach relaxed. Of course a man like Blair would want a child, would hunger for one. She remembered him at the Christmas party the previous year, with the little girl whose father had wanted a boy.

"I don't care if it takes a long time." She drew her

fingertips over his hard, broad mouth. She winced. "It's just… I don't know how long I…well…"

The anguish in his face made her feel guilty.

She pressed close into his arms and hugged him, held him. "It's all right. If I, well, if the spot is anything…it would be stupid to get pregnant. I'd be putting the child at risk, too." She lifted her head and met his worried gaze. "I was just afraid and grasping at straws. I don't want to force you into something you're not ready for." She felt guilty for what she'd said. He hadn't mentioned marriage, and here she was going on and on about a baby. It wasn't right to put him in that position. She loved him, but it was likely a physical need rather than an emotional one that had led him to carry her into his bedroom. She had to face that. He knew she was desperate for something to hold on to, and he was humoring her. It might be nothing more than that.

He smoothed her long blond hair and felt powerless. He was more than ready for fatherhood; that wasn't the problem. He started to speak just as his cell phone rang. He let her go and went to the bedroom to answer it.

"Yes?" He paused, listened, glanced at Niki. "Yes, that's fine. I'll bring her. Thanks."

He hung up. "That was Trevor. He'll meet us at the hospital at one this afternoon."

She swallowed, her embarrassment replaced by her terror of the CT test and what it might mean.

"All right," she said.

He took her hand and led her back to her own room. "Get dressed and we'll have breakfast," he said. "We'll face it together, Niki. Okay?"

She nodded. "Okay, Blair."

He walked away and left her at the door, his heart breaking in his chest. He should never have let things go this far. She'd been a virgin. That gift should have belonged to her husband, to a younger man who could give her a rich and full life. She was terrified, and he was trying to give her reasons to stay alive. He should have talked to her. Just talked to her.

Instead, in the fear of losing her, he'd taken her to bed. He was ashamed of himself.

But he prayed that her young life wouldn't end so soon. Even if he had to give her up forever, he just wanted Niki to live.

CHAPTER TWELVE

NIKI HARDLY TASTED what she was eating. Blair was quiet and morose. Guilt was written all over him. He blamed himself for crossing the line with her. But she'd invited that. She wanted a child, but only because it would have been his—because she loved him. Perhaps he thought any man would have done for that. She'd never confessed how she felt about him. She was afraid to.

But he didn't love her. She was sure of it. He'd slept with her not because he was in love with her, but because he'd been drinking and he wanted her. He'd wanted her for a long time. He'd been her best friend. Now he was something else: her lover.

She'd sacrificed all her principles to a man's lust. She was ashamed of herself.

"You aren't eating," Blair said curtly.

She looked down at the perfect omelet with hash brown potatoes and toast. For some reason the omelet turned her stomach.

"I thought you liked omelets," he persisted. He was having pancakes with bacon. He hated eggs.

"I do. I'm just worried, that's all," she assured him.

"At least nibble on the toast, will you?" he persisted.

She drew in a breath. "I don't want to go do the CT scan."

"Neither do I, but you can't run away from life. You have to face it, with all its unpleasantness."

She managed a smile. "I guess so."

He sipped coffee, frowning. "We've got several hours to kill. Suppose we go out to the battlefield."

"It's a long way, isn't it?" she asked.

He shrugged. "Not so far. We'll take the limo and give the tourists a treat," he added with a forced smile. "How about it?"

"I'd like that."

"Put your inhaler in your pocket," he said firmly.

She drew in a breath, and her gray eyes smiled at him. "It's already there."

He nodded.

IT WAS A long drive to Hardin, Montana, near where both the Crow Reservation and the Northern Cheyenne Reservation were located, but Jameson made excellent time on the long, lonely road. It was a sunny, pretty day. The scenery, while monotonous in some areas, was beautiful. Neither of them noticed. They were dreading the time ahead.

Hardin was known as the City with a Reason. The reason, given in an early twentieth-century brochure, was progress, due to its being a shipping point for agriculture. Niki thought it was charming. The Little Bighorn battlefield was only fifteen miles away.

Blair locked Niki's fingers into his as they walked slowly up the hill to the Little Big Horn monument.

"After the battle, Custer and his men were hastily buried in shallow graves. Predators and the heat made identification a very messy business. They marked Custer's grave with a tent and blankets and rocks, but the year after the battle, when his body was to be transferred to West Point, the tent and blankets and other markings were gone. The first time they thought they had Custer's body, the identification was questioned. The second time they were pretty sure they got it right. A hank of red-gold hair was still attached to the skull, and Libby Custer identified it as exactly the color of her husband's.

"The bodies were scattered by predators, weren't they?" she asked, recalling the television special she'd watched.

"Yes. So they allegedly buried Custer at West Point," Blair pointed out. "But they could only find a few bones, and I think they weren't even positive that they were all his. So probably pieces of him are still here, along with the men who followed him."

She turned to him. "What do you think really happened?"

"I think he was killed very early in the battle, probably when he and a few men charged across the river into the village. One of the Cheyenne said that a white officer fell in the river, and his men carried him up the hill, to the last stand. Logically, if the officer hadn't been Custer, they'd have left him in the river. Natives were charging the soldiers from all sides. It doesn't make sense that they'd risk being killed to recover a body, unless it was their commander's and they didn't think he was dead."

She nodded. Her eyes swept over the rolling countryside. The wind blew constantly. "It's so lonely here."

He smiled, and his fingers tightened around hers.

"Not so much," he teased, indicating dozens of people milling around the monument, taking photos and wandering along the trail that led through the battleground itself.

She leaned against him with a sigh. "It's still lonely here."

He let go of her hand and slid his arm around her, holding her close. "On June 25, 1876, it was a very busy place. Echoes of the day of the battle reach even into our time."

"Dad says we had a cousin who fought here."

He chuckled. "I had a distant cousin who fought here, as well." He leaned down. "But mine was Cheyenne. I imagine yours was on the other side."

She laughed softly. "I imagine so. Cheyenne?"

He nodded. "One of my French ancestors married into the tribe."

"Were your ancestors fur trappers?"

"That, and mountain men."

She stared out over the battleground. "I'm glad I wasn't here when this happened. I can only imagine how the wives felt. And to leave the men lying out here, all that time, away from their families who loved them…" She broke off. "Poor Mrs. Custer, waiting for them to send her husband's remains back home, and not even sure they had them right."

"It was a different time, and far away from the sensitivities of people in power."

"Archaeologists have made a lot of discoveries in the past few years," she said. "I watched a special about it on television."

"I don't watch television," he chuckled. "I buy DVDs. I hate commercials."

"But how do you know which products to buy, if you don't watch the commercials?" she teased, looking up at him. "You could miss out on something earth-shattering!"

He brushed his mouth over her forehead. "I had something earth-shattering last night," he whispered, and when he lifted his head, he wasn't smiling. "The most beautiful, erotic experience of my entire life, Niki. I'll remember it until I die."

The words touched her. "So will I," she said, and then recalled that it might not be that long, in her case.

"Don't worry so much," he said, tugging her closer. "We'll handle it. Whatever happens, we're in this together."

She laid her cheek on his broad chest and closed her eyes. "Okay."

JAMESON DROVE THEM back to the hospital in Billings. Niki was taken to radiology, where she put on a gown in place of her blouse and bra, and the technician went to work. It only took a few minutes.

When she was done, she went back out to Blair in the waiting room. He slid an arm around her. "Finished?"

"Yes," she said. "I filled out all the paperwork before they took me back," she reminded him. "They said the doctor would contact me later with the results."

He grimaced. The next few hours were going to be a nightmare.

They walked around town and went into shops, just looking at things. Blair was preoccupied.

Niki paused at the baby department of a department store and winced. When she saw Blair's expression, she slid her small hand into his and drew him away from it, back to the sheets and pillowcase aisle. His expression had told her things she didn't want to know. She wanted a baby, but he was just making the best of it. Nothing had hurt quite so much.

He didn't say anything, but the set of his features was eloquent as he let her pull him along with her.

She looked at a pretty comforter on the shelf, and suddenly she remembered something he'd told her once, when they were at Yellowstone.

She turned and looked up at him, horrified. "You said Elise smiled, all through it," she said, flushing. "Your first time together, I mean."

He nodded. In spite of his misery, he smiled. "And now you understand, don't you?"

"She didn't feel a thing," she said.

"No. I don't think she ever did. At times, it was like she forced herself to be with me." His face hardened. "My pride could only take so much of that, so we spent most of our marriage apart."

Niki couldn't imagine a woman who wouldn't want him in bed. He was everything she'd ever dreamed of. The memory of the pleasure they'd shared still echoed in her body as she stood close beside him.

He lifted an eyebrow. "Why are you staring at me?" he teased.

"I was thinking she had to be crazy," she said.

He lifted both eyebrows. "Why?"

"Not to have stayed with you," she explained. She averted her eyes to his chest. "You're a wonderful lover," she whispered unsteadily.

His chest swelled with pride at the words. He knew that she'd enjoyed him; it had been obvious. But it was nice to hear it, as well. He drew her head to his chest and closed his eyes. "So are you, sweetheart," he whispered back.

"I didn't know a thing."

He lifted his head and searched her soft gray eyes. "What you know doesn't matter. It's what you feel that matters."

She drew in a shaky breath. "I could live on last night for the rest of my life," she confessed.

He touched her mouth with his forefinger and groaned inwardly. He didn't want to think about what might lay ahead of them. If he lost her now, he might as well be buried beside her. He had no reason to stay alive if Niki wasn't somewhere in the world.

"Niki," he began slowly, just as the phone vibrated madly in its holder on his belt. "Just a sec." He pulled it out, checked the number, grimaced and answered it. "Coleman," he said. He waited, hesitated. He stared at Niki as if he'd had a revelation. "Yes. Of course. We'll be right there."

He hung up. "It's Trevor. He wants us to come back to the hospital right now."

"Oh, dear," she began worriedly.

"He says he has good news," he replied. His face lit up. He picked her up and whirled her around in his arms, laughing. "He says it's not cancer, honey."

"Oh, my gosh!" she exclaimed.

He kissed her hungrily, right there in the middle of the store. It was such a relief. He put her down quickly, though, before other shoppers paid too much attention to them. He caught her hand. "Let's go!"

DR. TREVOR MANNHEIM was waiting for them at the front desk. He took them into the hospital administrator's office, a courtesy from the administrator himself, and closed the door behind them.

"Okay, this is what we've got," he said, and began to speak. "You've got a tiny nodule in your right lung, the size of a BB, which I've seen very often in my practice. It's almost always benign," he chuckled, "and unlikely to grow. We'll need to keep a check on it, CT scans annually. But I'd bet my life that it will never be anything to worry about." He looked at Niki, who was beaming, and shook a finger at her. "And that, young lady, is why we have diagnostic tests, so people won't worry themselves to death about possibilities."

She hugged him, shyly. "Thank you for my life."

He flushed bright red, then laughed. "You're very welcome." He shook hands with Blair. "I wish I had time to take you out for drinks and talk about old times." He checked his watch. "But I have a consultation coming up on a test that had a very different result than this one. I have to head home."

"My jet's fueled and waiting at the airport for you," Blair said. "Thanks, Trevor. You don't know how grateful I am."

"Oh, I have some small idea," the older man chuckled when he saw the way Blair looked at the young woman beside him. "Take care."

"You, too."

BLAIR TOOK NIKI back to the house, with Jameson at the wheel of the limo. They ate lunch in the dining room, but neither of them was talkative.

"I need to take you home," Blair said quietly.

She looked up, wincing. "What? Why?"

He pushed his plate aside and lifted his coffee to his mouth. It burned his tongue, but the pain made it easier to say what he needed to say. "I got drunk and did something I never should have with you. I'm sorry. It should never have happened." He ground his teeth together at her expression. "You're going to be fine now. You got a second chance. Now you have to do something with your life."

"You don't want me?" she faltered.

His eyes closed. "No." Lying through his teeth. Of course he wanted her to stay. But he was back where he'd been before, with the age difference killing his conscience. That, and the very real possibility that he was sterile. After all, Elise had never gotten pregnant with him. Niki wanted a child so much! He drew in a steadying breath and stared into her eyes. "I'm too old for you. That hasn't changed, even though I'm over the moon that you don't have something fatal."

"I see." She toyed with her coffee cup. "And you don't...want something permanent with me."

"That's exactly it," he said. He averted his eyes. "I've been thinking about Elise lately. She needs help. I still think she's being blackmailed. I want to go and see her and find out what's going on."

She swallowed the last of her coffee. "You still love her, don't you?" she accused with her eyes on the table. "But she didn't want you, in bed..."

"That could change," he lied. He wanted to make her leave. He had to make her leave. Now she had hope; she had a future. He'd had his one perfect night with her. He could live on it forever. But she was

young. She needed a man who was her age. She'd
wanted him, been curious about him as a lover. That
had been wonderful. But it wasn't enough. He couldn't
give her a child. She'd tire of him. She'd walk away.
He could only give her half a life, and he'd be left
bleeding to death inside as he was forced to give her
up to someone younger. He knew that was in the
cards, even if she didn't. He had to let her go.

She drew in a long breath and forced a smile to
her lips. "Don't worry, I won't try to make you feel
guilty. Thanks for taking care of me, and for calling
Dr. Mannheim in to consult."

"You're welcome."

"I guess I'll go home and go back to work, then,"
she said.

She looked at him with aching need but turned
her eyes away before he could see it. She went to the
guest room to pack. She tried not to think of what had
happened in his bedroom last night, of the terrible,
sweet glory of fulfillment. He'd wanted her violently.
She'd almost thought it was love. But he'd said once
that he could take her and walk away without regret.
Maybe she could learn how that worked. She had no
other choice.

SHE WAS BACK at home in hours, driven there by Jameson
in the limousine and deposited at her front door. Her
father met her at the door and hugged her half to death.

"You idiot!" he raged. "Why didn't you tell me
what was going on?"

"I was scared to death. I didn't want you to be worried until I knew what I was up against. Blair has this
wonderful friend…"

"I know. He called me on the way to France," he added, "and told me the whole story."

"France?" she asked.

"He's going to see Elise." He let her go and his jaw hardened. "Damned fool. She'll chew him up and spit him out all over again. He should just leave her alone and let her handle her own problems."

"He thinks she needs help," Niki said wanly. "You know how he is."

"Yes, I do. Well, he's a grown man. I guess he has to live his own life. I had hoped…" He broke off with a smile. "No matter. I'm just glad you're home and all right."

"So am I."

Edna came out of the kitchen, beaming when she saw Niki. She hugged her. "You should have told us!" she cried.

"Well, I'm fine now, so it's water under the bridge," she assured the older woman. "What are you cooking? I'm starved! Jameson fed us a nice lunch, but that was hours ago."

"I have beef stew and homemade strawberry ice cream," Edna said smugly. "It's a celebration, isn't it? So I fixed your favorite foods."

Niki hugged her harder. "Oh, it's so good to be home!"

IT WAS GOOD to be home. But strange things were happening to her. By the end of the second week, she couldn't bear to look at an egg, cooked or uncooked. She felt nauseous at the oddest times. And she was so sleepy that she could hardly stay awake.

She was sure it was some virus she'd picked up, so she ignored the symptoms. She went to work during the day and helped Edna at home or watched television with her father in the evenings. A new man had taken Dan Brady's position in the office. He was nice, but he had a fiancée. Niki was glad. She didn't want to date anyone anymore. Not at all.

Tex drove her back and forth to work while her car was being serviced.

"You're sure quiet these days," he teased.

She laughed. "I've grown old," she returned, gray eyes twinkling.

"Is that what it is?" He stopped to make a turn onto the main highway. "We're all happy that you got a good diagnosis on that test," he added. "Lots of worried people around here, until we knew you were going to be all right."

She smiled. "Thanks, Tex."

"What are friends for?" he asked.

She leaned her head back with a sigh and closed her eyes. "Wake me up when we get there, if I nod off," she murmured. "I can't seem to stay awake these days."

He laughed. "Lot of that going around. We've been moving bulls to summer pasture. Hard work and long hours. Nobody complains about insomnia, that's for sure."

"I'll bet."

He hesitated. "You been moving bulls to summer pasture, too?" he asked with a grin.

"Feels like it." She smiled, but she didn't open her eyes. She was trying not to think about Blair, and failing miserably. He'd made it clear that he didn't want her. She had to come to grips with the fact that he was never going to want her, except in bed.

Her conscience bothered her about that night. There were extenuating circumstances, but she felt guilty just the same. She'd lived by the rules all her life. Now that she'd broken a major one, she was uneasy. She wished with all her heart that there had been a baby made out of that perfect interlude, but Blair had said it would be a long shot.

It was probably for the best that she didn't get pregnant, since he didn't want commitment. It wouldn't have been fair to force a child he didn't want into his life. Especially now that he was thinking about going back to Elise.

She remembered how much he'd loved Elise at first, how happy he'd been when they became engaged. Niki thought he'd never really stopped loving her. She knew how that felt. She was never going to stop loving Blair. But she could learn to live without him. She had no choice.

ELISE STARED AT Blair with horror. "What do you mean, who's…who's blackmailing me?" she stammered, flushing.

"You know what I mean. Spill it."

She bit her lower lip. She was beautiful, and she knew it. Usually she teased and cajoled him, but he'd taken the wind out of her sails the minute they sat down in this exclusive restaurant.

She grimaced. The waiter came to take their drink orders and passed out menus. When he'd gone, Elise looked at him over the table with set features. "It's a woman," she confessed miserably. "She's threatening to go to the producer and, well, tell him things. He's very religious, rigid in his views…"

"Tell him what things?" he asked. She hesitated. "Come on," he said quietly. "You know I never tell anything I know."

She swallowed. The waiter was back with drinks. She took her martini, thanked him and drank the whole thing down in almost one gulp. Blair, nursing a whiskey and soda, stared at her in surprise.

"You must have guessed," she muttered. "I mean, you had to know that I didn't really care for it when we went to bed together."

"I knew."

She let out a long breath. "I don't like men. Not that way. I never have." She averted her eyes. "I was trying to get someone out of my system. You were smart and rich and sexy, and I thought I'd try it with a man. But I just couldn't do it." She sighed. "I wish I could have been what you wanted me to be. I was selfish and cruel."

He moved his water glass around on the tablecloth. "I hoped you might want to stay with me, at first." He smiled. "I kept thinking you might get pregnant and it would settle you down."

"There was no hope of that. I was on the pill," she confessed, oblivious to his shocked expression. "I don't want children. I never did. It must have occurred to you that I never missed my monthly while we were together."

Elise was too absorbed in her misery to see the shock her revelation had caused in the man across from her.

He sipped water that he didn't even want. "When you never got pregnant, I thought I might be sterile," he bit off.

"That was unlikely. I just made sure that I couldn't conceive. I knew we wouldn't be together for long." She swallowed. "I don't like men. I like women," she confessed without looking at him. "I knew when I was ten. My father beat me up when he found out. He was horrified that someone might know the truth. I had to hide it until I left home."

He nodded. "You're a lesbian."

She was shocked and couldn't hide it. "You knew?"

"Yes. I hired a private detective to investigate you. The day the divorce was final, he gave me his report." He didn't add that he'd gone half-crazy at the revelation and gotten drunk. That was when Niki had come with her father to take him home with them. He'd never told them why he was so upset.

"I couldn't tell you. I've hidden it all my life. I thought I could try to be what my family wanted me to be, with you. But I couldn't. I just…didn't feel anything. This woman, I loved her. Loved her more than anything in the world. We were together for two years. Then she got killed in a car wreck and I was lost in my grief. That's when I met you." She searched his face. "I'm sorry, Blair. I should never have married you. I started drinking, I tried drugs—I was horrible to you when you were sick because I was stoned out of my mind overseas. I did go to rehab, but it was too late for us. I know you can't forgive me. I don't deserve forgiveness, but…"

"You can't help what you feel, what you are," he said quietly. "I wish you'd told me when we first got married. My pride took a hell of a blow."

"I can imagine." She breathed harshly. "Well, I'm

being blackmailed and there's nothing I can do except pay her off."

"The hell there isn't." He picked up his cell phone, checked his numbers and speed-dialed one. She listened while he outlined the problem to a private detective, got names from her and gave the man an assignment.

"You'd do that for me?" she stammered. "After the way I've treated you?"

"Of course," he said simply. "I'll stop her. Don't worry."

"It's the part I always dreamed I could play. I know I can make it in theater. I just need this one chance to prove it." She stared at him and winced. "I'm so sorry!"

"It's all right."

She searched his eyes. "You look miserable. It's that girl, Niki, isn't it?" She smiled sadly. "I thought so," she added when his face gave it away. "You should stop worrying about your age and go get her. She's been taking care of you for years. Women don't do that unless they love deeply."

"I chased her away," he said curtly.

"Then win her back," she prodded.

He sighed. "Too late for that, I'm afraid."

"Blair, if you love her, you'll find a way to get her back," she said gently. "You have to at least try."

He leaned back in the chair. "You're different now."

She managed a smile. "I met someone. She's everything I dreamed of. Sweet and caring and supportive." She shifted uneasily. "I guess it turns your stomach, to hear me talking like this."

"No, it doesn't," he said surprisingly. "People are what they are. I don't think we have the right to judge."

"You really are a nice man," she said quietly. "I hope things work out for you."

"Not likely. But I'll make sure that things work out for you. How about another martini?"

She smiled. "I'd like that. Thanks," she added.

He shrugged. "What are friends for?"

LATER, ALONE IN his hotel room, he downed two glasses of whiskey. He'd honestly thought he was sterile. He'd told Niki that a baby would be unlikely. He just didn't tell her why.

He hadn't been able to make Elise pregnant. But learning now that she was on the pill changed everything. He'd had unprotected sex with Niki, in the belief that he didn't need to use anything. What if he'd made her pregnant? He'd hoped to give her a choice, to let her go to someone younger, a man who would be a better bet to give her a child. He'd pushed her away. Again. Now there was every possibility that she was carrying his child, and she wouldn't tell him, even if she was. Or, worst-case scenario, she'd terminate it to spare him a child she didn't think he wanted. He hadn't even told her he loved her, that he wanted her forever, that he wanted a child.

Dear God, he thought miserably. What was he going to do? He made the same mistakes over and over again, trying to protect her. He put his head in his hands and groaned. He had no idea how to try to save the train wreck of his life.

NIKI FELT HEALTHIER than she ever had. She used her meds religiously, but she started going out again. There was a newly divorced man who worked as a vice president in the company. He was older than she was, but very nice. He loved to tell Niki about his ex-wife. Which was fine, because she loved to tell him about Blair. Not that she mentioned his name. She just told him that there was a man in her past that she'd loved who couldn't love her back. He understood all too well.

They had supper at a Latin club in Billings. He could do the dances, and he taught her. She blossomed as she got used to being out in the world, taking part in it. All her years in college, she'd hidden in textbooks and studying. She hadn't wanted to be around people. Blair had accused her of hiding, and he was right.

But she wasn't hiding anymore. She bought clothes that flattered her slender figure, in colors that suited her, and she wore them to work. Of course, they were a larger size because she seemed to be gaining weight. She had her hair styled and learned to use makeup. She took a class in public speaking, of all things, at the local community college in Catelow. It helped with her shyness and taught her how to debate. She was blossoming. It would have helped, of course, if she wasn't sleepy all day and getting nauseous at the oddest times. It must be some stubborn virus, she told herself.

"I can't get over the change in you," her father said with a grin. "You've matured, Niki."

"It was about time, I guess," she laughed.

"I like your new friend."

"Devlin?" she asked, smiling. "Me, too. He's great company, and he can really dance."

"So I hear." He toyed with his coffee cup. "Is it serious?"

She hesitated.

"Sorry, I won't pry," he said after a minute.

She smoothed her fingers over her own cup. "There's only Blair," she confessed heavily. "If I live to be a hundred, there will only be Blair. But he's gone back to Elise…"

"What?"

His surprise was obvious. "Didn't he tell you?" she asked with a wan smile. "He said he'd made a mistake by kicking her out of his life, and he wanted to try again. That's why he flew to France."

Her father's expression was too complex to classify. "Good Lord." He swallowed coffee, burning his tongue.

"Why do you look so surprised?" she asked.

He scowled. "Don't you know about her?"

"Know what?" she asked with a faint smile.

He started to tell her what he'd found out from Blair, but it wasn't really his secret to tell. It should come from Blair, who was positively wallowing in misery and asking all sorts of odd questions about Niki lately.

"He thought someone was blackmailing her," she recalled.

"Someone was. Blair put a stop to it."

Her heart fell. "I guess he does still care about her."

"He cared enough about you to come rushing down here the minute he heard you were in the hospital," he reminded her. "And he was ready to beat the hell out of Brady."

"I caused a lot of trouble," she said. "I'm more sorry than I can say."

He reached over and patted her hand. "We all understand where your mind was, honey," he said softly. "You wanted to spare us the trauma of cancer treatment. But as you see, it wasn't what you thought."

"I'm so glad," she said fervently. "I was scared to death. Blair was wonderful to me. Then, when we knew I wasn't going to die, he shot me out the door like a bullet."

"He thinks you're too young for him," he told her. "I thought like that, too, once, when I loved your mother." He smiled sadly. "I took a lot of convincing. I even set her up with a colleague of mine, hoping she'd get involved with him. Of course she had eyes for no man except me, but I couldn't see that."

She sipped coffee. "My situation is a little different. Blair's still in love with his ex-wife. Like this nice man I date from work." She smiled sadly. "I guess we take what we can get from life and try not to want things we can't have."

"Things were going well between the two of you, before we went to Mexico."

She managed not to flush and give the show away. "We were friends then," she said.

"And now you're not?"

She glanced deliberately at her watch. "Have to go. Mr. Jacobs is going to be out of the office, and I have to get there early. His phone rings constantly, especially when he's not there to answer it," she laughed.

"I try to lose mine," he said wistfully. "Oh, the wonderful old days when all phones were connected by a wire to walls. Work is far too portable nowadays."

"That's what Mr. Jacobs says," she laughed. "See you tonight, Dad."

"Have a good day."

She climbed into her car and drove to work, trying not to dwell on what her father had said about Blair helping Elise. She wondered when they'd announce their remarriage. She wished she didn't care so much.

CHAPTER THIRTEEN

"WHEN ARE YOU going to see a doctor?"

Niki grimaced as she glanced at Edna from the sink where she was washing her face after being deathly ill again first thing in the morning.

"I've just got that virus," she prevaricated.

Edna walked into the room and closed the door. "You're pregnant, and you know it," she said gently.

Niki's face contorted. Tears rolled down her pale cheeks. "He's gone back to Elise. What am I going to do, walk into his house and tell him he's going to be a father, when he's discussing remarriage with his ex-wife? Wouldn't that be a fine wedding present!"

"Niki, he cares about you..." she insisted.

"I pushed him over the edge, because he felt sorry for me." She lowered her eyes to the wet washcloth that she'd bathed her face with. "It's not his fault. I was scared and desperate. I had some crazy idea that I could have a child before they did surgery and started treating me for cancer. But there isn't any cancer, and I don't know what to do now."

"I thought it might be something like that. He's a man who loves children, you know," she added.

Niki drew in a long breath. "He doesn't think he can father a child, Edna," she said quietly, staring at the sink. "After all, Elise never got pregnant. He might not believe it was his, even if I told him."

"He told you that?" she exclaimed.

"Well, no. He told Dad he thought he was sterile, and Dad told me. There's another problem." She glanced at the housekeeper while she bathed her wet eyes. "Blair told Dad that Elise had been on drugs and that was why she acted the way she did. She's back to normal and going to be an actress. You know that Blair was crazy about her."

"I do," the older woman said gently. "But honey, it's his baby. He has the right to know about it."

"Well, he's not going to. Not from me."

"Child, you can't hide it forever," Edna said.

"I know that. I've thought that I might move down to Colorado or Arizona and get a job with another mining company."

"You don't think your father would find out? Or that he wouldn't tell Mr. Coleman if he did?" Edna exclaimed.

Niki grimaced. "I guess it does sound a little farfetched."

She pursed her lips. "Your emotions are all over the place. You aren't thinking clearly."

"I'm not really sure that I am pregnant," Niki said stubbornly. "It takes weeks to tell, doesn't it?"

"It takes one day, with a blood test. You should see a doctor and make sure."

"Doctor Fred would call Dad. Then he'd call Blair."

"You could go to a doctor in another city," Edna persisted. "Babies need a lot of prenatal care," she added worriedly. "You need tests and vitamins and regular checkups."

Niki knew that. She was almost certainly pregnant, but she wasn't brave enough to tell anyone. Especially Blair, who would hate her if she caused him to lose Elise.

She was going to swear Edna to secrecy when the nausea came back. She assumed the position in front of the toilet and tried not to think of the smell of eggs.

WHILE NIKI WAS throwing up, Edna went back to the kitchen to make chamomile tea to ease her stomach. Just as she reached the dining room, Blair walked in the door. He was somber and quiet, and he looked as if his world had ended.

"How is she?" he asked Edna worriedly. "She's all right now, isn't she?"

Edna had a thought. Her eyes twinkled. "Let me show you how she is, Mr. Coleman. Follow me."

She led him to the bathroom and cracked the door.

Blair's expression underwent a remarkable transformation. His sad, hopeless face disappeared and changed into one of absolute exultation.

He put a finger to his lips, went into the bathroom and closed the door. Niki was too sick to be aware of anything. She heard footsteps.

"Edna, can you...wet me another cloth, please?" she asked wearily, leaning her head on her arm over the toilet seat.

Water was running. Then a wet, cool cloth was pressed into her hand. A big, husky man knelt beside her and turned her pale face to his.

"Niki," he whispered huskily. "Niki!"

She couldn't even protest. Tears ran down her cheeks. He didn't look worried or sad. She'd never seen such an expression on his broad, leonine features.

"Blair…oh, God…!" The nausea came back.

He didn't leave her until she was finally able to get up from the toilet. He helped her to the sink, helped her wash her face and use mouthwash. Then he picked her up like the treasure she was and carried her into the bedroom. He dropped into the big armchair by the fireplace and cuddled her close, holding the cloth to her forehead.

"I didn't know how to tell you," she began unsteadily. "Dad said Elise never got pregnant, and you thought you might be sterile. I was afraid you might not even believe it was yours!"

"Of course I know it's mine, honey," he said softly. "Elise finally confessed to me that she was taking the pill the whole time we were married."

She caught her breath. "And she didn't tell you?"

He shook his head sadly. "We're going to have a baby." He drew in a long breath, and his face radiated joy. "I can't believe it," he chuckled. "I just can't believe it! What a delicious surprise!"

She flushed with pleasure. He brushed back her disheveled hair. He smiled tenderly, his black eyes fascinated with her. He smoothed down her blouse and over her still-flat stomach. His big hand rested there with joyous possession.

"You aren't…mad about it?" she asked worriedly.

He bent and kissed her eyelids, closing them. "Oh, no, I'm not mad, baby."

She relaxed and let him take her weight. "I'm so sick," she moaned.

"Have you been to Doctor Fred?"

"I was putting it off," she said on a weary sigh.

"He can give you something for the nausea. You'll need vitamins, as well, and tests... A baby," he whispered huskily, and his whole face contracted. "God, it's Christmas!"

She searched his face with wide, fascinated eyes. "You really don't mind?"

He laughed softly. "Do I look as if I mind?"

He didn't. He looked years younger, full of life and hope.

"Not really," she said finally.

He curled her close and laid his cheek on her soft hair. "It will have to be a rushed wedding," he said, thinking out loud. "And nothing public, or we'll be swamped by the press. I have enough trouble with reporters when they're not prying into my private life. You'll need a gown, and I have to get rings..."

Her head fell back on his shoulder. "You want to marry me?" she asked, disbelief on her face.

He traced her soft mouth. "I've always wanted to marry you, honey," he said huskily. "But there was the pesky age thing. Then, when you started talking about children, I remembered that Elise had never gotten pregnant, and I was afraid that I was sterile. I was afraid to take the test."

"That sounds familiar," she sighed.

He kissed her tenderly. "We're both cowards," he teased.

She laughed softly. Her small hand went up to stroke his hard cheek. "Yes, we are."

He caught the hand in his and kissed the palm. "We could have the service here, if we can find a minister who'll marry us. Otherwise, it might have to be a justice of the peace."

"Why?" she asked, puzzled.

"Some ministers still won't marry a divorced man to another woman," he said simply.

"I would really like to be married by a minister," she said. "But I don't mind if we have to do it the other way."

He kissed her palm again. "I'll ask around. Your father might have some ideas."

As if on cue, her father suddenly opened the door. "Edna said you were sick…"

He stopped dead at the sight of Niki lying in Blair's arms in the big chair. He stared at them both, and wheels were turning in his head. All of a sudden, he grinned.

"Morning sickness?" he asked, and beamed at them.

Blair laughed. Niki flushed.

"Well!" Todd exclaimed. "And here I thought I'd never get grandkids! Listen, you two have to get married…"

"That's just what we were discussing," Blair said. "We'd like to be married here, by a minister."

"I have a friend who's an ordained minister," Todd said. He's not overly conventional. Suppose I ask him for you?"

"The sooner, the better," Blair added when Niki suddenly scrambled off his lap and went running back to the bathroom.

"Sorry," Blair told Todd before he followed her. "I'm getting into the daddy role as quickly as I can."

Todd just laughed.

BLAIR DROVE NIKI to the doctor's office in his luxury rental car and sat holding her hand in the waiting room until she was called back. Even then, he wouldn't let go.

Doctor Fred pursed his lips at the sight of Blair holding Niki's hand. He put two and two together with amazing perception.

"Morning sickness?" he asked.

Niki burst out laughing. "How did you know?"

"He's a dead giveaway." He pointed at Blair. "He's got baby fever. There's no cure, I'm afraid."

Niki was beaming. "I'm so happy!"

"I noticed. Okay, let's get this show on the road," Morris said. "Blood test first, then the exam, and then we'll talk. You staying?" he asked Blair.

He hesitated when Niki blushed. "Maybe I'll sit in the waiting room and daydream while you examine her," he said. He kissed her forehead with a chuckle. "If you tell us she's not pregnant, I'm jumping off the roof," he told the doctor. "I swear."

"I'll keep that in mind. I promise," Doctor Fred chuckled.

Blair left, winking at Niki before he left the room and closed the door behind him.

"Well!" Doctor Fred exclaimed. "If anybody had told me that Blair Coleman would be that excited about impending fatherhood, I think I might have fainted."

"Me, too," Niki said, shaking her head. "I didn't know how to tell him. You see, his first wife never got pregnant, so he thought he was sterile."

"I think we can probably discount the sterility theory, if the tests substantiate the morning sickness," the doctor said. "Now. Let me get the nurse in here, and we'll do a quick exam."

NIKI WAS FLOATING on air when they left the building. "I can't believe it," she said excitedly. "I suspected, but it could have been so many other things."

He tightened his grip on her fingers. He looked very smug. "Yes, it could have. But you said on the way over here that the eggs started off the nausea. I hate eggs." He looked at her stomach. He chuckled. "He hates eggs, too."

"He?" she teased.

He slid an arm around her shoulders as they walked toward the car. "Honey, there hasn't been a girl in my lineage in five generations," he said softly. "I would love a little girl. But a boy is much more likely."

She looked up at him as they reached the car, with her heart in her eyes. "Please tell me you're not just pretending to be pleased, making the best of a bad situation. Even if you have to lie."

He traced her soft mouth with his fingers. "I don't lie that well," he reminded her. He searched her soft gray eyes, loving the flush in her cheeks, the radiance of her face, the subdued beauty of her in the afternoon light. "I'm overwhelmed," he said finally. "Of all the things I've experienced in my life, this is easily the most profound. We made a baby, the first time." He smiled tenderly at her blush. He bent his head and touched his lips to hers. "It was a hell of a first time, too."

"Oh, yes," she agreed, sliding her arms around him.

He drew in an unsteady breath. "We have to go shopping. I want a couture wedding gown for you.

Something we can hand down to our children and their children."

Her eyes searched his, hungrily. "I was so afraid to tell you."

"I know." He hugged her close and rocked her. "I thought I might be sterile. I know how much you want children. When I thought I couldn't give you any..."

She pulled back and looked up at him with shock in her whole expression. "You thought it would matter?" she asked.

He scowled. "Of course."

She reached up and touched his broad, sexy mouth, his square jaw, his lean, hard cheek. "I want the baby because it's yours," she said hesitantly. "That's really the only reason I want it so much."

His heart skipped a beat. He just stared at her.

"You must know that I...that I love you," she stammered. "I mean, I've done everything except wear a sign for years...!"

She had to stop because he was kissing her. His hunger was immediate, devouring, out of control. He didn't even notice amused eyes turning toward them in the parking lot as he lifted her in his arms and groaned as he ground his mouth into hers.

"I'm sorry, but...it hurts," she moaned into his mouth, protesting the crush of his chest.

"It hurts?"

"My breasts are very sore," she whispered, flushing again. "It's part of the symptoms..."

"I'm sorry, honey! So sorry!" He eased his hold and kissed her mouth, her nose, her closed eyelids. "I wouldn't hurt you for the whole world."

"I know that. I wasn't complaining, exactly. Well, not about being kissed," she laughed softly.

He swung her around with a slow, warm smile and kissed her tenderly before he put her down.

There was a fine tremor in his big arms. He stared at her with an expression she didn't understand.

"We have to go shopping," he said, repeating what he'd told her earlier. "Suppose we fly down to Dallas?"

"Okay," she agreed, stars in her eyes. She frowned. "Why Dallas?"

He grinned. "Neiman Marcus," he said with twinkling black eyes. "A gown, and wedding bands for both of us," he added.

"You're going to wear one, too?" she asked, surprised.

"I belong to you, don't I?" he teased.

Her face radiated the joy she felt inside her. "Yes, you do," she said, and she smiled up at him with her heart in her eyes. He might not love her, but he was fond of her, and he wanted her and the baby. It was more than enough to start with. Love, she reminded herself, could grow if it was properly fed.

THE DEPARTMENT STORE was enormous, Niki thought, as she and Blair headed toward the couture section. She still felt a little nauseated, but it was fading. She was fascinated by all the gorgeous dresses. None of them seemed to have price tags, and she remarked on it to Blair.

"I own an oil corporation," he whispered back, amused. "You can have anything in the store. And I mean anything."

She searched his black eyes. "I wonder if they have rawhide necklaces," she teased.

He chuckled. "We could ask."

"I'll worry about getting a wedding dress first."

"Be sure to get a veil to go with it," he said, and his face was somber and tender.

"A veil?"

He nodded. He moved closer, touching her cheek with the tips of his fingers. "It's an old tradition. One that I love. Elise wore just a short purple dress," he added curtly. "With you, I want the works. Especially a veil that I can lift when the minister marries us," he added in a husky, deep tone, "so that I look upon your face for the first time as a bride, before anyone else in the world sees you that way."

Tears ran down her cheeks. It was the most romantic thing he'd ever said to her. "Oh, Blair," she whispered, overcome with emotion.

His own eyes were misty. He averted them quickly. "Get something beautiful."

"I will."

He glanced down at her hungrily. "You glow," he said softly. "*Maste*," he added in Lakota. "Sunshine."

She smiled, her insides as radiant as her face.

"May I help you?" a saleswoman asked gently, smiling as she approached.

"Yes, please," Niki said. "I want a wedding gown. Something unique. And a veil, too," she added, with a glance at Blair.

"I think we have just the thing," the woman said, not missing the interaction between the two of them. "Come with me."

"WELL, WHAT DID you get?" Blair asked when the dress was bagged and concealed from his eyes, while he paid for it.

"Something beautiful," she replied. And it was. White with oceans of lace, a keyhole neckline, with tiny puff sleeves, imported lace, a fitted waist, flowing A-line skirt and a long lace train behind. In addition, there was a veil that reached to her waist in front, secured by a tiara. It was the most beautiful thing Niki had ever dreamed of. And now it was hers. To marry the man of her dreams. "Thank you," she added softly.

He chuckled. "I can't see it yet, I guess?"

She shook her head and smiled. "Tradition."

"Ah, well. Come on," he said when he'd thanked the saleswoman and pocketed his credit card.

"Where to next?" she asked excitedly, holding his big hand.

"The jewelry department. But first…"

He led her to the lingerie department, not the least embarrassed as he pointed her toward the most expensive peignoir sets.

He paused at an off-white set with a low, lacy bodice. "What do you think?" he asked huskily.

"It's beautiful." She bit her lip and looked up at him. "Blair, the wedding gown is white…"

He put a finger over her mouth. "You've been mine for two years. I've been yours for two years. A piece of paper and an official pronouncement are nice, but I haven't had a woman since the divorce."

She was shocked, and looked it. "But…you went to Europe. Janet was there, and later, Elise…"

"I only want you," he said simply. His black eyes flashed as he looked at her. "White."

She sighed and the light came back into her face. She nodded and smiled. "White."

LATER, THEY WENT to the jewelry department. The rings were horribly expensive. She saw the price tags and hesitated.

"Money is no object, honey." he whispered in her ear. "Besides, these are a lifetime deal. No returns. Which means you can't ever leave me."

"As if I could ever leave you," she said involuntarily, looking up at him with tenderness.

A faint flush colored his high cheekbones before he averted his face and pointed at a set of rings. "Could we look at those?" he asked the salesman.

"Of course, Mr. Coleman," the man agreed with a grin. Blair was a rare customer, who always knew exactly what he wanted and could afford anything in the case.

"He knows you?" Niki asked while the salesman went to get a measuring stick.

He chuckled. "This is where I commissioned that orchid brooch I got you for Christmas the year I spent it with you and your father."

"I see."

He pushed the wedding ring set toward her. "What do you think?"

The diamond was a canary-yellow diamond. Blair wanted to buy her a three-carat one, but Niki wanted something a little more subtle, so they settled on a two-carat stone. It was set in an eighteen-karat gold band. The wedding band itself was studded with canary diamonds.

"They're beautiful," she whispered.

"They remind me of you," he said. "They look like the sun captured in gold. Sunshine."

She leaned against him. "I like them very much."

"So do I." There was a man's wedding band with three large canary diamonds in a wide gold setting. He tried it on. It fit. So did both of Niki's.

"Amazing," the salesman said. "I think that's a first."

Blair looked down at Niki. "A good omen, I'd say."

"So would I," she agreed.

The salesman boxed them up, accepted Blair's credit card and completed the purchase.

As they were walking away, Blair's phone rang. He answered it, chuckled and informed the person on the other end that he was shopping for his forthcoming wedding. There was a pause. He grinned again and thanked the caller.

"The credit card company, just making sure it was me," he said with a grin.

"You spent a fortune in there," she said, faintly worried.

"Outfitting my beautiful, pregnant bride," he whispered, and bent to kiss her. "I'm the happiest man on earth right now."

"I'm definitely the happiest woman," she whispered back.

NIKI SHOWED HER wedding gown to Edna, who was almost overcome with its beauty. "My goodness, it must have cost a fortune," she exclaimed.

"It did. He insisted. It's going to be an heirloom," she said with a rapt smile.

"He'll take care of you," Edna said suddenly. "And you'll never want for a thing, as long as you live."

Except for love, Niki thought privately. Blair did want her, and the child, but he'd never once said that he loved her. She didn't expect it. One day he might grow to love her. It gave her something to hope for. Meanwhile, she'd make him happy, no matter what it took.

WEEKS LATER, THE minister married them in the living room at her father's house, under an artificial arbor thick with white silk roses and ivy. When Blair slid the wedding ring onto her finger beside the engagement ring, tears threatened. When he pronounced them man and wife, they raced down her cheeks, hot and wet.

Blair lifted the veil very slowly and pushed it back over her long, pale hair. He studied her with an intensity that made her heart race. He kissed the tears away before he touched his hard mouth hungrily to hers for one long minute. And they were married.

The house was full of people, along with a photographer, one reporter who had an exclusive story and Mr. Jacobs and his wife and little girl. Doctor Fred was there just long enough to see Niki married before he was called away. Tex grinned and kissed her cheek. The ranch's cowboys filed through to offer congratulations.

"It was the nicest wedding I've been to in a very long time," her father sighed as he kissed his daughter's forehead. "And I must say, it's about time you two got your act together," he added sternly, with a quick glance at Blair.

Blair sighed. He smiled at Niki. "I just had to get my priorities in order," he remarked, filling his eyes with his lovely new bride. "I suppose age isn't as important as other things," he added quietly. His eyes dropped to Niki's flat stomach, and his high cheekbones flushed with feeling. "I'd given up hope of ever having a child of my own. My God, what a beautiful surprise!"

Niki beamed. She still worried that he might feel trapped, despite the fact that he'd denied it. But the look in his eyes couldn't be faked. She felt absolutely cherished.

"I guess a granddaughter is out of the question," her father said, smiling at them.

"It would be a very long shot," Blair had to admit. He grinned. "Boys are nice. One of my vice presidents has three. He plays soccer with them." He drew in a breath. "I guess I'll need to work out in the gym more so that I can get in shape."

"For three boys?" her father teased.

Niki laughed. "Or four," she mused, with a wicked smile at Blair.

"We can get the cowboys to learn soccer so they can help you out," Todd said. He grimaced. "I guess you'll both be living in Billings," he added with a touch of sadness he couldn't help.

Blair looked smug. "Not really. I bought the old Vinings ranch down the road a couple of weeks ago," he added, surprising his best friend and his wife. "It needs some work, though, but it's going to be a showplace. I like horses. I thought we might raise purebred quarter horses. I have a livestock manager hired, and a ranch manager ready to interview." He glanced at

Niki, who positively glowed. "We can move in next week, if things go according to plan. Meanwhile," he said with a tender smile, "we're going to be lying on a nice beach in Jamaica on our honeymoon."

"I'll love that, living close to Dad and Edna," Niki said warmly. She ground her teeth. "Oh, gosh, my job!"

Just then, Mr. Jacobs joined them. "Nice wedding," he said, shaking hands with Blair and pausing to kiss Niki on the cheek. "Congratulations. I guess I'll be losing my best assistant ever here," he added with a sigh, glancing at Niki.

"Afraid so," Blair chuckled. "I'll want her with me most of the time. Especially now."

"Especially now?" Jacobs asked.

Blair was beaming. "We're pregnant," he said, clasping Niki's hand closely in his.

"Congratulations again!" Jacobs chuckled. "You lucky devil. Kids are wonderful. God knows, I love mine." He glanced toward his daughter. She was leaning on a cane beside a nice-looking brunette, who was Jacobs's wife.

"I hope they find something that can help your daughter someday," Niki said softly.

Jacobs nodded. "They're coming up with new treatments all the time. But she has a wonderful attitude. She's always smiling, despite the pain and disability."

"You're a sweet man, Mr. Jacobs," Niki said. "I'll miss working for you."

He grinned. "Thanks. I hate to lose you. But I don't hate losing the health nut," he added with a sly glance at Blair. "I forgot to tell you about him!" he added quickly, when Blair glowered at just the mention of the man. "Dan quit his job and went to work as manager of a health-food store out in California!"

Niki and Blair burst out laughing.

"At least now he has an excuse for handing out helpful advice," Niki agreed.

"May he hand it out anywhere but Wyoming," Jacobs replied.

"Amen," Blair seconded.

THE PLANE TRIP to Jamaica was a long one. Niki was asleep when their flight touched down in Montego Bay.

"Time to wake up, sleepyhead," he teased softly. "We're here."

"Gosh, already?" She yawned behind a small hand and stretched. "I slept all the way, I guess. Sorry."

"I didn't mind. Gave me a chance to catch up on some work." He indicated the laptop he'd just put away in his briefcase.

When they finally got through customs, Niki was wilting, and Blair quickly got them a cab to the hotel, which was right on the beach.

"It's lovely!" Niki exclaimed when they checked in and were escorted to their room. The glass patio door opened onto the beach beyond. The room itself was huge and luxurious, with paintings on the wall and modern furniture and a Jacuzzi in the huge bathroom.

"All the comforts of home," Blair agreed. He came up behind her and pulled her into his arms, nuzzling her neck with his lips. "Tired?"

"Terribly," she moaned. She turned to him. "I'm

so sorry…" She looked as if she could barely keep her eyes open.

He smiled complacently. "It's the baby, honey," he said softly, and bent to kiss her. "He's growing. The nausea is better, though, isn't it, with the pills?"

She nodded. "Much better. I think the prenatal vitamins will help with the fatigue, too, but it's early days yet."

"Don't rush it. I want to enjoy every single minute of this," he said, his voice deep and husky with feeling. "I never dreamed I could make you pregnant," he whispered at her mouth. "I wanted to, so badly!"

"You thought you were sterile."

He lifted his head and nodded. His expression was solemn. "Elise apologized for that. She was on the pill and never told me." He rocked her gently in his arms. "She apologized for marrying me, too. She was trying to get over the death of her significant other. Drugs, pills, booze—you name it, she did it. I didn't realize that, either. It was why she was so cold to me when I got sick and ended up at your house, with you nursing me."

She hated the mention of the other woman's name. Her face closed up. "You loved her once," she said. She looked up at him worriedly. "If you hadn't known I was pregnant, you might have gone back to her… Why are you laughing?"

He kissed her hungrily. "Because going back to Elise was never an option."

"It wasn't?"

He lifted his head, and his eyes were soft and quiet. "Honey, there's something you don't know about Elise."

"What don't I know?"

He brushed back her long, pale blond hair. "She's a lesbian."

CHAPTER FOURTEEN

NIKI STARED UP at him with her heart in her eyes. "Oh, Blair, I'm so sorry," she said, not knowing what else to say.

He caught her hand and brought the palm to his mouth. "It's all right. I haven't had feelings for her in a long time," he confessed. "It isn't something she could help, you know. People are what they are."

She nodded. "She must have been in terrible pain when she married you."

"She was. She'd been badly treated by her father, when he found out that she didn't like men in that way. I think she struggled with her identity all her life." He kissed her nose. "You know, that first night, when I held you in the easy chair in your living room, after your blind date tried to hurt you—I was sorry that I was engaged, despite what I thought I felt for Elise."

"Really?" she asked, all eyes.

He nodded. He traced her soft mouth with just his forefinger. "You made me hungry, and not just physically. When I was sick, and you went against your doctor's orders to nurse me, and Elise wouldn't even come back to the States to see about me, I realized what a mistake I'd made. I divorced her soon after that."

"I remember." She smiled sadly. "You got drunk

on my graduation day, and Dad and I brought you home with us."

He sighed. "I'd just found out that Elise was a lesbian. And I was debating my conscience at the time, as well," he said, not wanting to admit that his hunger for Niki had helped provoke the drinking.

"Why?"

He studied her. "That can wait a little longer." He scooped her up and carried her to the bed. He put her down and pulled the cover and sheet back. "You need sleep," he said softly. "I'll have room service bring up supper when you wake up."

"Where are you going to be?" she asked as he rummaged through her suitcase for a gown. He brought out the beautiful white lacy one that they'd bought together.

"Walking on the beach," he replied with a smile. "I don't have the luxury of free time very often." He pulled off her shoes and slacks and blouse and then her bra. He stared at her pretty, pert breasts with delight. He smiled. "You're darker, here," he whispered, bending to put his mouth tenderly against the suddenly hard tips. "They're more sensitive, aren't they?" he added when she gasped.

"Yes," she agreed.

He slid the gown over her head and pulled it down before he put her under the covers and smoothed her long blond hair out on the pillow. "My sweet angel," he said quietly. "You are so beautiful, Niki."

"I'm not beautiful," she scoffed, flushing.

He chuckled. "It's in the eyes of the beholder, precious," he reminded her. "Do you need anything before I go?"

She shook her head. "I'm sorry I'm so tired."

"We'll make up for it later," he teased. "Okay?"

She smiled sleepily. "Okay."

"Sleep well."

He turned the lights out and went out the patio door onto the beach, where the waves were washing up on the shore. He felt like the luckiest man on earth.

WHEN NIKI WOKE up hours later, Blair was lying beside her on the bed, wearing tan Bermuda shorts and a yellow knit shirt. He looked very handsome, with his black hair thick and clean and wavy, and his broad face freshly shaven. He smelled of soap and light cologne, and Niki thought he had to be the most gorgeous man in the whole world. His chest was broad, and curling black hair peered out of the opening at his throat. She remembered how it felt against her bare breasts and blushed in spite of herself. Her eyes lowered to his legs like tree trunks, muscular and faintly feathered with hair.

He was chuckling softly at her intense scrutiny.

"I can't help staring at you," she confessed. "I think you're gorgeous, Blair."

"I think you are, too," he replied. One lean hand brushed back her own hair. His eyes were soft and tender on her wan face. "Feel rocky?"

"Just a bit," she said. "The fatigue is the worst."

"It will get better," he said. "I read this book," he added. "All about the early stages of pregnancy. Those vitamins, in time, will make you think you can lift the front end of a semi." He chuckled. "And the morning sickness will go away soon, too." He leaned closer. "As long as you don't try to eat eggs," he teased.

She rolled over toward him and curled up in his arms. "I'm glad that you aren't angry about the baby," she said. "I was scared to death that I might not ever have a baby. I sort of pushed you off balance..."

He was laughing. "I was already off balance. I wanted you to the point of madness two years ago. It hasn't gotten better in all the time between, either."

She turned her head on the pillow so that she could look into his eyes. "Really?"

He traced her mouth with his forefinger. "Really. I got more out of kissing you than I ever got out of sex with anyone else."

"Wow. Really?"

He laughed. That was what she'd whispered after their first intimacy. "You make me feel ten feet tall."

She moved closer, tracing her fingers along his jawline. "And you make me feel beautiful."

"You are beautiful, Niki," he replied, drawing her close. "Inside and out. And you can't possibly imagine how much I want this baby. I want it almost as much as I want you," he said.

She smoothed back his hair at his temple. "I thought you loved Elise, that I would never be able to make you forget her. And then there was Janet," she added sadly.

"Janet." He kissed her forehead. "I took her out trying to forget how it had been with you on the beach," he confessed. "I was so hungry for you that I could hardly bear it. Janet was a diversion, honey. Only that. I could have married her years ago if I'd wanted to. It was always only friendship on my part. Nothing more."

"We were friends," she pointed out.

He nibbled her lower lip. "I was trying to protect you from me."

She laughed softly, because he was smiling. "Why?"

"Because we're so far apart in age," he said. His face grew solemn. "But then we thought you had cancer, and I realized that nothing guarantees us another day of life, that I could outlive you. It was a staggering reality." He winced. "You don't know how I felt, when you told me about the spot on your lung. That's why I got drunk and took you to bed, Niki. You didn't have to push me over the edge. The trick would have been keeping me out of your bed. I was desperate for you."

She smiled lazily. "I noticed."

He sighed as he kissed her nose. "Life is unpredictable. We have to live it one day at a time and not worry away the future. I'll take care of you," he added tenderly. "All my life, Niki. As long as I live. I'll cherish you."

She moved closer. "And I'll take care of you." She brushed her mouth against his and smiled at the instant response.

He drew her closer. "Do you think…" Niki suddenly sat up in bed and held her hand to her mouth. He let her go and followed her mad run into the bathroom, reaching for a washcloth even as she rushed to the toilet.

"Oh…damn!" she groaned as she lost what little food was in her stomach.

He bathed her forehead with cool water and smiled. "We'll get through it together, honey," he said from beside her. "It will get better. I promise."

LATER ON BLAIR ordered food from room service for them. Niki was able to keep a little soup down. Blair fed it to her spoonful by spoonful, watching her as if she was the most fascinating thing he'd ever seen.

"Is my nose on backward?" she teased.

He chuckled. "I've never been around a pregnant woman," he explained. "Every minute of it fascinates me."

She was pale and lethargic, without makeup, still wearing the nightgown he'd put her in. He didn't seem to mind a bit. She loved the expression on his face.

"It fascinates me, too," she replied. "I've always wanted children. But after I got to know you, the only ones I wanted were yours. I used to dream about it." She stopped eating. "What if this is just a dream, Blair? I'd rather die than wake up!"

"So would I," he said gruffly.

"You could pinch me, just in case," she said.

He bent and kissed the tip of her nose. "I do not torture pregnant women," he informed her haughtily.

She smiled from ear to ear and accepted the last spoonful of soup.

That night she slept close and warm in his arms, curled into him like a treasure, safe and cherished. He might not truly love her, she thought, but he cared for her a great deal. It made her happy that he wanted the baby. But it was worrying that she was too sick to offer him the physical part of marriage. She hoped the nausea would pass soon, that she'd feel the way she did that one unforgettable night in his arms.

THE NEXT MORNING Blair tried to finish breakfast in between constant business calls. She knew that it followed him everywhere. He spent much of his time delegating chores, answering questions, positioning

management personnel. He saw Niki watching him
with a tiny, loving smile and forgot what he was saying. The caller had to prompt him to answer the question. He did, then ended the call. He turned his phone
off and tossed it onto a table near the patio window.

"I hate the damned cell phone," he muttered. "You
can't make people leave you alone as long as it's turned
on."

She moved close to him and pressed herself into
his arms. "You're a high-powered businessman. You
have a lot of people who depend on you to keep the
corporation running," she said simply.

His broad chest rose and fell. "I guess so." He
kissed the top of her head. "You're very tolerant. You
should be yelling at me for letting business interfere
with our honeymoon."

"Okay. Consider yourself yelled at," she laughed
softly.

His arms contracted. "Life is so uncomplicated
when I'm with you," he said, trying to put a feeling
into words. "Easy. I live in a state of constant turmoil
at work. People are short-tempered. Executives com-
plain. Subordinates argue. Then I take you for a walk
on the beach, and all the stress goes away. Just being
with you is... I can't explain it."

She smiled, pleased. "I'm not a stressful person,"
she said simply. "I don't challenge you or try to com-
pete with you." She pulled back and looked up at him
with her heart in her eyes. "I love you," she whispered.
"I could never do anything that would cause you pain
or upset you." She winced. "Well, I did a few times,
like the hiking trip, and then being so stressed about
the chest X-ray," she backtracked.

"None of that was your fault, baby," he said softly. "You were scared to death, and your emotions ran away with you. That wasn't like you to do anything that would cause trouble for other people." He brushed back her hair. "My mother was like you," he said. "Quiet and loving and gentle. She had a temper, and she could argue when she needed to. But she was wonderful company. Like you."

She smiled. "My mother was like that, too," she said. "Dad loved her so much. I thought I might lose him, too, after she died. He ran wild."

He looked down at her. "I know how he felt," he said huskily. "When I thought you had cancer, had to face the fact that I could lose you..." His face clenched. "I pushed you away because I thought you'd need someone younger, a few years down the line, that it wasn't fair to saddle you with a husband so much older. It never occurred to me that I might survive you." His eyes closed and opened, agony in his expression. "Nothing mattered after that. If the cancer had killed you, I wouldn't have had a life. I wouldn't have wanted to live."

Her heart stopped in her throat. Her mind went back to her time in the hospital, when Blair had stayed by her side, had refused to leave her even to sleep. He'd hired specialists, taken care of her, been willing to marry her even if she was facing a death sentence. When he realized she was pregnant, he'd acted as if he'd won the lottery. He couldn't wait to marry her. He read everything he could find about pregnancy, wanted to be part of every second of the experience. And after all that, she hadn't realized how much he cared.

He kissed her eyelids closed. "You looked, but you didn't see, did you, Niki?" he whispered.

She shivered in his arms, pressing closer, so that her body was completely against his. "No. I never dreamed…" She swallowed hard. "I thought, maybe, it was just desire."

"If all I'd wanted was one night with you, it would have been easy enough to seduce you, baby," he whispered at her ear. "I wanted much more than a night."

"You took care of me," she said. "You were always nurturing me, doing whatever I needed you to do, always there when I was sick."

"I always will be. As long as I live." He hugged her against him, hungrily. "You took care of me, too, when I got bronchitis. You risked your own health to do it. I knew then that you felt more than friendship for me."

"I never knew," she whispered.

He laughed softly. "When you want to take care of someone that badly, it's a little more than friendship. Then on Christmas morning, when the little girl who wanted a doll hugged me, and I saw the light in your eyes—" he paused, swallowing hard "—I started thinking about babies. I'd never wanted one so much."

Her face brightened. "I wanted one, too, Blair. But only yours. Nobody else's."

He bent and kissed her. "I pushed you away so brutally after Mexico." He sighed. "I knew you were dating the health-food nut, but I thought maybe you really cared for him. He was younger, more suited to you, or so I thought." His face hardened with the memory. "Truth is, he landed you in the hospital. I couldn't get to you fast enough. He's damned lucky he didn't get more than a punch. I wanted to strangle him!"

She drew her fingers down his cheek. "You never left me, while I was in the hospital," she recalled. "You wouldn't even leave me to sleep. You can't imagine how it felt, to know you cared that much. I thought you'd gone for good, that you didn't want me."

He drew her palm to his mouth and kissed it hungrily. "I couldn't have left after that," he said huskily. "I was afraid that I'd lose you. Especially when you told me about the X-ray." He closed his eyes. "I've never known fear like that in my life."

"Neither have I," she confessed. "I just went overboard, thinking I was going to end up like Mama did."

"I wanted one night with you, to keep in my heart, in my memory, for the rest of my life." He stared into her eyes. "It was the most perfect night I've ever had."

"For me, too, even though it was my first time." She nuzzled her face into his throat and held on tight. "Nothing you can read prepares you for how it feels."

"It felt like explosions inside me, like swallowing joy," he whispered. "Never like that. Never in my whole life."

She smiled against his throat. "I hope we can have another one, once I can stop throwing up," she moaned.

"It will pass," he promised. He lifted his head and smiled. "I've read all the books. I know what to do for you, even for backaches when you get bigger."

"I'm going to look like a pumpkin in a few months," she said, staring up into his black eyes as she smiled. "Will you mind?"

"Hell, no," he murmured, nuzzling her cheek with

his. He chuckled. "I'll take dozens of photos and put them on my desk at work."

"I'll do the same with photos of you."

"And I plan to limit some of those business conferences. I won't travel as much, especially while you're carrying our baby."

"Our baby." She slid her hand up into his wavy black hair, loving its thickness. "I was so afraid that you'd think it wasn't yours. I knew that you said Elise couldn't get pregnant…"

"I didn't know about her birth control pills," he replied. He smiled. "But, honey, exactly how would I think the baby was someone else's? I was your first lover," he whispered. His voice deepened. "I remember every sweet second of it. I'd never have doubted it was mine."

"You wouldn't? But why?" she asked, honestly curious.

"Because you love me, Niki," he said quietly.

She smiled. "Yes, I do. So much!"

"I thought I'd found love twice in my life," he said. "Both times were false starts, because I didn't really know what love was." His arms tightened around her. "I found it in the oddest place. In a quiet, shy young woman who played with me and made me hungry for a family, for a place to belong."

She smiled against his chest, her eyes welling with tears. "You have a place to belong. You belong to me."

He nuzzled her ear. "And you belong to me, my darling."

"I'm so tired," she said. She smiled at him, and then her face contorted. "Oh, gosh…!"

He picked her up and carried her into the bathroom just in time. He went to get a washcloth, wet it and brought it back. She pressed it to her lips and her forehead. She started crying.

"Honey, what's the matter?" he asked worriedly.

"It's our honeymoon," she wailed. "And I'm going to spend it kneeling in front of a toilet!"

He laughed tenderly. "You're pregnant," he mused. "It sort of goes with the condition. I don't mind. I really don't." He took the cloth and bathed her face with it. "In sickness and in health, baby," he said softly. "I took a vow."

"I'll take care of you, if you need me to," she promised.

He felt warm inside, not only at the words, but at the love in her voice when she spoke them. He was the richest man alive, and it had nothing to do with money.

"I've been alone all my life until now," he said quietly, brushing back her hair as she finally got up and flushed the toilet.

"So have I, really, except for Dad and Edna," she replied. "I feel awful."

He picked her up gently and carried her back to bed. He put her down on the coverlet while he searched for her new yellow nightgown.

"It's daylight," she said.

"You're sick," he replied, smiling. "You can get up when you feel better."

He pulled off her long dress and tugged the pretty yellow frilly gown over her head. It was one of the ones they'd bought together at Neiman Marcus.

He tucked her in. "Need something to drink?" he asked gently.

"Is there any ginger ale in the minibar?" she asked.

"I'll check." He found one can of it, opened it and handed it to her.

"Thanks," she said, smiling up at him. She sipped it, finding that it calmed her stomach quite nicely. "Blair, can you find my pills in the little suitcase? There should be two bottles—one's vitamins and the other is nausea medicine."

"I'll check." He dug them out and handed them to her.

"I forgot to take the nausea pill this morning," she said with a sheepish smile. "It's new."

"It's all new, isn't it, honey?" he asked, his face radiant. "For both of us."

"You said that after Elise, you never wanted to marry again."

He sat down beside her, his fingers teasing around one pretty breast in the deep neckline of the gown. "That was how I felt. Until Elise, I never wanted marriage."

"Not ever?"

He shook his head. "Then even before the divorce, I wanted you. I would have died to have you. But you were so damned young!"

She smoothed over his fingers, coaxing them into the deep neckline. "Love doesn't have an age limit," she said simply. "I'd have loved you if you'd been my age or older than you are. It's what's inside you that I love, Blair. It has nothing to do with the outside. Even if the outside is utterly gorgeous," she added, eating him with her eyes.

His high cheekbones flushed, but his black eyes twinkled. "Gorgeous?"

"Oh, yes," she said. She grimaced. "And I wish I felt like doing something about it."

"Sick again?" he asked gently.

She sat, swallowing for a minute. She took the nausea pill and lay back. "It's dreadful to feel this way on a honeymoon in paradise," she groaned.

"You'll feel better. When you do, we'll go tour the island, even if we have to carry a pail with us," he added with a grin.

She laughed at his expression. "Okay."

"And that's what I love about you," he said softly. "I've never known anyone as easygoing as you are."

"You are."

"Only with you, baby," he replied, and he was serious. "Most of my executives hide when they see me coming. I'm temperamental. Or at least I was," he added. "I think marriage might lighten my mood."

She beamed. "I'll work on that."

He chuckled. "See if you can sleep for a bit while I finish taking care of business," he added, picking up the cell phone. "I'll go outside to yell at subordinates, okay?" he asked, bending to kiss her forehead. "If you need me, I'll be close by."

"Thanks, Blair."

He kissed her eyelids. "My sweetheart," he whispered. "You look so beautiful, Niki, even pale as a sheet and without a trace of makeup."

She kissed his hard cheek. "My gorgeous husband. You're beautiful to me."

He made a face, winked at her and went out the sliding glass patio doors with the phone.

NIKI ENDED UP dozing again after the last bout of nausea. When she woke up, Blair was lying on his side, propped on an elbow, just watching her. He was wearing tan shorts. His broad chest was bare, and he was barefoot. She caught her breath just looking at him. His chest was broad and muscular, covered with curling black hair. His legs were like tree trunks, muscular and finely covered with hair. Even his feet were attractive, big and tapered.

"I could spend hours just looking at you," he confessed softly. "You're so beautiful, Niki."

"I was just thinking the same thing," she mused. "You're gorgeous."

"How do you feel?"

She stretched. "Much better." She rolled over into his arms and pillowed her head on his chest with a little sigh. "Are you finished yelling at people?"

"For today," he chuckled. "I shut the damned thing off. Business gets tedious."

She smoothed her hand over his chest, loving the play of muscles when she touched him. He was warm and strong. She turned her face and kissed the skin under the thick hair. He stiffened a little. It amazed her to find him vulnerable. That made her bold.

She raised up, resting her chest on his, and kissed his mouth. Her nightgown was low-cut, and the top of her breasts pressed warm and soft into his chest. He looked at her with laughing black eyes.

"Are you trying to seduce me?" he asked.

She pursed her lips. "Mmmmmm," she murmured. Her small hand tangled in the thick hair over his chest and moved slowly down. His body tautened even more. "What a delicious thought," she whispered.

He laughed softly. "Go ahead. I'm easy."

"Are you really?" she whispered. She moved her mouth warmly over his. She loved kissing him. His mouth was broad and chiseled and warm. She teased it with her lips until he nibbled at her own mouth, and she was lost.

He turned her slowly until she was under him, his hands going to the straps of the gown. He lowered them very gently, brushing his chest over her naked breasts until she gasped with the sudden pleasure.

He tossed the nightgown over the side of the bed. It was followed in quick order by her panties and his own clothes. His mouth smoothed over her soft breast, his tongue sliding gently against the hard nipple. She arched up, and he chuckled before his mouth began to move down her body. It went from her neck to her calves and back again, up her sides, to her back, all over her. And all the while he touched her, arousing her to such a fever pitch that she was almost in tears when he finally turned her onto her back and slid between her long, trembling legs.

He touched her gently between her legs. "Yes, you're ready for me."

"Ready?" she asked, concentrating on the slow movement of his hips as he began to enter her.

"Your body produces a very effective lubricant," he whispered over her mouth. He pushed down gently and felt her envelop him. "You see? It makes it easy for me to go into you."

She flushed, because the intimacy was still very new. "I see."

His mouth moved onto hers, teasing, exploring, while his hips rose and fell in a slow, easy rhythm

that very quickly caught her up and made her whole
body tense with each downward movement.

"We have to learn to please each other," he whispered. "First times are difficult. But it gets easier as
we go along. Do you like this?"

His hips moved from side to side, and she shivered and cried out.

"Yes, that works, doesn't it?" he teased. "How
about this?"

The movements were quick and hard, and she
began to moan and dig her nails into his arms. Even
that first night had been nothing like this. She shivered with each movement of his powerful body, felt
him so deep in her body that she thought they might
be joined forever. He was far more potent than he'd
been the first time. She arched up to him, her eyes
wide open with pleasure and surprise.

"You…you're…more than last time," she gasped.

"Much more," he whispered, holding her eyes.
"Men are more potent at times. This is definitely one
of them." He moved down. His body shuddered, and
he whispered huskily as the pleasure bit into him,
"Oh, God, honey, I don't think I can…hold it…much
longer!"

"You don't have to," she said, moving with him.
She gripped his shoulders hard. Her body trembled.
"Please, now!" Her voice broke on the word as pleasure bit into her like a knife. She cried out with each
quick, sharp, deep movement of his body, watching
him the whole time.

Her eyes on him intensified his pleasure, which
was already monstrous. His hands gripped the pillow
on either side of her head, and he gave in to the pas-

sionate hunger. "Oh, God, baby, oh, God, it's like…
dying…!" he choked.

Her eyes closed on the fierce pleasure he gave her.
She felt his body arch down into hers as she was almost swept away in the overwhelming pleasure. It was
nothing like before. She convulsed under the driving rhythm of his hips, shuddered and moaned as
her whole body seemed to liquefy with molten heat.

She didn't think it could get any better, but it did.
Just as she climaxed, he moved down against her, and
she shot up into realms she'd never dreamed existed.
She sobbed into his shoulder as her body moved involuntarily up toward him, pleading, hungry, insistent.

He shuddered one last time, and she felt him throb-
bing inside her. Her hands smoothed over his damp
back, holding him close. He tried to spare her his
weight, but she pulled him back down again.

"No," she whispered. "I like to feel you lying on
top of me like this. I love your weight on me."

"You feel like silk to me," he murmured breathlessly. "Was it too quick?"

"You're kidding, right?" she laughed huskily. "It
was wonderful, that first night. But it was nothing
like this. I thought I might die…of pleasure," she said,
flushing. She slid her legs around his, loving the intimacy. "It feels so good, being with you like this."

He rolled over onto his back and took a deep, long
breath.

She pillowed her cheek on his hairy chest and
smiled. "Tired?"

"Deliciously tired," he mused.

"Me, too."

"Want some ginger ale?"

"That would be nice."

He moved away, got to his feet, padded to the mini-bar and found her a ginger ale. He opened it on the way back while she lay on her side and watched him with wide, soft, curious eyes.

"Oh, Blair," she whispered. "You really are gorgeous. I am a very lucky woman."

He laughed. "I'll have to start working out more, so that I don't start drooping too soon."

She sat up and curled her arms around his neck. "You don't have to do anything of the sort," she said quietly, her eyes loving on his face. "I love you so much, Blair. More than anything in the world."

His high cheekbones had a faint flush. He handed her the ginger ale. "If I started counting my blessings right now, I'd be old and gray before I finished," he said. He searched her eyes hungrily. "You're my world now, Niki. My whole world. It's just you and me. Forever."

She sat up, beautifully nude, and studied him.

"Looking for hidden treasure?" he mused, laughing at her.

"Oh, something like that," she said. "I was thinking…"

"Thinking?" he asked as she moved toward him, climbed onto him, her knees going on either side of his hips.

She lifted up and positioned him, delighted to find that he was more than ready to accommodate her. She slid down onto him with a soft gasp. "I was wondering," she whispered, "how it would feel…if we did it like this."

His big hands helped her, because she very quickly

became too weak to keep it up. Pleasure overwhelmed her, so suddenly that she felt as if she dropped from a great height.

"Blair!" she cried out, shivering in pleasure.

"Oh, it's good like this," he breathed, moving her hard against him, impaling her. "Good, good, good…!"

"Yes…" Her voice trailed away into a smothered scream as the intensity shot her up like a rocket. She shuddered and shuddered and wept. Pleasure almost as deep as pain racked her slender body, while Blair held her hips and went into her so hungrily that she felt blind, deaf, dumb from the utter joy of it.

"Now…" he choked. "Now, now…!"

He cried out, a hoarse, deep groan that echoed in the room, combining with her high-pitched moans as they climaxed together.

"Dear God!" he moaned at her ear when they were able to breathe and speak again.

She clung to him, weeping. "It's…it's… I can't even find words!"

"Paradise," he whispered. "That's what it is, Mrs. Coleman," he added, using her married name for the first time. He looked down into her wide, soft gray eyes. "Paradise."

She smiled slowly, her body perfectly attuned to his, her eyes blinded by the love on his face. "Paradise," she agreed.

THEY WENT HOME a week later, tanned and so much in love that they became quickly inseparable. They moved into the house next door to the Ashton ranch, and Niki's father and Edna were frequent visitors.

The long months of her pregnancy ended in a very quick delivery. Blair barely made it to the hospital with her before their little boy was born. The baby looked up at them with blue eyes.

"Our son," she whispered.

He kissed her and then the baby's tiny forehead. "You don't need to die to find heaven," he said softly, looking into her eyes. "If you're very lucky, you find it right here on earth. Like I have." His mouth smoothed over hers tenderly. "I love you so much it hurts, Niki," he whispered unsteadily. "Oh, God, honey, I'd die for you!"

Tears stung her eyes. "I'd do the same for you," she whispered.

She looked up at him with eyes so full of love that they almost blinded him.

"I will never leave you," she whispered, chipping away at that tiny fear that still showed sometimes in his black eyes. "Never."

He swallowed, hard. His mouth brushed over hers hungrily. "I'll take care of you all my life."

She smiled tenderly. "And I'll take care of you, my darling, all my life."

She drew his face down to hers and kissed him. It was still magic to her, to love and be loved so much. And to have a child, born of that love, a living symbol of it, really was heaven on earth.

She let him go and shifted the baby in her arms, kissing his soft head with wonder. "We still haven't discussed names," she said.

"I like Todd," he said softly. "For your father."

"Yes, I like that, too, for his middle name. What was your father's first name?"

"Jacob."

Her eyes softened. "Jacob Todd Blair?" she suggested.

He smiled back. "It sounds good."

"It sounds very good." She touched her fingers to his lips. "I've loved you since I was seventeen, you know," she told him softly, laughing at the shock on his face. "I just had to grow up enough to convince you I was old enough for you."

He touched his mouth to hers. "You convinced me," he said on a husky laugh. He searched her eyes hungrily. "My little hothouse orchid. I love you insanely."

She felt warm inside, cherished and secure. "I love you back, insanely," she whispered intently.

His mouth crushed down on hers for a few heated seconds until the baby moved restlessly in his mother's arms. They both looked down at him then, their hands locked together over his small body. And they beamed.

* * * * *

For a long moment, Ella feared she'd gone too far.

Then the storm clouds faded from Ben's eyes and his voice turned smooth again. "I am like my father. Always have been. Something a nice girl like you would do well to remember."

Even through her knit mittens and his overcoat, she could feel the tension in his muscles. "That sounds like a warning."

"I said you were intelligent from the get-go."

She moistened her lips, even though doing so just made them colder. "I felt a lot safer with Randy's flirting than I do right now." She could not fathom the insanity that made her admit it aloud. Maybe it was the way she couldn't drag her eyes away from his.

"Much as I disliked seeing him flirt with you, you were definitely safer."

Her chest felt so tight it was hard to breathe. She

imagined she could see her own reflection inside his eyes. "Ben—"

He took a step back and pulled her hand once more through his crooked arm. "It's getting cold standing here, and Bonita's chocolates are waiting."

She figured that the famed street would be spectacularly beautiful during warmer months. And it wasn't without charm now, with snowflakes drifting around them, dusting the buildings and the snowplowed street with a fresh coat of white.

Maybe someday she'd visit Boston while the trees were green and the flowers were in bloom.

But now she was here with Ben.

She exhaled and fell into step with him again.

They eventually reached the chocolatier's shop, which was set down a short staircase from the street level and was smaller inside than she'd envisioned. But the very air was sinfully redolent of chocolate confections and she couldn't help but admire the beautiful displays behind the glass-fronted cases. "I'm gaining weight just looking."

A woman wearing a pristine white apron and a black bow tie appeared, and Ben gestured at one of the larger boxes on display. "Give me one of that size and fill it with anything chocolate that has a nut in it. It's for my secretary and she doesn't touch chocolate without nuts. Nothing fruity, either."

The clerk plucked an empty box from under her counter and tucked shimmery white tissue paper in it before deftly beginning to fill it with chocolates of every size and shape.

"Your secretary is a lucky woman," Ella said dryly,

because she'd noticed the tastefully discreet price tag that was even more enormous than the box itself.

"Indeed, she is," the clerk agreed. She stopped near Ella to select several round confections topped with walnut halves. "Would you like a sample of anything?"

"Oh." Ella shook her head. "I couldn't."

"Sure, she could." Ben stepped next to her, touching her shoulder as he leaned over to examine the displays.

"Your husband is right." The clerk's hand hovered over the trays of precisely arranged chocolates. "Perhaps a white ganache or an almond praline?"

Ella opened her mouth to correct the clerk, but Ben's hand moved to the back of her neck, scorching even through the scarf, and the words caught in her throat.

"Give her one of those Manhattan truffles."

She almost did a double-take at the quick wink he gave her. Instead, she just felt heat course down through the rest of her from the source at the back of her neck. When the clerk set a silver foil cup containing a glossy round truffle on top of the glass, she quickly picked it up and sank her teeth into it, biting off half.

Dark, heady chocolate dissolved blissfully on her tongue, but it was nothing compared to having Ben slip the other half of the truffle out of her fingers and pop it into his mouth.

She actually felt faint and considered tearing off her coat to run into the snowy outdoors for relief.

"There's a first," Ben murmured. "Our first whiskey truffle together."

The clerk fit the lid in place on Bonita's chocolates before sliding the box toward Ben across the glass. "You sound like newlyweds," she said with a benevolent smile. "I can always spot the newlyweds. Can I get you anything else?"

"Pack up a dozen of these." He flicked the empty foil cup and slid a credit card toward her in exchange.

"My pleasure." The clerk took the card and greeted a customer who entered behind them before moving toward her cash register.

Ben's hand fell away from Ella's neck and she moved near the door where she had a slim hope of catching her breath while he finished paying for his purchases.

The snow was falling even harder when they went up the short flight of stairs to reach the street level. "Why did you let her think we were married?"

"It's the theme for the day, evidently."

"Yes. Karma for you lying to Randy about being my fiancé."

She was grateful to see Johnny and his car waiting at the curb and aimed straight for it.

The driver opened the door for her, and she ducked her head and climbed in, sliding across the seat for Ben to follow. Once Johnny closed the door after Ben and got back behind the wheel, she sat forward to offer him one of her Manhattan truffles.

"Don't mind if I do, miss." He plucked a round truffle from the small box and popped it in his mouth before pulling out into the traffic that hadn't lessened a speck despite the snowfall. "Back to the hotel, sir?"

"I thought we'd hit Little Italy for dinner, but it's still early."

"Already be a line forming outside of Giacomo's," Johnny said. "Always is."

Ella pulled off her mittens and unwound her scarf, since the car interior was toasty warm and she still felt like she was burning up from the inside. "What's Giacomo's?"

"Best Italian joint in the North End." Ben set the large bag containing Bonita's chocolates on the seat between them while he pulled out his cell phone and studied it. "They don't take reservations and there's hardly any space inside, but it's worth the wait every time." He returned his phone to his pocket, then pulled open his coat and dropped his scarf in the bag with the box of candy. "Give Ms. Thomas the city tour, Johnny. And turn down the heater. We're roasting back here."

Ella couldn't help but wish that the cause of his overheating had less to do with the town car's heater and more to do with her.

At least then he'd be sharing her discomfort.

The warm air blowing from the heating vents disappeared and Johnny launched into his role of tour guide again as he drove through the city, pointing out landmarks, some famous and some so obscure she felt almost certain he was pulling her leg. He ended in the North End, dropping them off at Ben's request on Hanover Street in front of the restaurant where a line of people stood outside on the sidewalk, not seeming to care about the weather as they waited.

It took the better part of an hour, but eventually it was their turn to weave their way through the closely set tables crowded inside the small restaurant. They sat at a table for four with two strangers and Ella's bemusement only increased from there. Wine. Seafood.

Pasta. It was loud and noisy and delicious and so close that Ben's knees were pressed against hers beneath the table the entire while.

And for the first time since she'd met him what seemed so much longer than a mere week ago, he seemed to actually relax, not checking his phone for the entire time.

After the filling meal, she expected Ben would want to return to the hotel, but again he surprised her, choosing to walk to a nearby pastry shop where he insisted she try a cannoli. And even though she was positively stuffed, she managed to consume half of the delicious cream-filled dessert before begging off. "I'm going to explode," she told him plaintively, "if you keep feeding me like this."

He smiled and finished the cannoli the same way he had her chocolate truffle. Then he pulled her out of the pastry shop and down the street a few more doors into a dimly lit pub, where she sat on a high bar stool at the crowded bar and Ben stood so close beside her that she felt engulfed by him.

It was more intoxicating than the wine, the food and the desserts could ever be.

Her head was already spinning so she was grateful when Ben, looking amused, ordered her a soda in place of the cognac he'd ordered for himself.

When they finally climbed into the rear of the town car and Johnny dropped them off in front of the hotel, it was after midnight.

"Thank you, Johnny," she said when he opened the car door for her yet again. "I feel like I had a personal tour guide."

He beamed. "My pleasure, miss."

Ben shook the driver's hand and Ella couldn't help wonder if there'd been an exchange of cash in the action. The snow had stopped falling when they'd had their dinner, but now the night was even colder, an icy wind cutting easily through her layers, and she hurried inside the hotel.

At that time of the night, the gloriously beautiful lobby was nearly deserted and when Ben pressed the call button for the elevator, the doors slid open immediately.

Feeling unaccountably edgy, she pushed the button for her floor and moved to the back of the car, leaning against the wall. He might be able to put aside the things they'd said on the street outside of the chocolatier's, but she wasn't finding it so easy.

Ben hit the button for his own floor and the doors glided shut, closing them in alone. "Tired?"

What she felt was wired. And he was the single cause of it. But she shrugged her shoulders, leaving him to interpret it however he chose. "Johnny should have been tired. But he didn't seem to be. I hope he gets paid well by the hotel."

"He doesn't work for the hotel. He has his own business. Employs ten other drivers the last time I asked."

"Impressive." She looked at the floor display. The elevator seemed to be crawling. Even though they had the entire car to themselves, Ben had chosen to lean in the corner less than a foot away from her, his hands stretched out against the rail that ran the perimeter. The glossy shopping bag from the chocolate shop hung from his thumb that he tapped slowly against the rail. The rustling the bag made as it swayed sounded loud, but not as loud as the thumping inside her chest. "Thank you for dinner and…and everything."

He inclined his head slightly, his eyes typically unreadable. "Now you can say you've seen at least a bit of Boston."

"Yes." She stared down at the carpeted floor and moistened her lips, wishing the elevator would hurry up. When the doors dinged softly a moment later, she automatically stepped forward, only to feel Ben's hand clasp her arm.

Her eyes flew to his face, but he was looking at the elevator doors, and she realized they were opening to admit more hotel guests and they hadn't reached her floor yet at all.

She subsided, and Ben tugged her even closer when the elevator continued to fill with the increasingly boisterous group until her back was pressed against his chest as she stood directly in front of him, his hand on her waist through her coat.

She stood stock-still, even though she had the worst desire to sink back into him.

The other guests were clearly celebrating and they tumbled out again a few floors later. Alone again, Ella had no reason to remain plastered against Ben and she gave him a smile that felt awkward and tight as she stepped away. "Looks like they were having a good time."

His eyes were hooded again. "You don't have to be afraid of me, Ella."

She started. "I'm not afraid of you!" She looked at the floor display again. She felt like an absolute idiot and didn't like it one bit. "Maybe *you* should be afraid of me," she muttered, proving that she was still fueled by too much wine, sugar and the intoxication of *him*.

Before he could respond—if he even wanted or intended to—the elevator stopped again, this time at her floor, and the moment the doors opened, she stepped off. "Good night, Ben."

Then the doors closed again and Ella's shoulders slumped.

She hauled in a deep breath and made her way to her room on legs that felt like mush.

Ella presented herself at Ben's suite the next morning exactly two minutes before nine. She wore her navy skirt once again, this time with a silky white tee, and she left the blazer behind.

Ben answered her knock and seemed thoroughly back in his usual mode, with his cell phone at his ear with one hand and a newspaper in his other. He gestured at the dining table in his living area. "Breakfast. Help yourself."

She didn't have to ask if Randy was already there; she could see for herself that he was not. She crossed the room and studied the breakfast selection laid out on the sideboard. Ben had enough food there to feed a dozen people, and she filled a plate with fluffy scrambled eggs, two slices of crispy bacon and a blueberry muffin of decadent proportions. Then she sat at one end of the gleaming table and tucked in.

She felt famished and blamed it on fruitlessly chasing Ben through her dreams all night long. It was just as well that he didn't join her at the table, instead pacing around the living area as he made one call after another, clearly conducting business as usual even from a distance. She hadn't finished even half of her food when they heard a knock on the door.

Ben gave her a look and went into the adjoining room, pulling the doors closed.

She huffed out a breath, trying to rid herself of her nervousness, and crossed the room to open the door. "Good morning, Randy."

Even though it was a Saturday, he was dressed in a dark suit and tie every bit as professional as Ben's. But unlike every time she looked at her handsome boss, the effect from Randy was totally wasted on her. She invited him in, gesturing at the breakfast spread across the room. "I hope you're hungry. Mr. Robinson has a small feast here."

Randy's gaze was frankly curious as he entered the suite and looked around. "Is he here?"

She didn't want to lie outright, even though this entire exercise was based on pretense. "He's on a call," she said. "He'll join us if he is able." She led the way to the dining area. "Can I pour you a coffee or some juice?"

He glanced toward her plate. "Is that your breakfast? Finish eating. I can pour my own coffee."

He seemed insistent, so she returned to her seat and a moment later, he joined her, sitting opposite her. "Pretty sweet suite you've got here," he said cheerfully as he tucked into his own breakfast.

He probably figured she'd shared the room with her "fiancé," and even though she hadn't, she still felt her face warm. "Yes, it's very nice. Thank you for coming again. I hope it wasn't too inconvenient."

His lips twitched. "Nothing's too inconvenient when it comes to Robinson Tech."

Her conscience nipped again and she rose to refill her own coffee cup. "Do you live near here?"

"My folks have a place in Back Bay. Too high rent for me, though," he added ruefully. "I have an apartment in Watertown."

With that conversational door opened so conveniently, Ella sat and cradled the china cup between both hands. "Do you have any brothers or sisters?"

He shook his head. "Mom always said she wanted more kids, but she had a lot of trouble carrying me."

"That's too bad."

He nodded around a mouthful of toast that he chased with coffee. "I was born really prematurely," he said eventually. "Just twenty-six weeks. I spent the first four months of my life in the hospital."

She hid her dismay. Even before Antonia had left Robinson Computers, Gerald had left the country on a business trip. Ben's notes about his father's schedule and whereabouts during those years had been carefully reconstructed. If Randy had been born several months early, there was no possible way that Gerald Robinson could have fathered him. Not when he and Antonia were in different parts of the world when their child would have been conceived. "Well, I'm glad things turned out okay for you," she said. "My, um, my little brother was also premature," she confided. "He has cerebral palsy."

"That's gotta be tough."

"It's a concern, of course, but Rory's the tough one. He's overcome a lot. Mostly his CP affects his legs." She smiled. "He wants to design computers someday."

"Then you're marrying into the right family."

Ella laughed because he expected it. She took a

few more sips of coffee, then excused herself and went to find Ben.

He was in the bedroom, sitting at a desk near the windows with another view of the outdoor terrace. The newspaper was unfolded on top of the desk and his cell phone was sitting on top of that. But she had the distinct impression that he'd been staring out the terrace when she'd interrupted.

She kept her eyes diligently away from his unmade bed, but it was difficult. "He's not your brother." She kept her voice low, even though she'd pulled the doors closed after her.

"How do you know?"

She relayed the information. "There's no way he could have been conceived when his mother was still interning for your father. The dates are just too far out of line, knowing he was so premature."

"Maybe he wasn't early. Nearly thirty years ago? Babies were regularly claimed as 'premature' to explain away a birth that came a little too soon after a wedding."

"I'll see if I can find the hospital records. A long hospital stay like he's described is more than just glossing over a baby made a few weeks before the I do's. Which there weren't anyway, not right away. Even though Randy says his mother and Ronald Bell met in Colorado Springs, don't forget that I couldn't find any record of their marriage until they moved to Massachusetts years and years later. I don't know whether or not Ronald Bell is his natural father, but for your purpose, it's not important anyway. What *is* important is that Gerald *isn't*."

He scrubbed his hand down his face before he

reached out and grabbed his phone. But all he did was tap the edge of it against the newspaper covered desk. "Fine."

She wasn't sure if he was dismissing her or not. "What should I tell him now? The poor guy thinks he's got a crack at working for Robinson Tech."

"Tell him the job requires relocating. Maybe he'll lose interest."

Ella shook her head. "He won't." But she left the bedroom, leaving the doors closed again. She rejoined Randy at the dining table and picked up the fancy, silver coffee server. "More?"

"Sure." He held out his cup and she refilled it before topping off her own. "Do you mind if I ask how many other candidates you're considering?"

"Three." It was appalling how quickly she came up with answers, but that was the number of individuals currently on her latest list of baby mama suspects. "I do need to tell you that relocation would be necessary. Is that—"

"—not a problem," Randy assured.

"Right." She started to sit when she noticed the French doors opening again, and Ben appeared.

Randy noticed, too, and immediately stood, extending his hand. "Mr. Robinson. Good to see you again."

Ben gestured at the food. "I hope you helped take care of getting rid of some of this stuff."

Randy grinned. "My starving student days are still fresh in my mind. I try not to pass up too many meals that are offered to me."

"You've got an impressive resume. And Lester Tomlinson speaks highly of you."

"He's BRD's vice president." Randy looked surprised.

"I know." Ben's gaze traveled over Ella for a moment before returning to Randy. He pulled a card from his lapel pocket and handed it to the younger man. "Give my secretary Bonita a call on Monday. We'll set you up to come to Austin. Get a close-up look at what we've got to offer you."

Randy eagerly took the card and he smiled brilliantly at Ella. "Thank *you*!"

Ben looked vaguely amused before he walked Randy toward the door of the suite. "Might want to save the thanks—working for Robinson Tech is more of a calling than a job."

Randy's smile didn't waver a watt. "I'm up to the challenge, I promise."

Ella sat down at the table, cradling her coffee, and waited until Ben returned once Randy was gone.

He gave her a glance before pouring himself a cup. "What are you looking at me like that for?"

Warmth bloomed inside her chest as she watched him. "You're a softie," she said. "You're going to give him a job."

"We give lots of people jobs," he said dryly. He plucked a slice of bacon from the heated dish and ate it with his fingers. "Even more jobs with our latest expansion. I am *not* a softie."

He was acting as if he hadn't done anything at all out of the ordinary, when she knew just how far from ordinary this situation had been. "Actually *giving* him a job had never been part of your plan."

"Plans change. Aside from trying to flirt with my HR rep, he's got skills."

"You're not worried he'll go around telling people you're engaged to me?"

"I'll make sure he won't." He sounded unconcerned and polished off the bacon slice before wiping his fingers on a napkin. "So Randy's off the list. Who's next? Someone in Chicago, you said?"

She scrambled a little to keep up with the sudden shift. "Uh, yes. Chicago. Nancy Belgard."

"She was with the advertising firm my father once used."

"Yes. I have the notes in my room if you want to go over them."

He shook his head, glancing at his watch. "Later."

She immediately rose and moved the used plates to the sideboard. The food she and Randy had eaten hadn't made a dent in the generous buffet. "It'll only take me a few minutes to get ready to leave for the airport."

"A commendable trait, considering my experience with most females. But we don't have to race back to Austin all that fast. The sky's clear and there's still plenty of the city that you haven't yet seen. Not to mention Cambridge. And your water taxi ride, of course."

He hadn't said a word the night before about more sightseeing. "That's very generous of you, but—"

"I'm not generous, Ella. I'm selfish. I want what I want when I want it."

She watched him over her coffee cup as she took a long sip. It *was* really good coffee.

When she was finished, she set the empty cup next to the used plates. "Saying something doesn't make it so, Ben," she said as she headed for the door. "So far, the only selfish thing I've seen you do was eat the other half of my truffle yesterday. But if you selfishly want to show me more of this fabulous city, I suppose I can suck it up and go along." Smiling impudently, she pulled open the door, only to gasp when he followed her and reached above her head to push it shut again.

"I *am* selfish," he said flatly, and planted his mouth on hers.

* * * * *

Don't miss FORTUNE'S SECRET HEIR by
New York Times *bestselling author Allison Leigh,*
available January 2016 wherever
Harlequin® Special Edition books
and ebooks are sold.
www.Harlequin.com

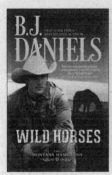 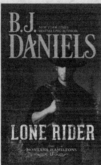 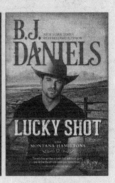

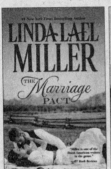

REQUEST YOUR FREE BOOKS!

2 FREE NOVELS
FROM THE ROMANCE COLLECTION
PLUS 2 FREE GIFTS!

YES! Please send me 2 FREE novels from the Romance Collection and my 2 FREE gifts (gifts are worth about $10). After receiving them, if I don't wish to receive any more books, I can return the shipping statement marked "cancel." If I don't cancel, I will receive 4 brand-new novels every month and be billed just $6.49 per book in the U.S. or $6.99 per book in Canada. That's a savings of at least 19% off the cover price. It's quite a bargain! Shipping and handling is just 50¢ per book in the U.S. and 75¢ per book in Canada.* I understand that accepting the 2 free books and gifts places me under no obligation to buy anything. I can always return a shipment and cancel at any time. Even if I never buy another book, the two free books and gifts are mine to keep forever.

194/394 MDN GH4D

Name	(PLEASE PRINT)	
Address		Apt. #
City	State/Prov.	Zip/Postal Code

Signature (if under 18, a parent or guardian must sign)

Mail to the **Reader Service**:
IN U.S.A.: P.O. Box 1867, Buffalo, NY 14240-1867
IN CANADA: P.O. Box 609, Fort Erie, Ontario L2A 5X3

Want to try two free books from another line?
Call 1-800-873-8635 or visit www.ReaderService.com.

* Terms and prices subject to change without notice. Prices do not include applicable taxes. Sales tax applicable in N.Y. Canadian residents will be charged applicable taxes. Offer not valid in Quebec. This offer is limited to one order per household. Not valid for current subscribers to the Romance Collection or the Romance/Suspense Collection. All orders subject to credit approval. Credit or debit balances in a customer's account(s) may be offset by any other outstanding balance owed by or to the customer. Please allow 4 to 6 weeks for delivery. Offer available while quantities last.

Your Privacy—The Reader Service is committed to protecting your privacy. Our Privacy Policy is available online at www.ReaderService.com or upon request from the Reader Service.

We make a portion of our mailing list available to reputable third parties that offer products we believe may interest you. If you prefer that we not exchange your name with third parties, or if you wish to clarify or modify your communication preferences, please visit us at www.ReaderService.com/consumerchoice or write to us at Reader Service Preference Service, P.O. Box 9062, Buffalo, NY 14240-9062. Include your complete name and address.

HARLEQUIN®

SPECIAL EDITION

Life, Love and Family

Save $1.00

on the purchase of

FORTUNE'S SECRET HEIR

by Allison Leigh, available

December 15, 2015, or on any other

Harlequin® Special Edition book.

Available wherever books are sold, including most bookstores, supermarkets, drugstores and discount stores.

Save $1.00

on the purchase of any Harlequin® Special Edition book.

Coupon valid until June 30, 2016. Redeemable at participating outlets in the U.S. and Canada only. Not redeemable at Barnes & Noble stores. Limit one coupon per customer.

52613193

5 65373 00076 2   (8100)0 12112

HSECOUP1215